LOVERS OF
TOMORROW

*To Monica —
my greatest friend
in Plaza South*

Peggy Hmaeko

Books by
Peggy Hinaekian

Of Julia and Men
The Girl from Cairo – A Memoir
Collection of Short Stories and Essays-
Of Humans and Animals

LOVERS OF TOMORROW

A Romance Novel

Peggy Hinaekian

Copyright © 2022 by Peggy Hinaekian.

ISBN:	Softcover	978-1-6698-1794-9
	eBook	978-1-6698-1793-2

All rights reserved. No part of this book may be reproduced or transmitted in any form or by any means, electronic or mechanical, including photocopying, recording, or by any information storage and retrieval system, without permission in writing from the copyright owner.

Any people depicted in stock imagery provided by Getty Images are models, and such images are being used for illustrative purposes only.
Certain stock imagery © Getty Images.

Print information available on the last page.

Rev. date: 04/07/2022

To order additional copies of this book, contact:
Xlibris
844-714-8691
www.Xlibris.com
Orders@Xlibris.com
841496

CONTENTS

Mina 1
Gary 6
Mina 8
Coup D'etat in Egypt 14
Lebanon 17
War in Egypt 23
Return to Egypt 27
The Journey 29
New York 32
Gary 36
Life without Gary 37
Rifaat 39
Vako 41
ROBERT 45
Paris 49
Visit to Cairo 51
Shoukry 55
Beirut 71
Manhattan 75
Fashion Design 77
Vera 80
Mina 84
Europe 89

Rome	95
Geneva	103
The Apartment	110
Adam	114
The Office	119
Vera's Arrival	121
Bernard	126
Friends	130
Geneva	132
The Accident	134
Norbert	137
Marcel	140
The Office	143
Summer	146
Louis	148
The Murder	153
Louis	155
Geneva	157
Marcel	159
Geneva	161
Adam	163
A Horrible Evening	166
Hunter	170
The Divorce	173
Louis	176
Marbella	185
Madjid	192
Manhattan	195
Louis	202

Fabio	206
Dogan	209
The Office	211
The Father	215
This and That	219
IOS	224
Socrates	226
Gary No. 2	229
Tuscany	232
Shoukry	244
Rome	247
Shoukry	253
Rome	257
Note from The Author	259

LOVERS OF TOMORROW
A Romance Novel

The story of Mina, a young Middle-Eastern woman living in Manhattan in the 1960s with her husband. She works as a Secretary at the United Nations, but has aspirations of becoming a fashion designer.

After eight years of marriage, she divorces her husband and returns to Egypt to visit her family whom she had not seen since the Suez Canal War of 1956.

She meets Shoukry, a pilot in the Egyptian Air Force. She has a torrid love affair. He asks her to marry him but she refuses because her goal is to pursue a career in fashion design in Manhattan.

Miina becomes disheartened with her jobs in the designing field and, on a whim, decides to go to Switzerland where she will have a better quality of life by working for the United Nations.

Her sister and parents join her in Geneva. She meets several men and has affairs with some of them but does not fall in love. She only cares for Shoukry and can't forget him.

One summer, she goes to the Tuscan coast for vacation with her family.

While dining in a restaurant, she sees Shoukry there with a woman. She realizes that the woman is his girlfriend. She is extremely jealous and contrives to snatch him away and try to restart their relationship.

"Lo, I am drunken with love!
I wake but my heart sleeps."

Sayat Nova

MINA

Mina's life took another turn.

She shed her husband of eight years.

She had not expected it to happen so suddenly. She had visions of drifting away from him gradually, and then perhaps coming to a mutual understanding and asking for a trial separation again. They had been separated on mutual agreement for about six months three years prior, but they had gotten back together and the marriage had a new start.

No, that is not the way it happened. This rift had FINAL written all over it.

Gary was supposed to pick her up from an art show she was participating in at a Manhattan gallery. It was her first group show and she had put a lot of effort into it. She had six pieces exhibited, all in blues and reds—her favorite colors for painting. Those were not her favorite colors when it came to clothes, though. She was a beige and brown girl, hues which matched her honey blond hair.

When Gary came into the gallery, Mina noticed that he was upset. She felt bad vibes of what was to transpire. She was having a lot of those lately—major reason for wanting to separate from him, again.

He seemed to be in a hurry and was in a foul mood. "Aren't you ready?" he said, interrupting her rudely while she was speaking with a potential client. Mina flushed and was taken aback. She felt humiliated vis a vis the client. She wished she could sink down through a hole on the floor and disappear.

Damn Gary, she thought. *He is spoiling my spiel. Can't he see that this show is extremely important to me?*

"Sorry, I have to go," she managed to tell the client who looked surprised at the intrusion. "I'll call you with more information about the piece you like. Please give me your phone number."

With that said, she took out one of her business cards from her pocket and scribbled down the man's name and phone number. She then grabbed her purse and coat, went out of the gallery with Garry, and followed him to the car. He had parked illegally. Reason for his hurry, she surmised. In his impetuous and brusque movement of going through the door of the gallery, one of the pockets of his vest had got caught in the door handle and ripped. Well, that was the last straw for him. He was fuming. Mina could literally see the vapor coming out of his nostrils.

"Look what happened! It's all your fault!" exclaimed Gary getting in the car. He drove off before she even had time to properly adjust herself in the passenger seat.

Fuck you, she thought. They never used foul language to each other but she seemed to be using the F word frequently in her thoughts.

Mina was seething but she bridled her temper. She did not want to make a fuss in the car. Gary drove frantically and they arrived home in fifteen minutes flat. She felt nauseous and anxious but, nevertheless, she decided to confront Gary. She was fed up with his temperamental behavior, especially in public.

After taking off her coat, she went into the kitchen, took out a bottle of Shiraz and poured herself a glass. She was not in the habit of reverting to alcohol in moments of distress but she did, this time. She had seen people in the movies do just that.

She then stormed into their bedroom. Gary was removing his clothes and watching TV at the same time. It was evident that he was late watching a game. He was addicted to the sports channel. It was always this game or another. She was not into sports at all. Maybe tennis, now and again. One of her girlfriends had told her that she chose to marry a man who was not into sports because she hated sports. The friend had made a good choice. Mina had not been that lucky.

Mina shouted at Gary. "This is the last time you'll vent your anger at me, especially in public. What you did is unpardonable. I've had enough of your volatile moods and rude behavior."

"I was parked illegally and you were taking your sweet time. I've always asked you to be on time," he retorted, glaring.

"I was talking to a potential client. You know that during these precarious months of financial uncertainty, they are not queueing up at my door."

"That's no excuse. You should have been ready. I didn't want to miss my game."

"I don't give a hoot about your game. The TV seems to be the most important thing in your life. It's always hockey, football or some other darn game. I'm not at your command. I'll not tolerate your uncouth behavior any longer," Mina said in a composed manner.

She sat down on her vanity chair.

"What are you going to do, leave me?" asked Gary looking at her sarcastically while taking off his vest.

"Yup, that is exactly what I'm going to do."

"Leave me, then. See how far you can get, all alone in New York."

"No problem. I can always find someone to share the apartment with me."

"Go, then," he barked.

"No, you go!" she exclaimed defiantly. "I paid for all the furniture and appliances, so just take your precious belongings and your sorry ass out of her and disappear from my life."

There! She'd said it.

Mina was surprised at her own outburst. She hated quarreling, but her patience had been exhausted. Gary's behavior at the gallery was the limit. No man was going to hinder her career path. Her art meant everything to her. She wanted to succeed in becoming a reputable artist with exhibitions all over the world. This New York exhibition was her first group exhibition in the United States. It was just the beginning—and beginnings were important.

Mina sat down on the bed and, toying with her wine glass, looked at Gary apprehensively, following his every move, waiting to see what he would do. Was he actually going to leave? He had threatened to do so a few times in the past when they quarreled but he had never left. Gary suddenly became silent after her outburst. He sat in his favorite armchair in the bedroom and, putting his hands on his face, looked down at his shoes, breathing heavily.

As though he can find a solution by looking at his shoes, Mina thought. *He is too quiet, what is he going to do?* She asked herself anxiously. She felt a little scared of his upcoming reaction. She hoped he would not be violent. He had never been before. He finally got up from the armchair, fetched a suitcase and started to pack a few things. Mina stared at him and realized the time had come for their final breakup.

They had not gotten along well for a long time now but they had not quarreled much lately. They were not having the violent quarrels of the early days. That was thanks to her being more tolerant in order to keep peace in the marriage. She had tried to create times of peace and companionship but it had been difficult. The problem was they hardly ever enjoyed each other's company anymore and they bickered over inconsequential things.

This last piss match was the turning point.

Without looking at her, Gary picked up his suitcase and a coat and went out of the house yelling over his shoulder.

"You won't see me ever again. You can manage on your own paying the rent and everything else. I'm leaving," he snapped and walked out the door, banging it shut. Mina jumped up from her thoughts. He was gone. Gary had left. Now what?

Mina never imagined such a final showdown. She was stunned. Her cushy earth had shattered, or had it? She was surprised at her own outburst. She had never before talked to Gary in that resolute manner. She had never even shouted at him before. She was usually more accepting of his volatile temper. Yes, Gary had a short fuse and she always tried to pacify him. She hated marital squabbling. Her parents did that sometimes and she always left the room when that happened. She preferred peace at any cost rather than belligerent confrontation. It was almost impossible to take back hurting words once they were spoken. She was very careful not to indulge in that.

Now, eight years after being married, Mina had done the unthinkable. The unthinkable as far as their families were concerned. Their families—in fact, the whole Armenian community—thought this was a love match made in heaven. They did not know the true story, the endless squabbles and disagreements. Their sex life had also become rather tepid. At first it had been exciting and wonderful. It was new and full of surprises. *What do you expect after being with the same guy for years?* Mina asked herself. *Was this the case with all married couples?* Her married girlfriends never talked about marital sex. They were quite inquisitive before getting married but, afterwards, they shut up like clams.

She tried to digest the fact that she had finally gotten rid of her husband. Their fights had never become physical, though. *Thank God for that,* Mina thought, because she would never have tolerated physical abuse.

And now she felt physically, emotionally and mentally exhausted. She tried not to feel panicky. She was prone to panic attacks.

Mina was very much in love with Gary at the beginning of their relationship, but as time went by she became disillusioned with the idea of marriage and the constant togetherness. There were no longer any surprises. The thrill of being together evaporated, vamoosed, little by little. Gary started getting on her nerves. Was it because she was meeting other, more interesting men at the workplace? Was it because Gary had been the only guy she had gone to bed with? Or, was it because she just wanted to experience freedom which she had never had? She had gone from parental control to a marital one. She had never been actually free to do what she really wanted. There had always been some opposition.

"You're too young." "You have no experience." "You're too naive." "You're too impulsive." On and on it went.

During the first separation period, Mina had visited her family in Cairo. Only part of her family—her parents and her younger sister, Vera. She had also visited Beirut, where her older brother, Ted and older sister, Gita, lived. They had moved there with their respective families some years ago when the first signs of trouble started in Egypt just before the 1952 Revolution and the expulsion of King Farouk. They were lucky in having been able to do so.

GARY

Gary had not really wanted to leave Mina. He did not know why he had acted so impetuously. After slamming the door, he took the elevator to the garage, got in his car and started driving through the night. He didn't know where he was going. He couldn't believe what had happened. Had he been too hasty? Too demanding? Should he have let her continue talking to the client at the gallery? Mina had never been so resolute with him before. This was a new Mina. Was she perhaps unfaithful to him? They had not had sex for over three weeks now. *This is not normal for a young married couple*, he thought. Every time he had made some overtures, she had invented a pretext. It suddenly dawned upon him that she had not been affectionate with him lately, although she was extremely affectionate with their Maine coon cat and always talked to him as though he were her child. She talked more to the cat than she did to him. Gary thought it was stupid of him to be jealous of a cat.

"*If she has a lover, I'll take a lawyer and fix her ass,*" he told himself. Just thinking of the probability made him furious. At this point, he was fuming and his heart was racing. He banged his fists on the steering wheel out of frustration and drove around until he calmed down but he did not return to the apartment. At other times, when he had left their home after a dispute, he had not packed a suitcase but had just driven around to let out steam and had returned eventually during the wee hours of the morning. And the next day, they had pretended that nothing had transpired. This time, however, she actually pronounced the word "GO". He could not return home. He would lose face if he did. He drove around for about an hour then called his friend Steve, who was a bachelor, and asked him whether he could crash with him for a few nights.

Steve was surprised when Gary related to him what had transpired. Gary then started drinking to forget the unfortunate episode. He was breathing heavily and was agitated.

"You're leaving Mina? I can't believe it," said Steve.

"Yup, after what happened, I can't go back unless she implores me to do so."

"I'm sure, when you have both calmed down, you will think otherwise."

"I really don't know what to do. She is too independent. Perhaps she has a lover."

"Hey, man, I don't think so. She is not the type. Yeah, I know some women may deceive you with their angelic airs, but Mina is not angelic; she is a straightforward woman from what I have seen. You are not in Egypt any longer, where you can perhaps chain your wife to the stove, ha, ha, but nevertheless I don't think Mina would cheat on you."

"I really don't feel like laughing. Cut it out."

"You remember Sarah…." continued Steve.

Gary interrupted him. "I'm in no mood for this. I couldn't care less about Sara. I'm going to bed."

Gary had a restless night. He tried to drown himself in alcohol but all it did was make him sweat and become even more agitated. *Fuck Mina*, he kept repeating to himself. Why had things deteriorated so much? He went to work the next day, feeling like shit and thinking of Mina the whole time. He wondered whether their relationship could still be salvaged. He thought she should make the move for a reconciliation since she had banished him from their home. Banished was too strong a word, perhaps. Her "GO" had been so emphatic. She had never appeared so decisive. She almost had venom in her stare. He had never seen her like that.

Gary hoped Mina would call.

MINA

Mina tried to analyze her feelings after Gary's departure. This was a new beginning for her. The only thing she was sure of was that she was now FREE. But freedom had also its drawbacks. She wondered whether she been too hasty in chasing Gary away. Did she feel relief? Did she feel scared of being alone, without a man?

She told herself to think positively and an imperceptible smile crossed her lips when she realized that, being free now, she could do as she pleased.

From the time she was fifteen years old, she had not been without a man. She met Gary at a dinner dance at the Armenian Social Club, when she was sixteen and he was seventeen. He was her second boyfriend. The first one, Dick, was a childish crush. Nothing had actually transpired between them. Nothing could have transpired. It was strictly taboo for Armenians to smooch and fool around, unless the guy had serious intentions. If a girl fooled around, she would be considered tainted and no guy would marry her if she separated from her boyfriend. The men wanted "pure" girls.

What bullshit. Mina hated that mentality.

She had been infatuated with Dick, but she fell in love with Gary. Gary was the real thing.

Even as teens, they had a tempestuous relationship, quarreling and making up all the time. Mina was really in love then and Gary adored her. She wanted to be with him all the time. She thought about him constantly during school. She waited for the phone to ring. She wanted to be in his arms and feel his kisses. Kissing was done clandestinely, of course. They had serious plans. Plans to get married eventually when they were both of age. *How can I wait four years?* Mina asked herself.

What had happened to their relationship? Where had all the thrills gone? Would this happen with every man she would take up with in the future? Maybe she was not made to be married. How can her passionate love for Gary disappear into thin air after just a few years of married life. When she asked these questions to her girlfriends, they were not of much help. They were mum about their relationships. Middle Eastern girls did not talk freely about their marriages. They pretended everything was fine.

They were still living in Egypt then. Although, before getting married, she craved for Gary's presence all the time, after getting married, Mina wanted to have some moments alone. But Gary overwhelmed her with his constant presence. She didn't want to see him all the time. What bothered her most was sharing the same bathroom. She hated to see him brushing his teeth, for instance. Somehow, he was slowly getting on her nerves. Her moods changed often though. She had highs and lows. When her libido was high, she craved him and she felt cuddly. When she was painting she hated being interrupted and he always did that, asking her a stupid question out of the blue. Was there something wrong in the way she felt? She tried to talk to her mother, who was also somewhat her confidante. Not in sexual matters though. She did not talk to anyone about sex.

"You are imagining things that are not there. Don't be so volatile," her mother admonished her.

"I'm not imagining mom. I sometimes feel I don't like him at all."

"I told you several times not to get married. You were too young and you didn't listen for any advice."

"Yes, ma."

"Also, he was too young for you."

"Yes, ma."

"A girl needs a much older man."

"Yes, ma."

Her older brother was of no help when she asked him for advice.

"I don't understand anything about women," he kept repeating, shaking his head with a puzzled look on his face. Mina thought he was too immature anyway and the woman he was married to was not the right one for him. Solange was a Lebanese/Armenian girl and her family was wealthy. She was spoiled rotten, was too bossy and a control freak but good-looking which was what had attracted Ted in the first place. She put on phony airs of belonging to the upper classes. Ted was weak and too much under her influence. *Maybe she is giving him good sex,* Mina thought.

Her older sister, Gita, who was happily married with two kids, did not offer any advice.

"I'm the wrong person to ask," she said. "I am content staying at home and looking after my children. I have no ambitions. I want to take it easy in life and not run around like a crazed dog. Happiness is here with me, now. You, on the other hand, are always looking for something else. You're never satisfied."

Her younger sister, Vera, was too young (three years younger than her) to give her any earth-shattering opinions. She was having her own troubles juggling her boyfriends—clandestinely. She was only seventeen and had a secret Muslim boyfriend, much older than she was. Their parents ignored this fact. Vera kept it a secret. She only confided in Mina.

Mina remembered the time when, just before getting married, they had rented an apartment. She was so happy then. *It's perfect,* she thought, as she toured the apartment, feeling as though she had wandered into a film set. She had hugged Gary and he had kissed her passionately. This was going to be their love nest and they would have endless evenings of sex. Yes, sex was very much on her mind, then. She was curious and was waiting impatiently for the wedding night. There had been a lot of fooling around, exploring each other's bodies but no real sex. There had been no penetration.

Mina thought the reason she felt unsure about her emotions towards Gary lately was because she was meeting other guys and getting somehow infatuated by them. Some had even made a pass at her but she never encouraged them. Therefore, she had continued her semi-comfortable relationship with Gary. In any case, she did not think she would ever fall in love again— that consuming type of love that only happens to the very young, like the one she had with Gary at the beginning. She was no longer immature. She now had a head on her shoulders, or so she thought.

Should she have continued to make a go of the marriage? But, how could she rekindle a romance that was no longer there? Her brain was like a watermelon full of seeds, like the Egyptian kind. She remembered how, in Cairo, they dried the seeds in the sun, then roasted them and cracked them open with their teeth, munching on them at the movies. Instead of popcorn they had watermelon seeds. The floor of the theatre was a disaster at the end of the film projection.

She was still a virgin when they got married. Armenian girls do not have sex before wedlock. Well, not only Armenians but most girls in the Middle East. Some accidents were reported but they were hush hush. Some unwanted pregnancies also occurred but abortion was easily obtainable. The Government did not interfere in women's choices. Her cousin's father was a gynecologist and also an abortionist—a good one. There had never been any problems.

Mina did not know why she thought of the past so often and not of the present. She did think of the future, though. She remembered a quote by the Dalai Lama about man not enjoying the present because he is so worried about the future. Mina was indeed worried about the future. She was avaricious. She wanted to be somebody and start on her life path. According to her, as long as she was still a secretary, her life had not started. Being a secretary seemed to be the only job available for women in the 1950's. She wanted more than that. She wanted to be a model, a fashion designer, an artist/painter, an actress. Her dreams were multifold and daydreaming was her favorite pastime.

Sitting in her favorite recliner in her bedroom, Mina contemplated on her past life and reminisced. The sun was casting weird shadows on her housecoat and it was like a convoluted pattern which resembled the state of her mind, always churning, never at peace. She resolved not to indulge in self-pity.

Mina and Gary were both Armenians, born in Egypt. People kept their ethnic origins in Egypt and in most Middle Eastern countries. They had their own schools, churches, social clubs, sport clubs and they tended to navigate through their own circles. The ethnic minorities were a big chunk of the population in Egypt, owning major businesses and even holding positions in the government. Mina was curious about the other minorities and often tried to mingle with them for diversity.

Their parents were also born in Egypt. Mina's parents were avant-garde but Gary's not at all. They had the stubborn trait of the *Vanetsis* (people from the city of Van), which was in Armenia before the Turkish massacres of 1915, but is now in Turkey. The people from Van were known to be extremely set in their ways and unflinching. After all, they were descendants of staunch warriors defending their walled city against the Ottomans. They had succeeded for a short while and this was considered a small victory.

Gary never liked Mina's assertiveness. He liked her to be docile and complacent and not contradicting him, especially in public. In the beginning she was somewhat obedient but her true character had surfaced after a few months of being married. He had been surprised at the change in her. *He should have chosen another wife then*, she thought, when he admonished her. She certainly was not going to put up with the macho behavior of any man. She was very much into women's independence and was adamant not to be dependent on any man. She wanted her own income and not ask money from a husband all the time as she had seen Armenian wives do in Egypt. She believed in herself and knew she could achieve great things, but not in Egypt. She had great hopes of achieving them in the country of her dreams, which was America.

She hated so much taking Gary's last name when they got married. It was unpronounceable. But there was nothing she could do about it. She felt that she lost being herself. She was now someone else. Someone else's appendage. She liked her last name and would have liked to keep it. After all, she was an artist and artists do not change their names. She considered herself a real artist not a weekend dabbler. God, she hated those. Would Gary allow her to pursue her dreams?

Another thing she disliked was her official first name, Arminé. It sounded so archaic. It was an ancient Armenian name. She did not want to be associated with anything that was old sounding, so she changed it to Mina. Gary also changed his official first name, Garabed, to Gary. In that respect they were in sync.

COUP D'ETAT IN EGYPT

Mina's thoughts went back to her life in Egypt again and to the 23 July, 1952 Egyptian Revolution which changed their lives drastically. The burning of Cairo at the beginning of the year was a precursor to the Revolution.

There was a scuffle between the British soldiers and Egyptian police in Ismailia, a town on the west bank of the Suez Canal. After a two-hour confrontation, many Egyptian soldiers died. Consequently, there was widespread anti-British sentiment in the masses throughout Egypt. At that time, the population felt that something much bigger was brewing in the sidelines.

In 1952, Mina had just graduated from St. Clare's College in Heliopolis and worked as secretary to the Board of Directors at Eastern Tobacco Company in Giza. The company used to be owned by the Armenian Matossian Brothers, the largest manufacturers of tobacco in Egypt and they employed about 70,000 Armenians at one time. They then sold it to British American Tobacco which eventually became the Eastern Tobacco Company with a British Board of Directors.

Gary was a jeweler. He was also a designer of jewelry and had a lucrative business in this father's shop in the Khan Khalili Bazaar in Cairo. In Egypt and Lebanon, most renowned jewelers were Armenians. Mina did not really have to work for a living as her father's job was thriving at the time but she liked being around people and having her own money to spend.

The Coup d'Etat was fueled by powerful Egyptian nationalism and it was carried out by the Movement of Free Officers headed by General Mohamed Naguib and Colonel Gamal Abdel Nasser. Its main purpose was to decolonize Egypt from British occupation. It advocated political, economic and social change. In order to make those changes, it had to abolish the monarchy of King Farouk and establish a Republic. Egyptian monarchy was seen as both corrupt and pro-British. The Free Officers adopted an Arab nationalist and anti-imperialist agenda much to the chagrin of the large foreign population and the well-to-do Egyptians. Egypt had a vibrant, educated, elite class of people. The rich and powerful classes had accepted British rule. It was favorable to them and their businesses thrived.

On the fatal day of the Revolution, King Farouk was surrounded by the revolutionary guards in the Ras El Tin Palace in Alexandria and forced to abdicate in favor of his infant son by his second wife. It was a bloodless coup, and it was arranged that he sail away in his naval uniform on the Royal Yacht together with the Queen and his children. The King was only thirty-two years old but a life of gluttony had made him into a paunchy, balding man. He had reigned for sixteen years. The ethnic minorities, mostly Christians, had it good during his reign.

Cairo was a boiling pot of mixed ethnic groups that got along well together. The Revolution was the catalyst for these minorities to make plans to leave Egypt. Those with money abroad made it out easily, leaving most of their possessions behind, with the hope of returning some day when the situation got better. Quite a number of them went to Lebanon. The Jews with French, British and Italian passports went to their respective countries. Mina and Gary lost quite a few friends with this mass departure. The cacophony of the different languages in the streets gradually disappeared and life was not the same in Cairo. It has lost its multicultural identity. There was fear and apprehension for what would happen next. It was an unsettling period and there were all sorts of rumors.

The wealthy could make their plans but what about ordinary people, those who had no contacts or finances abroad? Armenians had Egyptian passports, if any, and they could not take up and leave, except to go to Lebanon on vacation. Luckily, Gary and Mina had some money saved and planned to go to Beirut and from there to the United States, "*inshallah.*" They were in a hurry to do so but had not yet made concrete plans.

The political situation was precarious and unsettling in Egypt, with the *Mukhabarat* (secret police) all over the place, arresting people who spoke against the regime publicly. When General Naguib became President, the new government changed the names of the streets from the Latin Alphabet to the Arabic one. So, if one did not read Arabic, one did not know one's whereabouts if one happened to be in a strange neighborhood. Most Ethnic minorities did not read Arabic and some spoke it badly. The Arabic language was poorly taught in the foreign schools or not taught at all. Even the local Egyptians, who attended these schools, had to take private Arabic lessons at home.

General Naguib became President of the Republic after the military coup. He was more conservative than Nasser. He did not last long, however. After a failed assassination attempt on Nasser in 1954, in which Naguib was implicated, the latter was placed under house arrest. Gamal Abdel Nasser then became President. He was a great orator and staunch nationalist and vowed to end British colonization. The masses adored him and followed his every word. He had charisma. He was also an avid reader and read books on past foreign and local leaders as well as novels by French authors.

Nasser nationalized many foreign-owned industries, like private banks, insurance companies, shipping companies and other basic industries. He wanted to achieve equality between the poor and the rich and he gradually installed an agrarian reform, nationalizing vast properties of the very wealthy, Muslim population.

Cairo drastically changed from being a European metropolis to a military-run city. The glory days of "Paris on the Nile" had disappeared.

LEBANON

Well before the 1952 Revolution, when there were rumors of dissatisfaction with King Farouk by the majority of the population, some people foresaw trouble brewing. It was then that Gita went to Beirut with her husband and two children. Gita's husband opened a photography shop and they were doing quite well. They seemed to be happily married and did not envisage to move from Lebanon. The same with Ted, who worked with Middle East Airlines, and was married to an Armenian/Lebanese woman, whom Mina considered to be a shrew. Likewise, they had no dreams about the U.S., this land of delights, where everything was possible, or so thought Mina.

At that time, Mina's older siblings urged the whole family to move to Lebanon.

Mina and Gary left Egypt for Beirut just in the nick of time before the borders closed during the Suez Canal crisis in the autumn of 1956. This was the third Middle Eastern war which involved Egypt. They left with the pretense of going on vacation to Beirut which was still allowed at the time. They could not take a whole lot of suitcases with them. They planned to return to Egypt a couple of times to take more stuff for their eventual departure to the U.S., if that ever materialized. Gary and Mina left Egypt with broken hearts. After all, they were born there and had made quite a good life for themselves. They had friends, a busy social life and enjoyed an enviable existence.

Mina's parents and her younger sister stayed behind to wrap things up but then they were caught with the Suez Canal War and were unable to leave. Up to the Revolution, Mina's father had a lucrative decorating business and was the decorator of pashas and wealthy locals. The mother was a high-class seamstress and had two employees. Theirs was a busy household. Gary's family had no intention of ever leaving Egypt. They had quite a few business interests in Egypt, with jewelry shops in Cairo, Alexandria and Port Said and were making a good living. They also owned real estate which was not yet nationalized like most large foreign-owned businesses.

Mina and Gary managed to find good jobs in Beirut. It was a bustling commercial town, with a lot of wheeling and dealing going on. It was easy in those days in Beirut. All that was needed were a few connections and Gary had plenty; friends of friends from Egypt. Mina found a secretarial position with SAS (the Scandinavian Airline System) and Gary found a job with a prominent jeweler. Most jewelers in Beirut were Armenians.

Lebanon was different from any other Middle Eastern country in that half the population was Christian and the Government was run by a mixture of Muslims and Christians. The largest Christian minority were the Armenians. Actually, the Armenian presence in Lebanon dated back to centuries and Armenians had become Lebanon's most prominent and productive community. Three Armenian political parties played significant influences on the diasporic communities. Mina's father did not belong to any political party and Mina hated the squabble between the three parties. It did not create unity.

Beirut's location was desirable, being between the Mediterranean Sea and the mountains. It was the playground of affluent people from the Middle East. Mina did not like the way they spoke Arabic though, with a sing song manner. What had attracted Gita and Ted were the tax incentives. Mina did not care that much for that city. The Lebanese were more of a show-off society and they thought they lived in Little Paris, as they nick-named their town. But it was certainly not Paris for Mina.

It was well-known that Cairo was the cosmopolitan metropolis of the Middle East, where there was an abundance of chic, glamor and wealth. Alexandria followed suit with a large number of Greeks and

Greek-owned businesses. Beirut was smaller and had one main street, Hamra, where most of the high-end boutiques and restaurants were located.

Despite all that Beirut offered, Mina definitely preferred Cairo—the Nile, the exotic nightclubs, some on houseboats on the Nile, the exclusive Gezireh Sporting Club, swarming with foreigners, and the Pyramids. Cairo had a certain mystery, charm and exoticism which Beirut did not. Beirut was more of a commercial city, whereas Cairo had grandeur, worldliness and, perhaps, some decadence which made it all the more exciting and interesting.

Gary and Mina appreciated mostly the coast line and the beaches of Lebanon. During hot summer days, they sometimes went to the mountains, which were not too far away, to get away from the heat. Most wealthy Lebanese had summer homes in the mountains. Although Lebanon had numerous archeological sites, they lacked the grandeur of those in Egypt. Beirut was as cosmopolitan as Cairo and the couple acclimatized themselves quickly. However, there was a *malaise* because they were temporary residents. They did not really belong.

Well, Mina thought, *if we can't get to the States, Lebanon is not that bad and it is still close to HOME. And, my parents and Vera can eventually come over and join us.*

Beirut was also a fun city and they had a good social life, a number of friends, mostly from Cairo. Nightclubbing was their Saturday night pastime with good bands from Europe and the Philippines. Mina's favorite was Bruno Martini, an Italian band they used to dance to at the Mena House Hotel night club situated near the Pyramids of Giza. Bruno played the piano standing up. He was so charismatic, Mina thought.

Mina and Gary applied for immigration to the United States with the help of ANCA (the Armenian National Committee of America) which helped Armenians settle in the U.S. and find sponsors and jobs.

In Beirut they shared a large apartment with two bachelors from Cairo. They were Gary's friends. They gave a lot of parties and life was indeed loads of fun.

"Lebanon is quite a free country and there are no travel restrictions here. Why don't you stay here?" Some friends, who had opted to stay on, asked them.

"It is still a Middle Eastern country and women's professions are limited," Mina replied. "Staying here would not further my career in any way," she continued.

"What's your obsession about having a career?" Both male and female friends asked her. "Don't you just want to stay home and make yourself pretty and have an active social life? After all, your husband makes good money. You don't even have to work."

"You just don't understand," Mina told them. "I'm not like you. I can't sit pretty on my ass and lead an idle, aimless life. I have to be doing something creative with my time, otherwise I get easily bored." She got so exasperated with their comments.

They still did not understand her and rolled their eyes.

The beach was not far from their apartment. Women wore trendy bathing suits and wrap arounds. Some wore bikinis. It had just become the vogue in Lebanon, after Brigitte Bardot had started strutting around with skimpy ones at the beach in St. Tropez. Therefore, as Mina followed the latest fashion, she wanted to wear a bikini.

"I don't want you wearing a bikini and showing off your body. I don't want you to look like a *poz*," (prostitute in Armenian), Gary commented. He was very much the Middle Eastern man trying to control his wife's apparel and make up.

"Okay then, I'll wear a two-piece suit," Mina said just to appease him.

"If it does not reveal too much."

"Too much what, for God's sake? I don't have a lot of flesh to exhibit."

Mina did not like Gary having control over what she wore and she cajoled him into agreeing that she buy a couple of two-piece suits. He was in a good mood that day and agreed.

Mina rushed to buy a couple of suits that were more like bikinis and wore them, challenging Gary, who disapproved but did not forbid her. He was still in a good mood because he was having sex, sometimes charity ones but he could not tell the difference. He did not have that much experience in that domain. Before getting married, he had sex with prostitutes, which was mostly 'in and out.'

If Mina stayed in Beirut, she could probably be designing clothes for the elite but that would mean she was a seamstress. She did not want that. She wanted more. She wanted to be a real fashion designer in the U.S. She also wanted equality for women. Little did she know that women in the U.S. were not considered equal to men in the business world.

She wrote lengthy letters back home.

"If we don't make it to the U.S., you'll all come to Lebanon. At least the family will be united," she wrote.

"What is your father going to do for a job?" asked her mother.

"He can manage a hotel or something. He has experience in that." Among the many professions their father had was hotel manager of a small hotel in Helwan, a spa town not far from Cairo. After the Revolution, his lucrative business of interior decorating had gone downhill. The new clientele was the military and they did not pay well or didn't pay at all. He was having a hard time paying his employees. So, he took the job as Manager to the hotel in Helwan. It was owned by an acquaintance.

Mina was very close to Vera, more so than to Gita who was entrenched in being a perfect mother and wife. Well, Mina was a wife but perfect? She was not.

Vera was then working as secretary to the Philippine Ambassador in Cairo. One day a Philippine diplomat came to Beirut on his way to the Philippines and gave them all the 'real' news from Egypt.

"The atmosphere is deteriorating rapidly. There is a rumor that Egypt will be at war again. You're lucky you're out. If there is ever a war, nobody will be able to get out of Egypt for a long time. Nasser seems hellbent on de-westernization and de-colonization."

Mina's face fell. Not able to see her parents and sister? She realized that Egypt was losing its golden years and her carefree youth had already vanished. They had to overcome lots of hurdles to be re-united.

"Darn Nasser and darn the Middle East." She could freely vent in Beirut. There were no spies around like in Cairo where every word you uttered could be reported to the *Mukhabarrat*.

"Try to get to the U.S. because Lebanon does not look too safe either," the diplomat said with a serious demeanor. "You never know what can happen. The Middle East is like a time bomb. A new era of Arab nationalization is looming on its horizon."

WAR IN EGYPT

Mina followed politics in a haphazard way. She was not that much interested, except when it had to do with her day-to-day life.

She knew that since the establishment of Israel, Egyptian forces often clashed with Israeli ones at the border of the two countries. When the military took over the government in Egypt, they asked the British to end their military presence at the Canal but the British did not follow up on that. In those years, The British had their largest military presence at the Suez Canal. They would lose their bread and butter if they agreed to demilitarize.

The actual crisis started when the Israelis, in cahoots with the British and the French, invaded Egypt at Suez in the autumn of 1956. The British and French then followed suit much to the chagrin of the Americans who pressured the foreign powers to withdraw. They did not want another Middle Eastern war, with Russia surely getting involved this time. Egypt had veered closer to Russia after the Americans refused to lend money to build the Aswan High Dam. Up to that time, the Americans were always much loved in Egypt but their refusal to finance the dam changed the perception of the Egyptians. The foreign invading troops finally retreated but Egypt was not the same after that. It had changed drastically from a European metropolis to a military-run country.

Mina received letters from her sister every week while they were in Beirut. The letters were heavily censored, even the Armenian ones. Mina guessed they had hired Armenian translators at the censorship bureau. The letters were numbered to keep track of them. Sometimes she received no. 4 before no. 3. They were ten-page detailed letters, full of non-political news and even dialogue. They were extremely interesting. Her sister had turned out to be a good writer. She described her daily life, her work, and her boyfriends and stories about their Siamese cat.

Even though Egypt was at war, social life in Egypt had not deteriorated that much. The nightclubs and cinemas were open and Vera had a couple of boyfriends at her service. Both high-ranking Egyptian Army officers who took care of her entertainment needs. They took her to the movies, to nightclubs and invited her to parties. The Gezireh Sporting Club seemed to be a favorite place for a number of activities. This Club, which at one time had been exclusively for the wealthy Cairenes, had opened up to the high-ranking Egyptian Army officers who were the new elite in Cairo. Vera liked her job as secretary to the Philippine Ambassador in Cairo and enjoyed diplomatic privileges, meaning she could order stuff from abroad. She could not write about the unrest in Egypt, nor anything about the new order of things. People trickling into Lebanon gave them the rest of the inside news.

Although they were well off in Beirut, Mina and Gary did not relinquish their dream of going to the U.S. The only family Gary had in the U.S. was an uncle who was an anthropology professor in a university in Chicago. He had been an orphan of the Armenian genocide and his brother, now deceased, had found his way to the States in 1918. He had managed to bring his younger brother thereafter. He was the only contact Gary had. In any case, his uncle could not help them to immigrate to the United States. So, Mina and Gary made their application through ANCA (the Armenian National Committee of America) which was helping Armenians settle in the U.S. by helping them find sponsors and jobs. Many of their friends chose that route.

While waiting for their papers to come through, Mina and Gary continued working. They did not want to rent an apartment of their own because they did not know when their papers would come through. They intended to immigrate as soon as that happened. It would be a waste of money to buy furniture and household stuff.

How Mina hated being a secretary! Taking dictation from a boss. But that was the only type of job available for educated young women in the Middle East. She wanted so much to have a fashion design career. She did meet a wealthy Lebanese woman who asked Mina to design a couple of dresses for her. Mina was at first reticent but she then agreed and charged quite a bit of money. This woman referred her to others and Mina had a sort of second job. She had to cut the patterns and make the dresses herself. It was a full-time job but she did not dare leave her secretarial position. She also needed as much experience as possible being a secretary to land a job in the U.S. as soon as she arrived. Her dream career of being a fashion designer went on the second burner.

The favorite destinations for the Armenians were New York and Los Angeles. Mina and Gary opted for New York.

Mina thought the American immigration forms were hilarious. They asked whether you would indulge in criminal activities while in the U.S. or whether you were a prostitute and would continue on exercising that profession. *Who in his right mind would answer yes to these absurd questions?* Mina asked herself.

As there were many Armenians wishing to immigrate to the U.S. from Beirut, their papers took a long time to be processed. With Arab nationalism spreading in other Middle Eastern countries, Armenians in those countries were also hellbent to go the States. It was felt that the situation for Christian minorities was deteriorating in all of them. The conversation in the coffee shops and the social clubs was all about getting out and going to America or Australia—the latter being another chosen destination. Most of the news coming from relatives in the U.S. was good but there were some bad ones too. The biggest problem being that some elderly people did not know enough English to find a decent job. They were urged to take classes.

"Why the hell is it taking such a long time to get our papers?" complained Mina.

"They don't think our case is urgent," Gary replied. "We have our residence papers and jobs in Beirut. It's not like we are refugees or something."

"I'd like to go ahead with my life. I am already twenty-three years old. I'd like to have a proper career and not be a secretary my whole goddam life!"

"Yeah, but you have traveling privileges working for SAS."

"What privileges? Go to Sweden or Norway? Who wants to be in the freezing cold?"

"Don't complain too much. Life is not that bad in Beirut. We have the same kind of life as we had in Cairo."

"It's okay for you. You're a jeweler and will always be one wherever you go. I'm only an 'effing' secretary, a robot. I just follow orders given by idiot bosses."

It took them a couple of years since the onset of their application but they finally got the required papers to immigrate to the U.S. They had enough money to pay for their trip and also some money left over to settle down in the U.S. without being a burden on the AGBU (Armenian General Benevolent Fund) which helped Armenian immigrants in the resettlement process.

RETURN TO EGYPT

While waiting for their papers, Mina and Gary went back to Egypt a couple of times to bring over more of their possessions. Those trips were not a problem. The customs officials were super friendly when they entered Egypt.

"Welcome back to your country," they said with a broad smile.

Egypt was indeed their country. Going in was easy, but going out still created problems but there was always a way around obstacles in Middle Eastern countries. All you had to do is throw some *baksheesh* around here and there. Money could get you almost anything in the Middle East. Government officials, not being well paid, relied on the under-the-table perks.

As it was not allowed to take money out of Egypt, they bought quite a number of Egyptian made goods, like bedsheets, towels and brocade fabric to make dresses. They also took out jewelry of course, the clandestine way, hiding them in Mina's abundant curly hair or in Gary's shirt collars and bribing people, of course.

Reunion with the families was heart-wrenching and Mina almost felt like abandoning her wish of going to the U.S. the last time she visited her family. People who did not wish to leave Egypt kept telling them that they had all the comforts. Why leave? True, Gary could still get a good job as a jeweler. Jewelry buying was the favorite pastime of the Egyptians. Even the illiterate peasant women went around with 22 karat gold bangles on their wrists. Whenever their maid had some extra cash, she bought another gold bangle. She had about thirteen of them on her wrist. Gold was considered more precious than money. Besides buying jewelry for herself, Mina bought some to sell in the U.S. They needed money over there while looking for jobs.

Mina and Gary enjoyed themselves tremendously when in Cairo again. They spent their leisurely time going to the sporting clubs and night clubs and meeting friends who were still there. Social life was still quite active and night clubs were a very important feature of night life. Nothing had changed much in that domain since Nasser came into power. Religious Islamist zeal had not yet completely taken hold of the masses. Women were not veiled, and drinking alcohol was allowed in restaurants and nightclubs. The Egyptian high society did not follow the Koran to the letter. Cairo still seemed somewhat like a European city. It had not lost all of its cosmopolitan atmosphere but Mina could feel there was social unrest. The most drastic change being that businesses required that employees work in Arabic. Secretaries scurried to take Arabic lessons to be able to keep their jobs.

Mina had to admit that life was easy in Cairo with everything being done for her by her mom and the maid. She had no housework to take care of. But then, a little voice in her head told her she would have many more opportunities of making something of herself in the U.S. Did she not want to have her own business as a designer? Did she not want to be an artist? A world-known artist and not just a local Egyptian one?

She quickly brushed aside all the negative little voices that were nagging her and looked forward to a life with new horizons and, to achieve that, they had to go to the States.

THE JOURNEY

What a journey it had been—from Cairo to Beirut, which they considered as a stepping stone to the U.S.—two years in the "*m'as-tu-vu*" (did you see me) society and unfamiliar surroundings to which they adapted quickly. Different culture, different people, different dialect of the Arabic language. Luckily, they assimilated fast though and made some good friends.

However, it was now 1958, and Lebanon did not appear that safe and rumblings of a start of a civil war was gaining momentum. Mina hated doomsday prophecies though. She went to church and prayed. She realized that she only prayed when she wanted something from God. "That is not being a true Christian," the Sisters at the Franciscan College in Cairo had said.

"You have to pray to God every day, thanking him for your good fortune," they preached.

"What about bad fortune?" Mina asked them.

She got a stern look from the Sister of the class and she probed no further. She could never argue with the Sisters. They always had the final say in the matter.

After calling home to say final goodbyes to their respective families, they were on their way from Beirut to Naples first. It was Mina's first sea voyage. Her heart was beating like a hammer. She could not believe that she was finally making the journey to the U.S. where a new and exciting life awaited her. She knew her past and her present but the future was full of question marks. A lot of 'what if's'. As she was going up the gangplank, she feared the onset of a new bout of anxiety. She hoped she would not have a panic attack while on board. She was prone to having those. She took deep breaths to assuage her fears. Her mother had taught her to do that in time of crisis. And lots of crises they had had. She concentrated on what an incredible life she was going to have. They had lived three years in Beirut and now they were finally on their way to the U.S. Her impossible dream was coming true. She was optimistic about the future and was adamant to make good things happen to her.

They stayed in Naples a couple of days and gorged themselves with pizza. Mina felt a little out of place in a foreign country where people did not speak English, French or Arabic and she had some minor anxiety attacks. Gary had no such feelings. For him, everything was good. She took solace from Gary's comforting words. They were disappointed at Naples, however. It was the first European city they had ever seen. It was dirty and people were not well dressed like those in the trendy streets of Cairo and Beirut.

Naples is not my final destination so who the hell cares what it's like, thought Mina. They were careful not to get robbed as they had heard of quite a few purse snatching incidents in this city. They had also heard about being given the wrong change as they were unfamiliar with the Italian lira. Of course, they also knew about the Mafia.

Finally, their Naples stay was over and they boarded the Andrea Doria, a large Italian ocean liner bound for New York.

To economize, they had chosen to buy tickets for cabins below deck, in third class, which housed four people to a cabin. They could not share a cabin together. To do that they would have to be in second class but that was above their budget. Gary was with three other men near the engine rooms and Mina shared a cabin, on one floor above, with three other women. She felt as though she was in a dorm with the exception that her roommates were all older women and they snored. It was very depressing to be below deck, without any portholes. Mina had claustrophobia being cooped up in her cabin. The anxiety that tore at her for leaving Cairo and now Beirut, was overwhelming. She was sad and happy at the same time. Was she ever going to see Cairo and her family again? She gave herself a mental boost.

Their trip on the ocean liner was uneventful except for meeting an elderly American couple who taught them how to play Canasta. From then on, Canasta became their favorite card game. The food in third class was ghastly and, in any case, Mina could hardly eat because she was sea sick most of the time. They could hear the engines day and night in their cabins. Mina spent most of her time on deck wrapped up in a blanket to keep warm.

"I swear I will travel first class one of these years," she told Gary. "As soon as I make some money in the U.S. I will take an extended European vacation. I have not seen Europe except for Napoli, and that does not count."

"Don't set your sites so high, Cabin class will do also."

Mina was always a day dreamer, while Gary was more pragmatic.

Passing the strait of Gibraltar was quite a wonderful experience, seeing the splendid Spanish and Moroccan coasts on each side. Mina could see part of the Atlas Mountains in Morocco as they were passing through the strait, and the southernmost tip of Spain, Tarifa, an Arab coastal town. Morocco. That was another place on her agenda that she would explore after she made her fortune. Gary took dozens of photos.

NEW YORK

When they saw the Statue of Liberty on arrival in New York harbor, they were awestruck and happy to have finally made it. It was a balmy, breezy afternoon in September.

The ship docked at the harbor and there were hundreds of people waving to their friends and relatives. They had nobody to greet them.

They went through customs without a hitch and, lugging their umpteen suitcases, they took a taxi and landed in a cheap hotel on 34th street in Manhattan. Mina had one look at the room and she wanted to take the first plane back to Cairo. Gary was more relaxed and pacified her saying it was only for a week or so, until they could find an apartment and jobs.

Gary called a few people he knew from Cairo to get acclimatized to the terrain. One of his friends told him that it would be cheaper to live in New Jersey rather than look for lodgings in Manhattan which was super expensive.

After about a week in the cheap hotel, they finally found a two-bedroom apartment in the town of West New York, New Jersey, overlooking the Hudson River and the Manhattan skyline which turned to gold at sunset. Mina hoped her pockets would be filled with gold soon after.

The apartment had one bathroom and the second bedroom was tiny. Margie installed her painting studio in there.

"This will be the guest room, don't forget that," Gary told her. "So, don't mess it up too much."

"What guests are you talking about? We hardly know a soul in the U.S."

"Well, there is my uncle."

"Your uncle is quite wealthy and can afford to go to a hotel rather than stay in a tiny room without TV and sharing our bathroom."

After her comment, Gary did not bring up the guest issue anymore.

They had a few contacts in New York and one of them was the famous Armenian jeweler, Onnig from Cairo, who dealt with diamond dealers and jewelry makers in Manhattan. Gary quickly found a job through his connections on 47th Street in Manhattan where all the jewelers and gem dealers were located. They were both relieved. At least there would be some money coming in and they could now apply for permanent residence permits.

As Mina was fluent in both English and French, she soon found a job with the United Nations. Her job was boring but it got her permanent residence papers and she met some interesting people. The working environment was not that great. A lot of envy and back-stabbing from Latina secretaries. Mina knew how to take care of herself though and the bullying in the office did not bother her. What she liked most about her job was meeting foreign diplomats from all over the world. Some of them hit on her but she just flirted with them. This job was a beginning for her. She was hopeful to become a fashion designer later on. Being a model had gone down the drain thanks to Gary's opposition, although she had the figure for it.

Now, her real life began in the city of her dreams.

Speculating on her future as an artist, model, fashion designer, or actress, she started making nebulous plans in this most vibrant city in the U.S. Her first reaction to Manhattan was not encouraging, though.

"I really don't like all these skyscrapers and the crowds in the streets," said Mina.

"Well, you wanted to be in a big city. You can't have bigger than this. You'll get used to it," was Gary's response.

During the first few weeks their time was mostly spent with furnishing their two-bedroom apartment and going to the movies. They could not do without the movies. They also found a fantastic night club to go to on Saturday nights. It was called Chateau Madrid in midtown Manhattan, where the music was non-stop. They took up their favorite pastime—dancing. There were always good Cuban bands playing Latin American dance tunes which they both adored. There was quite a large Cuban population in New York—all escapees from the Castro regime and Cuban music was the thing in those days. They also saw a couple of flamenco shows which they put into practice in their repertoire.

All in all, Mina and Gary were happy and they soon made a few friends. Although Mina was working as a secretary, she had not given up on her aspirations. She had to make them happen, somehow. As modelling was a no, no as far as Gary was concerned—"you show off yourself strutting down a runway, which is hardly becoming for a young married woman," she wanted to take up acting. Gary was against that too. He thought all actresses got famous on the couch.

Mina felt constrained by Gary, who had become a control freak since they left Egypt. He had these tendencies in Cairo but Mina thought, once they were in a much more liberal society, he would change. Alas, she realized he had become worse.

Mina was very much into art. She visited museums and galleries whenever she had the time. Sometimes Gary accompanied her but, more often than not, she went by herself. She preferred it that way. She felt free to linger wherever she liked. Gary was always in a hurry to end a gallery visit.

"Come on, we've seen everything, why are you lingering?" he said impatiently.

"I would like to talk to the gallery owner, do you mind?"

Mina, therefore preferred to do the rounds on her own and take her time.

At this point in time she started to dislike Gary. Everything he did or said got on her nerves. She wanted to make her life more pleasurable and her marriage to work better but she did not know how. One thing she was sure of. She was no longer attracted to Gary and that was a big problem. She started faking in bed. A dissatisfaction had gotten hold of Mina and she was adamant to find a way to ameliorate her life. She also realized that they were fighting a lot again—over minor issues. Gary always flew off the handle at the slightest provocation.

Mina wanted more out of life. First of all, she did not have job satisfaction at the U.N. Being a secretary was not glamorous. It was being subservient. The memos she typed were boring beyond-belief. Sometimes she felt like a robot.

Secondly, she was looking for passion in her marriage. She had a nagging feeling inside her gut. *This man is not for you,* the little voice inside her head told her. She did not know how to make her life more pleasurable. They had few friends in this big city, and they rarely went out, except to the movies once a week and dancing on Saturday nights. That was the only time that Gary did not pick a fight. He was too busy watching the movie and too engrossed in the dancing. That part of her marriage was good but you can't dance the days away nor can you watch movies all day long.

Gazing out of the window, after Gary left, Mina realized that a big chunk of her youth had evaporated by being married to Gary. Volatile youth never again to return. No, she was not going to be the victim of circumstances. She had done the right thing in breaking up with Gary—for good. There was no going back this time. *I have to start thinking about divorce now,* Mina thought.

GARY

Gary felt something was wrong with Mina but did not know what exactly. He did realize that they were no longer having fun, that perhaps Mina did not love him anymore. He did love Mina but he did not like her rebellious side. He wanted her to be more docile. They were working hard and making good money but she did not seem to be satisfied. She looked unhappy. And, to top it all, she was not giving him sex when he wanted it.

He thought the problem stemmed from the fact that they did not have the easy-going ambiance of their lives in Egypt. Here in the U.S., it was all work and more work—money and more money. Well, they had both decided on coming here to make a new life but they soon realized it was no paradise. They were too young for marriage perhaps and were not ready to make sacrifices.

Grievances accumulated and this is when they had the big fight and Gary stormed out of the apartment, leaving Mina alone. He wondered how she would make out without him. They had one separation during their marriage and this one seemed a final one. They could not possibly have one separation after another. There was also the question of children. Mina categorically refused to have any. Gary thought she might settle down if they had a child or two. "I want a career, I don't want to be bogged down with children," she always said when the subject came up. They had not sat down and talked things over like a normal couple. Well, if there ever is a normal couple, Gary pondered.

LIFE WITHOUT GARY

Mina switched her brain to the present after reminiscing about her past for a long time.

When Gary left, Mina looked all over Manhattan for a suitable and affordable place. She found one apartment but she had to share the bedroom—a huge bedroom—with three other girls, all airline hostesses. They each would have a bed and a dresser and share the walk-in closet. Although they would hardly be in the apartment all together, as the hostesses would be flying at different intervals, Mina thought it would be too cramped and she did not like being in an all-girlie atmosphere. The bathroom would never be free and it would be a mess, full of clutter. Also, she could not bring her cat over in a crowded apartment. Finally, she rented a room in the home of an elderly woman, Mrs Pastore, who accepted the cat. This suited Mina fine because Mrs. Pastore was very accommodating and allowed her the use of the whole house and the kitchen.

"You can bring men friends over, if you like," she said with a chuckle, "but you can't go in the bedroom with them."

What men friends? She had not met any yet. Where would she meet them anyway? Most of the U.N. diplomats were married and she had a strict rule not to mingle with any man from the Office. It would be awkward.

The first week away from Gary, Mina felt rather lonely. She wondered whether she had done the right thing in shooing Gary away definitively. It was the first time in her life that she was alone, really alone.

She was in Manhattan, one of the liveliest cities in the world, with no husband and no family to enjoy it with. Not that she was doing much enjoying with Gary aside from their once-a- week movies and dancing. Well Gary was gone now and she had to survive. She was adamant to make a go of it. She wrote a long letter back home giving them the details of the break-up.

Mina analyzed her feelings. Did she feel relief? Did she feel scared? Did she feel capable to live as a free woman?

"You know Mina, you should not treat your boyfriend in that manner," her mom always told her when she was being impatient with Gary. "Men don't like independent women. And, in any case, you can't be independent in this country."

"That's ridiculous. I'm no one's belonging. I have my own opinion of things. This is my life and nobody else should govern it but me."

Another thing Mina hated was preparing food for one person only and eating alone. That is what she did in Mrs. Pastore's apartment. She was not a TV person so all she did in the evenings is paint and read. She did small paintings because she did not have a proper studio. Not having space for painting frustrated her.

Mina thought about the past a lot. Now she had to stop and think about her future. She was quite content living with Mrs. Pastore as she had all the freedom she wanted in the apartment. Mrs. Pastore was a curious old bird though, and she wanted to know every detail of Mina's life. Mina did not mind relating anecdotes from her life to her and taking advice.

RIFAAT

When Mina was working as secretary at the United Nations, she met a few fellows who asked her out. One of them was Rifaat. He was an Egyptian official assigned to the Middle East Department. She met him at the cafeteria. They shared the same table and started conversing. He was taken in by Mina, especially when he found out that she was an Armenian from Cairo.

"I had quite a few Armenian friends from the American University in Cairo," he said, and he mentioned a few names. Mina recognized only one name as he frequented the Armenian Social Club in Heliopolis.

Rifaat was a big guy, a pleasant and fun fellow, well-educated and quite wealthy. He wined and dined her which was fine with her, but there were no sparks flying around. He was a Muslim and she was a Christian, but religion did not matter that much to Mina if the person was not a practicing Muslim. And, Rifaat was not. Nor was she. She rarely went to church. However, she did not see any future with him. She knew very well that Middle Eastern men were the controlling type and Mina could definitely not be controlled. Even living abroad did not really change the mentality of the Middle Eastern man. It was inbred. Gary was an example.

Rifaat came to her office one day and seemed eager to talk to her. He asked her to have coffee with him in the Cafeteria.

"What's the rush? What's the matter?" Mina inquired.

"I have something to tell you," is all he said.

After getting their coffees and were sitting down at a table, Rifaat looked at Mina and took both her hands in his. He then proposed to her right there and then, telling her he could see little Rifaats running around them.

This is crazy. He can already see the children we will have even before we are engaged and he has taken me to bed, Mina thought and laughed to herself. Rifaat seemed rather serious and sincere about the proposal and Mina was taken aback. She had acted quite virginal with him and had refused any serious petting. Having lived in Egypt, a Muslim country, she knew that Muslim guys do not respect girls who are forward, not that she ever was with anyone—not even with Gary. Girls who succumbed easily were taken for granted and discarded. Middle Eastern men wanted "pure, untainted" girls. Well, she had been married so there was no question of her being pure.

"Oh, Rifaat," she said. "I'm not ready to get married. I'm not even divorced yet."

"I'll wait, it should not take that long," he said looking at her with doleful brown eyes.

"Please don't do that, I am planning on going to Europe in a couple of months to look for a job there," she lied on an impulse. She did not wish to hurt his feelings by telling him that marriage to him would be out of the question. After all, he was a nice guy and he had been very respectful in their relationship.

Rifaat's face fell. She could see the disappointment in his eyes but there was nothing more to say. Mina pitied him but there was no way she could console him. The relationship ended before it had even started.

Their coffee encounters were never the same after that.

VAKO

A couple of weeks later, Mina received a phone call from an old friend from Lebanon. He had also gone there from Egypt with the hope of ending up in the United States. He had just arrived in New York.

"How are you, guys?" Vako asked when Mina answered the phone.

"Fine, Vako, what a nice surprise. When did you arrive?"

"A couple of days ago and I got your phone number from Onnig."

"Did he tell you that Gary and I are separated?"

"No, he did not. What happened? I thought that was a match made to last forever. You guys went through a lot of trouble before you got married, with the opposition from his parents and all that."

"Yeah, I know, but things happen."

"I'm sorry to hear that. Do you want to tell me about it?"

"Not particularly."

"Do you want to go out for dinner tomorrow," he then asked.

"But, I'm not yet divorced," she told him.

"So what, you are no longer living with your husband so it would be okay. Don't worry, nobody is going to talk behind your back. In any case, we are no longer in Cairo, and there is no one around to talk badly about you. This is just a dinner."

Vako was a most ikeable fellow, average height and weight with a joyful personality. He was just an ordinary looking guy and he had never been married. He was about six years older than Mina.

Mina agreed to have dinner with him. He came to pick her up in a rented car. The restaurant was a Middle Eastern one and the food was excellent and his company, amusing. She had liked him in Cairo and she liked him now. They mostly talked about Armenians who were leaving Egypt and the latest news from Cairo.

"What are your plans?" Mina asked him.

"I think I will make my way to San Francisco. A friend wants me to go into business with him, the tile business. Seems it's quite lucrative. I know nothing about it, but I can learn. I am a fast learner. And, what about you?"

"I don't know yet. I am thinking about my future very very seriously."

Mina enjoyed Vako's company. She had a great sense of perception and she realized that he was attracted to her but did not know how to handle it. She was not prepared to make it easier for him.

"Would you like to go dancing?" Vako asked her when the dinner was over and they were leaving the restaurant. Vako was known to be a good tango dancer.

"No, not tonight. I'm rather tired. Perhaps another time, if you're still around."

In the car, he kept looking at her and touched her hand. She did not withdraw it. It would be rude. She liked his company and wondered whether he was going to ask her out again. Upon parting, he leaned over and planted a moist kiss on her lips. She was taken aback but it felt nice. Being kissed by other men was a strange feeling for her. Rifaat and now Vako. She started comparing them to Gary. Not much difference there. As she had been only with Gary up to now, she did not know how to handle amorous relationships.

They had a few lunches, dinners and movies and each time they got closer until finally Mina ended up in his apartment and, not surprisingly, she had sex with him. The first time with another man. It was quite pleasurable. They were together for a whole month. He was supposed to move to San Francisco soon, so Mina did not take things too seriously. It was just an adventure for her—trying another man in bed. He started to get quite romantic during the last week or so before his departure. Then, bam, during an amorous interlude in his bed, he asked her to marry him. She did not see this coming. She had in no way shown any love towards him and he had not told her he loved her.

"Vako! You can't be serious."

But he was serious. All she had to do was look into his earnest eyes.

"You must have realized that I love you, although I didn't come out and say it out loud," he said.

"I can't jump from one marriage to another so quickly," Mina told him. "I need some space, I would like to breathe a little. After all, I have been with Gary for such a long time."

"What are you going to breathe? You can still breathe while being married to me." They both chuckled then.

"In any case, I have not yet started divorce proceedings. This is too soon for me."

"I imagine in this country that would not be a problem."

Mina did not know how to respond. She did like Vako. In fact, she liked him a lot but not enough to get married to him. She also hoped that, while being semi-free from Gary, she would meet other fellows and expand her horizon for comparison purposes. She had to have some experience with men before plunging into yet another marriage. The sex was good but that was not the only criterion for a marriage. She was looking for fireworks. Neither Rifaat nor Vako had produced any sparks.

Before Vako left for San Francisco, he asked her again and again but Mina told him it was too soon. They wrote to each other quite often and sometimes he called. He reiterated his love for her in every letter and always asked about her intention vis a vis his proposal.

It had been four months since Vako left and Mina was planning on going to Europe to investigate life over there. She finally told him her plans and also told him, very gently, that marriage was on the back burner for the time being.

"Maybe, I could come with you," Vako suggested in a phone call.

Mina nearly panicked. That is not what she wanted. She had wanted to put more distance between them. She disliked clinging men. "You have a good job where you are; why on earth would you want to come to Europe?" she asked.

"To be with you, you dopey," he said.

Mina wanted to buy some time before definitely refusing his offer of coming over, but she didn't want to be her usual blunt self. She didn't want to hurt his feelings. He was a nice guy, after all.

"Be patient. I'll let you know how I get along. No need for you to follow me yet."

Time passed and Mina became more and more non-committal in her letters. He finally understood that she was reluctant to pursue the issue of marriage any further and he gave up asking her about her intentions. They still corresponded sporadically and remained good friends. Mina had told Vako that she was going to Europe but she had not made any specific plans just yet. This was just a tactic on her part to distance him.

ROBERT

Mina was more or less satisfied with her social life. After Vako's departure, Rifaat also went away. He had been called back to Egypt for another assignment. He sent her postcards now and again, asking about her prospects. Mina did not divulge much in her replies.

Mina met a few other guys at work—nothing extraordinary. They were quite young, eager and hot and bothered. She preferred older, worldly and more suave men. She also went to a few parties but most guys got drunk and tried to rub themselves against the girls. That was not Mina's scene. She no longer accepted party invitations after a couple of disappointing experiences.

There was one guy at the office that she really liked. His name was Robert. He had never been married and he was already 41 years old. *He must be very choosy,* Mina thought. Robert was a journalist, covering U.N. affairs. He had a quirky sense of humor which she appreciated tremendously. He was not a heartthrob in the looks department but he made up for it with his humor. He made her laugh and she needed that badly. She had heard somewhere that women fall for men who make them laugh. That did not happen to Mina. She liked him but did not fall for him.

After a few dinner dates, Mina invited him to her place for an after-dinner drink. Actually, he expressed the desire to be invited. All they had done up to then, were a few chaste kisses on the cheeks in the car while saying goodnight. He had looked at her lustily, though, with those droopy grey eyes of his.

Mina wondered what Robert's next move would be. She knew something was bound to happen soon. When he came over, they sat on a couch in the living room and exchanged pleasantries. At one point, Robert got hot, hot in his suit. So, he took off his jacket and moved closer to Mina. She suspected what was about to happen next. The first real kiss. It was pleasurable but it did not get out of hand, although Robert was making moves towards more intimacy, trying to touch her boobs and saying such things like, "you smell divine, show me your bedroom."

She laughed and said Mrs. Pastore would find out and she did not want to trespass on her kindness. Mrs. Pastore had said, "no men in the bedroom."

"Okay then, how about lying down the couch," Robert came out with.

"You're kidding me, right?"

"No, I'm not. I don't think your landlady would hear us. Her bedroom is on the other side."

"Absolutely not," Mina said and drew away from him.

"You're so sexy and attractive and I've got an unquenchable desire to make love to you," he said.

"We hardly know each other."

"What I know is enough. Are you playing hard to get?"

"No, of course not. I don't play games. I just don't feel at ease, that's all."

Robert was good natured and, lucky for Mina, he did not insist.

However, the next time they went out to dinner, he took her to his place. He had a one-bedroom apartment on a high floor in the upper East Side. It was minimally furnished and looked pristine. After they had an after-dinner drink of a Vodka liqueur, Mina did not refuse his advances this time and the inevitable happened. She enjoyed the lovemaking. She wondered whether she would fall in love with him. This was not love at first sight. It was just a pleasurable sexual interlude. She started to compare the three men—Gary, Vako and Robert. Many more sessions followed in the bedroom. Robert was not overwhelmingly better than the other two in that department. *Would there ever be a man overwhelmingly better?* she wondered.

A few times Robert came out with "you're adorable, I can't get enough of you," which boosted her ego.

Mina was bored working at the U.N. All this secretarial stuff was not for her. She tried to get a designing job but she was unsuccessful. She decided to take a break and visit her family in Cairo so she asked her boss for a lengthy vacation period. One of the perks of working at the U.N. was the lengthy vacation time. Three weeks was her due, as she had only worked for six months. She made a request for a few weeks more without pay.

Her boss was rather a dour individual and a workaholic. "It is out of the question," he told her, emphatically.

"Give me at least another week, unpaid. I'm going all the way to Egypt. I have not seen my family in ages," she implored.

"I can't allow that. This is a busy conference season and we are short of secretaries."

"I'll quit then," Mina said impulsively and gave her notice. This was the second time she was being so resolute in her life. She was beginning to enjoy her independent streak.

She could easily get another job on her return. No big deal. Secretarial jobs were a dime a dozen. She still had hopes of landing a fashion design position on her return, though. She had to concentrate on that seriously.

The next time Mina saw Robert, while they were having dinner in an Afghan restaurant, she told him about her plans of going to Egypt.

"Oh shucks. When did you decide that? Isn't this too sudden?"

"No, it's not. I miss my family and I've been thinking about this trip a lot lately but I just didn't know how I would manage it."

"How long will you be gone?"

"A few weeks or until such time as I get bored over there. I gave notice at work, so there is no absolute necessity to return at a specified date."

"I hope you won't forget me, babe."

"Why, Robert, I would never do that," she said flirtatiously.

"I am sure you will meet some hunks and 'goodbye Robert' it will be."

"I'm keeping my room, so I will play it by ear. I'm so homesick. I am dying to see Cairo and my family again. I will also pass by Beirut to see my older sister and brother, of course. I'll write."

"You better write, babe. I have your photo in my wallet and I will certainly not forget you. You'll always be on my mind. Are you planning on getting a divorce in Egypt?"

"Won't have time. I'll deal with that on my return."

"It better be soon. Can't stay away from you for a long period."

"Robby, I'm not disappearing, you know. I'll be back soon."

They had one last session in bed before his departure.

That was that.

She was flying away from all her men. She had no intention of settling down yet. They were nice guys but they did not make her swoon over them. And she wanted to have that feeling. The only difference was that Robert was very cozy in bed. He had bulk. Vako was a little too thin and Gary, too wiry.

She did not bother calling Gary to inform him of her plans. He had not made any effort to contact her, *so the hell with him*, she thought.

The first thing Mina did was send her cat over to Cairo. He would be better off over there keeping Mickey, their other cat, company. She did not want to leave him in New York with a friend or in a shelter.

She then made detailed plans for her trip but she had no clear vision of what she would do on her return to Manhattan.

She took two suitcases packed with her clothes and gifts. She also packed up her recording machine, her favorite item. She had always wanted a recorder since she was in Egypt. She had saved money in the U.S. and bought one and she spent time recording herself singing and talking and writing some kind of a journal. She even recorded Robert who was greatly amused speaking into it. He had a melodious voice.

PARIS

Mina's first stopover was Paris, to meet Jeannot and his wife. She knew Jeannot since she was a child. She even had a crush on him when she was fourteen but, when she met Gary, her infatuation disappeared. She considered him like a cousin, now. His uncle had been engaged to her mother but when her mom broke off the engagement because she found out he was a liar, the families stayed friendly. Mina never asked her mom details of her relationship. She was not that much interested in her parents' past lives. Jeannot wrote saying that he would pick her up from the railroad station. She took a cab from the airport to the station at the *Invalides* and waited for him to arrive.

Jeannot was late and Mina felt anxious waiting for him. She wanted to call him but she did not how to use the Paris public telephone system. She needed some change which she did not have. She did not know a soul in Paris. She hoped nothing had happened to him. A car accident or some such thing.

An old man was sitting opposite her in the waiting room. What Mina meant by old was that the man was over fifty. At twenty-six everyone over forty was old for her, even Robert. He struck up a conversation with her and she told him she was waiting for friends to pick her up. He suggested that she go to his place and wait there. Mina was surprised. Did he think she was that naive coming from New York? She refused of course and just then Jeannot and his wife showed up. Jeannot had put on some weight since she had last seen him a few years ago in Cairo. It was the first time she was meeting his wife. She was Dutch and quite pretty. She liked her.

Jeannot proposed that she stay with them on a couch in the living room. No, that would not do. She needed some privacy. They found her a stinky hotel in the Latin Quarter. She didn't have much money and could not afford a swanky place, much as she wanted to. She stayed three days in Paris. The weather was balmy with not a drop of rain. She saw all the touristy sights, went on a boat ride on the Seine, explored the Latin Quarter and the quaint shops, went to the Flea Market where she bought a couple of trinkets for gifts. She loved Paris and wished she were living there. She started to daydream again—her favorite pastime. She told herself to stop her wandering thoughts—one of her many flaws—her life was in New York now. Her family would be coming over eventually. She could not afford to waver at this juncture. Her mother had always admonished her by saying, "you flip flop all the time, girl, make up your mind once and for all, and stay put."

The second night at the hotel, she woke up in the middle of the night feeling some crawly things in her bed. She put on the light and lo and behold, her bed was swarming with four cockroaches, the smaller type, not those big brown ugly things. Nevertheless, she was disgusted. She took off the sheet and the bed cover and shook them over the floor. Then she stomped on them. She realized they were coming from the restaurant right below her room. This was her second experience with cockroaches in hotels. The first was in Alexandria, in a four-star hotel during her honeymoon. She sincerely hoped there would not be a third one. As they say in French, *jamais deux sans trois,* (Never two without three).

Her Paris trip ended and now she was finally on her way to Egypt.

VISIT TO CAIRO

A welcoming group awaited Mina at the airport. Her parents, her sister and a few neighbors. What a heartfelt moment that was. She was almost in tears. Happy tears.

The moment she stepped on Egyptian soil, she felt exhilarated. All that sun—it was blinding. And the smell of jasmine as they drove home. The villas on the road to their house had jasmine plants in their gardens. She was home at last after an absence of three years. Everyone started talking at the same time asking her a million questions in the cab. Actually, they took two cabs. One for people and the other for luggage.

There was also her precious recorder. She had lugged it all the way from New York, then on to Paris and now to Cairo. She had recorded Robert speaking and that was important for her to keep and to have her sister and mom listen to it. She wanted their opinion of him. Also, it would remind her of Robert when she felt lonely in Cairo, not that there would be any chance of that.

The apartment, that she had loved so much and so intensely, had not changed one bit. It had a peculiar odor, the odor of home, the odor of the various live plants her mom liked to have around, and also of home cooking which she had craved since having left. The first thing Mina did was go from room to room to get re-acquainted with them. She was still going to share a bedroom with her sister although there were plenty of other spare bedrooms. They would share the king size bed again as they had done before her marriage to Gary.

Mina was exhausted from talking and stumbled into the bedroom to take a nap. Her mother gave her a belladonna tablet to make her relax. This was the medication given for anxiety in Cairo at that time. She swallowed the pill and she soon fell asleep until she was called for the evening meal.

The family was gathered together in the small dining room anxiously waiting for her to relate the details of her life in New York. There was so much to talk about. She also wanted to know about the family stories and about the cats. Her adored cats. She had missed them so much.

Her mother had prepared all her favorite meals. Lamb Shish Kebab, stuffed grape leaves, garlic-baked potatoes, *mouloukhia* (a special Egyptian soup, made from dark green leaves – a vegetable only grown in Egypt) and to top it all, *baklava* for desert. Home-made *baklava*. Her mother prided herself for being the best *baklava* maker in the whole of Cairo. Mina swallowed several pieces *and the hell with my figure,* she told herself. After dinner, some of the neighbors came by and she had to relate her stories all over again. It was exhausting but it was a lot of fun getting re-acquainted.

Mina waited to be alone with Vera to ask about her love life. It seems she had a Muslim boyfriend from the military who was from a good family and he adored her. Vera told her that, after the takeover by Nasser, Egyptian military guys were all over the hotspots in Cairo. Mina's parents had accepted Fouad, as he was called, in their home because he showed a lot of respect towards them. Vera was still a virgin, of course. There was no way she was going to lose that before getting married, especially not to a guy who would consider her to be used merchandise and discard her on the wayside. Vera told Mina she would introduce her to him soon.

"In fact, we'll go to the Heliopolis Sporting Club tomorrow and you'll meet him. I want to introduce you also to all my friends. We are a fun group," she said, "a mixture of Armenians and foreigners."

"Are there any eligible guys you can introduce me to?" asked Mina.

"Plenty, my dear. Don't worry."

Mina had insomnia that night because of the jet lag and all the excitement of being in Cairo again and also because she had taken such a long nap.

Next day being a Saturday, Vera had no work and they went to the Heliopolis Sporting Club. Mina became a temporary member for the summer. Quite expensive by Egyptian standards, but she had saved enough money to splurge during her homecoming.

Vera introduced Mina to a group of people seated at a table around the swimming pool and also to Fouad, who was a green-eyed, dark haired fellow, with a mustache and quite a bit older than Vera. Mina immediately saw why Fouad appealed to Vera so much. He was handsome, sophisticated, well-mannered and well-dressed. Among the seated group, she recognized one woman, Christine, a distant friend of theirs, who was divorced and who had caused a scandal in Cairo for being a divorcee. After all, she was Armenian and Armenians did not divorce for flaky reasons and it was rumored that her reason had been flaky. She had fallen in love with an Egyptian Military Air Force pilot. The romance had lasted about three months and she was now heartbroken and alone. Everybody seemed to know her story. Nothing could be kept a secret in Armenian circles. It was such close-knit community.

SHOUKRY

The Sporting Club became their hangout to meet friends. On one occasion, Vera pointed out Christine's ex-lover. He was sitting with a group of military guys with their foreign girlfriends. Parents of Muslim girls did not allow any dating in those years. The girls were only permitted to go out with brothers, cousins and other relatives.

"Gosh, Vera, he is so handsome," Mina remarked while scrutinizing him.

"Yup, he breaks the delicate hearts of women."

When he got up to go to the bar, Mina looked him over again. He had an imposing stature, tall, good physique, longish black hair and a prominent aquiline nose. All in all, an exciting-looking man. She almost salivated.

The guy happened to look her way as he was passing their table and their eyes locked.

"Can you introduce me to him?" Mina asked her sister.

"Don't worry, he'll come around."

And indeed, when Mina went in for a swim, he dove into the pool and swam towards her.

"I have not had the pleasure of meeting you," he said with a perfect British accent. *He must have been educated in England,* thought Mina. "My name is Shoukry," he continued.

"I am Mina and am new here. I live in New York now and have come to visit my family in Cairo after being away for about three years."

"Welcome home. How long will you be staying?"

"About a couple of months."

"Do you find Cairo changed at all?"

"Too soon to tell. I just arrived three days ago."

"I can show you around," he volunteered with a smile, showing a perfect set of white teeth.

"Looking forward to that," she said, smiling back. What better way of going around Cairo than being accompanied by a charming and gallant escort. Playboy or no playboy, Mina didn't care. Shoukry was a hunk and she was in Cairo to have fun.

The conversation went on smoothly in between swimming laps. They did not discuss politics. Mina did not wish to get into it, especially with someone from the military. She liked him quite a bit. He had two sisters, both unmarried. His parents were still alive and they all lived together in a big villa in Zamalek—a trendy section of Cairo where most diplomats had their residence. *His family must be wealthy*, thought Mina. The custom in Egypt was that unmarried children—no matter how old—lived at home. The young men usually had a *garçonnière* for their amorous escapades, either on their own or shared with friends. He had gone to school in England and had also attended Sandhurst Military Academy for his military training. *Yes, they must be loaded. I wonder what his father does*, thought Mina. Her question was answered without her asking. He was a General in the Egyptian Army. Shoukry had travelled widely. He did not seem to be religious. Good thing because she couldn't stand religious types, no matter what religion. Religion to her was a private matter. His mother was Italian, born in Cairo. He had the combined look of an Italian playboy with a Middle Eastern twist.

Shoukry set a date to take her out to lunch at the Pyramids on the Saturday next. He had some time off that day. When Mina told her mother about the date, her mother flipped.

"You can't possibly go out with him," she said.

"Why is that?"

"Because he was Christine's lover."

"And so?"

"What is she going to think?"

"He is no longer her lover, so what does her thinking got to do with anything?"

"It is simply not appropriate. You know Christine well and it will be an affront to her. She will feel humiliated."

"Nonsense. They are not together anymore. I am going to go out with him and you can't prevent me. After all, I am a married woman, well, separated, and on the verge of divorce, may I remind you."

"Don't come crying to me if people start talking badly of you."

"You know very well I don't give a hoot about what people say about me. I'll do as I please."

"You have always been the rebellious type and look where it got you. Married to Gary, because you were so much in love, and now you want out."

Mina left the room at that point. It was no use having an argument with her mother.

She went to the club every day to swim and meet her friends. It was within walking distance. She did not need a car. Her father did not own one either. Few people had cars in Cairo in those days. They went walking everywhere or took a cab if it was too far. Cabs were cheap. And to go from Heliopolis to Cairo, there was the fast, above-ground Metro.

Shoukry came to pick her up for lunch on Saturday. Mina opened the door herself before the maid could get to it. He was dressed casually in khaki pants and a pale blue linen shirt, open a couple of buttons, showing some chest hair. Mina liked that. She detested guys who shaved their chests. They looked too sleek. Shoukry looked good with his shiny black hair combed back and a stubble on his chin. He looked all male.

"You look ravishing," he said sizing her up and down and gave her a peck on her cheek. She felt a little blush coming to her cheeks. She was wearing a short jeans skirt and a fun T-Shirt with the word *Sauvage* printed on it in gold lettering.

"Are you really *sauvage?*" he asked with a grin.

"For you to find out," is all she said.

She had a whiff of a faint after shave when he was close to her. It was quite agreeable and she wanted more. She followed him down the stairs of the building and discreetly checked to see if any of the neighbors was by any chance in the balcony watching the goings on in the street. She did not see anyone. Good. His car was a yellow Triumph Sports car. He opened the door for her and it was rather difficult to maneuver getting in it as her skirt was too tight. Had she known he had a frigging low-seating sports car, she would have worn a loose skirt. Her skirt rose way above her thighs in her sitting position and she saw, from the corner of her eye, that he was gazing at her thighs—discreetly and perhaps lasciviously—or was it her imagination? Luckily, they were tanned.

It was quite a long drive to the open-air restaurant of the Mena House Hotel at the foot of the Pyramids. Almost everything was open-air in Cairo.

The Mena House was a beautiful hotel built in the latter part of the past century. It had been frequented by royalty mostly from England. Mina had often gone to the night club of the hotel with Gary. She loved the atmosphere. So old world. She put Gary out of her mind and concentrated on Shoukry. He was a charming companion. Masculine to the bone with an overpowering virility. She liked that. She liked that a lot and she listened attentively to his conversation, while looking at his sculpted lips and his stubble. Mina was fixated on them. She was happy she had found a suitable escort during her stay in Cairo and did not think any further. She hoped that he would indeed be her escort during her whole stay. A little voice inside her was interrupting his conversation.

I really like this guy, I hope I'm not falling for him.

"You are somewhere else," he said interrupting her thoughts.

"Oh, sorry, I was thinking of how I shall occupy myself while I'm in Cairo."

"Don't worry. I'll take care of that," he said with a grin.

"You can't do that, you're working, aren't you?"

"I can manage."

So, he was all set to be her *chevalier servant* (attentive escort). She was carried away with euphoria at the thought of being escorted by Shoukry all over town. Her mother would not be too happy to hear that, she thought. *Tant pis.* (No matter).

They ordered lamb chops, rice pilaf, salad and Stella beer. The Belgian beer was the most popular in Egypt. It was made in Cairo now.

It always made her a teeny bit tipsy and she was careful not to go into one of her flirtatious modes. Not yet, anyway.

Lunch was over all too soon and it was time to return home. He dropped her off at her doorstep, kissing her on both cheeks and told her he would call the next day to plan some outings. She liked the feel of his lips. They were warm and sensual.

When she got home, her mother looked at her inquisitively. Mina did not volunteer any information. Vera took her aside to learn the details of her lunch with Shoukry.

Mina told Vera that he fascinated her.

"I have not met anyone like him before. He is so masculine and sexy. He has a lot of charisma."

"Are you falling for him?"

"No, of course not," she lied.

"Then why do you have this dreamy expression on your face and in your eyes when you talk about him?"

"I certainly do not. I find him an extremely pleasant escort, with a car and money to take me around Cairo."

"Anyway, just be careful and think before acting which, I know, is quite difficult for you to do. You're so impulsive, you jump into situations without thinking ahead."

"That, my dear sister, is better than sitting on your ass, waiting for things to happen."

"Christine will be livid when she finds out that you have taken over her man friend. You see, he left her and not vice versa. She had plans of marrying him but I heard from a very good source that he had no such intention. I don't think he is the marrying kind so watch out, don't have any such inclinations," advised Vera. "From what I have heard, he is the eternal bachelor."

"For God's sake, I'm in Cairo for two months to have fun. I am not even divorced and I have Robert back home waiting for me. Shoukry will just be another amusing episode in my life, a summer romance."

"I don't think so. He's going to be more than just an episode, you watch and see."

The whole family went to the movies that evening and saw Witness for the Prosecution with Tyrone Power and Marlene Dietrich. Mina thought Shoukry looked a little like Tyrone Power, one of her preferred actors, except for his nose.

Shoukry called her every day and took her out whenever he was free. He was extremely courteous when he met her parents and they liked him. They even invited him home for tea—English type tea.

Vera then came out and told their parents that she was also going out with an Egyptian Muslim military guy and she invited Fouad over to the house to meet the parents. They also liked him but they were still quite apprehensive of their daughters' relationships with these two local military guys. It could be dangerous.

"What the hell is the matter with you girls? Aren't there enough Christian fellows around?" asked their mother. "Not that I have anything against these guys or their religion. After all we worship the same God. The rest is all ritual. They act like perfect gentlemen. Watch the neighbors, though, there will be some malicious talk. I heard from Eva upstairs that our dear relative downstairs is bad-mouthing you. You better watch your reputation, especially you Vera. You live in Cairo, don't forget. Your sister will be going away and gossip does not matter that much to her."

At that moment, Mina had a thought. *Could I stay on in Cairo and marry this guy?* Her mind was going around in circles. She was infatuated by Shoukry big time but she had some doubts about the fidelity issue. He was known to be a playboy and she didn't want to be another of his playthings. And yet, she could still envisage being married to him. He was so exciting. She didn't think she'd ever be bored with him.

When Vera was alone with Mina, they commiserated.

"I think Shoukry could very well transplant Robert. *Loin des yeux, loin du coeur,* as they say in French (away from sight, away from the heart)," Vera told her.

"Don't be silly," retorted Mina. Shoukry is Middle Eastern although his mother is Italian but he was brought up in Egypt. He may very well be modern-minded, but he is an Egyptian military man and some beliefs are encrusted solidly in the minds of Middle Eastern men, especially, preconceived beliefs about women— obedience, virginity, dependence, to name a few. Of course, the virginity issue would not refer to me as I have been married.

One question bothered her, though. What did Middle Eastern men think of divorced women? Did they think they were easy lays?

Mina had no time to think about Robert who wrote to her quite frequently asking her whether she was getting her divorce in Cairo and whether she missed him. She wrote back telling him that she had no time for divorce and of course, she missed him, which was not true with Shoukry being in the picture now. She was very much preoccupied with Shoukry.

Shoukry escorted her all over Cairo, going to the movies, dancing in all the favorite places that she had gone with Gary. The Italian bands were still performing in Cairo and she enjoyed herself tremendously. Dancing close to him, was absolute heaven. She liked the feel of his muscular body and the heat emanating from it. There were several smooching sessions in the car, some of them quite hot but Mina could handle them. Shoukry was always the gentleman. He did not force her to do anything against her wish and he did not go too far, although she wanted to. But she had to be careful how to act with him.

A couple of weeks later Shoukry told her that he had to go away for two weeks for some military training somewhere which he did not disclose. She did not insist in asking him the whereabouts. It seemed to be top secret. She was thus left alone without an escort. On the third day after his departure, while she was sitting at the edge of the pool at the Heliopolis Sporting Club, a fellow came up to her, said hello and introduced himself.

"Hello, I am Jose. You must be new here. I have not seen you before."

"I'm Mina. Yes, I am new but I am originally from Cairo."

They chatted for a while then Jose invited her to lunch. He was a Palestinian Christian, the son of the owners of the King David Hotel in Jerusalem before the Israeli take-over. When an Israeli terrorist organization had bombed the hotel in 1946, where the British had their headquarters, he had been taken out at the nick of time by relatives.

His parents had perished. Jose was quite an affable fellow but nothing to write home about. After Shoukry, no one appealed to her that much. Shoukry overshadowed all the men she had met up to now.

Jose invited her to go out with his group of friends and she accepted. They were mostly Palestinians living in Egypt. At one party, Mina got attracted to a medical student who was going to Miami for his medical degree. He happened to be the water-skiing champion of Egypt. The problem was that Vera was also attracted to him, and Mina did not want to be in competition with her sister, so she ignored him. He persisted on dancing with her, nevertheless. She did not encourage him one bit. It was only one evening. No big deal. Her sister could have him. Also, she had Shoukry to deal with and waited eagerly for his return.

The two weeks were over and Shoukry returned from his military training. The reunion was hot, in the car. Mina knew that it all depended on her whether they would ever advance further in that domain. He did not insist in any way. He had self-restraint and she was surprised.

"We're having a big party for *Eid Al Adha*," (a Muslim feast celebrating Abraham's sacrifice of his son to God), Shoukry told her the next day. "I am inviting about thirty people in my apartment."

"At your mother's?" asked Mina incredulously.

"No, of course not. In another apartment."

"You mean in your *garçonnière*?" Mina said with a quizzical smile.

Shoukry did not reply.

"Come on now, Shoukry, I know very well that almost all Mediterranean men who live at home—and most unmarried men do live at home—have a secondary apartment to carry on their amorous adventures."

Shoukry then laughed out loud.

"You know quite a bit about men, I see."

"I wasn't born yesterday."

Mina was finally going to meet Shoukry's friends. She wanted to make a good impression and got dressed to her teeth in a billowing pale blue organza dress which she had made back in New York. She put on high-heeled silver pumps, and a phony red rose in her hair. She also doused herself with "Je Reviens," her favorite scent and she was ready for the event. She was giddy with excitement.

"Wow," said Shoukry when he came to pick her up. "You look absolutely stunning. My friends will be envious of me." He drew her close to plant a kiss on her cheek. "And, you smell divine." She could feel the heat emanating from his body. She yearned for more.

Shoukry's friends were mostly army and air force officers with their foreign girlfriends or wives. The apartment was on the top floor of a building overlooking the Nile. The view was stupendous. The veranda was set up with a bar with all kinds of drinks. Upper-class Muslims were not averse to drinking liquor. It seemed to Mina that the Koran's rules only applied to the poor who followed them blindly. Also, the upper-class Egyptians did not take more than one wife.

The Hi-Fi blasted away with all the contemporary tunes and Mina was the center of attention. She only danced with Shoukry. He was such a good dancer, holding her close and moving smoothly to the rhythm. She surrendered her whole body to his strong, embracing arms and his stubble grazing her cheek excited her. She imagined them lying in bed with his stubble all over her body.

At about 3 am, when all the guests were gone, she wanted to help clean up.

"Don't lift a finger. The maid will take care of everything tomorrow. Come here," Shoukry said and took her by the hand.

For a moment, Mina thought he would guide her to the bedroom and her heart skipped a beat and she froze in her tracks. No, he did not do that. He took her to the balcony and they sat on a two-seater rattan sofa with plump pillows. The evening breeze was mild and the sky, a dark ultramarine. No stars. Their eyes probed each other. Shoukry then put his arm around her, turned her face around and kissed her passionately. Mina was tingling all over and the beat of her heart thundered in her ears. She hoped he could not hear it. Things progressed rapidly from then. The atmosphere got very hot indeed as Shoukry was kissing her and trying to fondle one of her boobs, but Mina stopped him.

"Shoukry, I'm not going to bed with you," she said.

"Did I ask you?"

"Why on earth are we in your *garçonnière*, then? The party has ended and it is time to take me home. I have no intention of being one of your many conquests."

"I'll take you home," Shoukry then said and rose up from the couch extending his hand to her. "Gather up your things and off we'll go," he said matter-of-factly. He looked very serious.

Mina was surprised that there was no persuasion on his part. Actually, she would have liked the romantic interlude to last longer but longer meant going to bed. And that she was not prepared to do. She was worried about her reputation with him. An easy lay means a slut in the Middle East. She didn't want to be remembered as such. Going out and having fun is one thing but going to bed with a local playboy, quite another.

There was an awkward silence and they did not speak another word while Shoukry drove her home. He came around, opened the car door for her and accompanied her to her doorstep. He then planted a moist kiss on her lips upon parting. "I'll call you," he said.

Mina had a difficult time falling asleep that night. She thought she was getting too attached to Shoukry. She decided to accept Jose's invitations to distance herself a little from Shoukry. The problem was that Jose was starting to get too sticky and Mina did not want to encourage him. She just wanted to go to parties. But how to refuse Jose's advances? *Life is too complicated,* she thought.

"Are you running away from me?" asked Shoukry at their next meeting.

"No, absolutely not, why do you ask?"

"Word reached me that you are going around with a Palestinian crowd."

"And so, what's wrong with that? I'm just having fun."

"So, that's all it is?"

"Of, for God's sake Shoukry, so I went to a couple of parties. Don't get so possessive with me, please. It's not as though I'm sleeping around."

"I'm not getting possessive but I'd like to be sure that my girlfriend, if you consider yourself as such, would have more consideration towards my feelings."

"Sorry," Mina responded sheepishly, looking down on her lap. She realized she should not have snapped at him. They did not pursue the conversation.

Mina knew she had to take a decision. Her departure was coming close. What to do about Shoukry? Her mind was in turmoil. She liked him so much. Actually, she realized that she was enamored of him, big time and she lusted for him. He was like a magnet pulling her to him. Could she let him go? Did she want to let him go?

They had some hot, intense smooching sessions, always in the car, in the frigging cramped sports car.

While they were dancing cheek to cheek to an Italian love song, during a dinner dance at the Auberge des Pyramids—another favorite night club, Shoukry broached the subject of her return to the States.

"Have you definitely decided to return to the U.S.?"

"I think so," Mina replied hesitantly, with a small voice.

"It's either yes or no."

Mina was silent for a while.

Shoukry then looked deeply into her eyes with those foxy eyes of his and holding her very close, whispered some endearments in her ear.

"You surely must realize that I am in love with you," he said.

Mina froze and did not know what to say.

"No comment?" he pursued.

"I'm taken aback, actually. I thought you were a playboy and playboys do not fall in love."

"You're mistaken. They do fall in love when they meet the right girl. And, I've met the right girl. Will you stay in Cairo and marry me?" he then asked looking directly into her eyes.

"What?" Mina was really surprised at the question and drew back from his embrace. She never expected this.

"But, I'm not yet divorced."

"A minor obstacle that can be easily resolved. I have connections in the government. Mina, you must have realized by now that I care for you very much. In fact, I'm deeply in love with you—something I have never experienced before."

Mina was speechless. She realized she was also in love with him. But could she marry him? That would mean giving up all hopes of a career in fashion design, and her relationship with Robert, who was no longer in the picture, anyway. Her feelings for him had gradually dissipated after having Shoukry in her life. The question was: Could she live in Cairo for the rest of her life? And what about her family? Her parents and Vera were planning to go to the U.S. as soon as she was firmly established there with a proper job. It was also their dream. How could she let them down? They depended on her. She seemed to be leader of the family.

"How do you feel about me?" asked Shoukry, holding her at arms' length.

"Oh, Shoukry, you have made my life so complicated."

"What's so complicated? If you love me, you say yes, you get your divorce and we get married. I'll buy a house in Garden City or Zamalek (two posh suburbs of Cairo) or in Heliopolis, if you wish to be close to your parents, and we'll have a great life together. You won't have to lift a finger. You can paint all day long. We'll also have kids and live happily ever after. How does that sound?"

"Oh, Shoukry, you can't imagine how I feel."

With that said she started sobbing quietly.

"Why are you crying?"

"You are such a great guy and it was so easy to fall in love with you. Yes, I do love you, but I have mixed feelings. I don't know whether I will ever be satisfied with my life if I don't pursue my career in fashion design. You see, that's a passion that I cannot give up. It is like cutting one of my hands off. I have always dreamt about it—to be a fashion designer in Manhattan. Also, you are a playboy and I'm a little scared of marrying a playboy. Who knows when you'll get bored with me and leave me."

"My God, Mina, how can you think that? I've given a lot of thought about this and I'm serious. Think it over," was all he said and they resumed their dancing cheek to cheek with not another word about the subject. The atmosphere was rather tense after that and Mina did not like it one bit. She hated making important decisions about her life. She hated having to make a choice. The evening ended too soon and he took her home. They kissed in the car and she melted in his arms. She wanted to say yes but could not. She just could not visualize her life in Egypt.

The next day, at breakfast, Mina made an announcement to the whole family. "Shoukry has asked me to marry him," she said and watched the expression on their faces.

"And, what did you say?" her father asked not looking up from his plate.

"Are you crazy?" her mother asked. "What about your plans of returning to the States?" Mina could see that her mother was probably thinking about their own future of reuniting in the States.

"She is utterly confused," said Vera with a smile.

"I gave much thought to this subject last night and, although Shoukry described a beautiful picture of love, marriage and kids, I think I will refuse his marriage proposal. I'd like to pursue a fashion design career in Manhattan. Also, there is Robert there. I don't know what to do with him. He is expecting me to divorce and to marry him. Of course, after meeting Shoukry, Robert is completely out of the picture. I have to tackle him gently when I get back. After all, he is quite a nice guy."

"You are again confronted with the same old problem," said her mother. "You don't seem to be able to put your life on track. You jump from one thing to the other."

"Leave her alone, it's her life," put in her father.

"I don't envy your predicament," said Vera. "You have gotten yourself in a fix and I really don't know what's best for you. Perhaps marrying Shoukry is not a bad idea after all. I know you are very much in love with him. It's written all over you."

"No, it's not." She did not want to admit how much she loved and yearned for him.

"Get married to Shoukry and stay here. Cairo is not such a bad place except for the fact that the ethnic minorities are leaving and we don't know what's store for us in the future," said her father. "I am not doing too badly with my work with the new regime. I've got some new clients, but you never know."

"You can't possibly think of marrying a Muslim," her mother retorted. "I repeat, I have nothing against that religion but it is different than ours. They expect a certain behavior from their wives. They don't like independent women and you're too independent."

"We have not been too religious, Mom. So, whether it is a non-practicing Christian or a non-practicing Muslim, it makes no difference. I couldn't marry a fervent Christian either. In any case, his mom is Italian, so that makes him half a Muslim," Mina said laughing.

"Everyone will be talking about you, again," said her mother.

"Have I ever paid any attention to what people say?" asked Mina.

"No, you never have," said Vera.

Mina got off the table then. "I'll tell you what I decide after I see Shoukry again tonight."

Shoukry called her and asked her whether she wanted to go to the Sound and Light performance at the Pyramids that night. Mina had never been to one so she gladly accepted his invitation. He came to pick her up dressed casually in jeans and an open-neck white shirt, smelling of faint after shave. He gave her two pecks on her cheeks. The atmosphere was rather tense in the car. They talked about banalities. She did not know how to broach the subject of his proposal but it had to be done somehow.

After the spectacular performance at the Pyramids, they went to the Mena House Hotel Night Club for drinks. Mina waited for Shoukry to broach the subject of marriage but he did not.

"Shoukry," she said after they had ordered their drinks, "the thing is I am in a dilemma. One part of me wants to accept your proposal because I love you also and the other part wants me to return to Manhattan to pursue a career in fashion design. I have wanted that since I was a teenager and I can't give it up now. Shoukry, I'm too young to be settling down and being bogged down in marriage. I'm not ready." She felt very uncomfortable saying this but it had to be said. He looked at her without any emotion on his face. She couldn't tell whether he was surprised or angry or what.

"Say something," she said.

"Well, Mina, it's your decision. I will not influence you."

"I wish you would."

"No, I don't think so. I don't want to be blamed for any regrets as a consequence of my insistence that you stay here and marry me."

Mina could see that he was hurt but there was no way she could console him.

He then took both her hands in his and looked straight into her eyes. A few tears welled up in them and Mina released one hand to wipe them off.

"Oh, Shoukry, I hate leaving you but I will have to go away, I'm afraid. Otherwise, I'll regret it all my life and I don't want to blame you."

"Okay then," he said "I'll take you home." With that said, he took her by the hand and they walked towards his car. When they arrived in front of her door, he embraced her and gave her a chaste kiss on her lips. She grabbed his face in her hands and kissed him passionately.

"Why did you do that?" he asked perplexed.

"Because I love you."

He did not comment.

"I will not take you to the airport on Sunday, as your family will be with you, so I'll say goodbye now. You have made your choice," he said. "It's no use saying anything more. It's also no use to correspond and write love letters to each other. It will get us nowhere. You know where I am, the ball is in your court."

He got out of the car and opened the door for her and accompanied her to her doorstep.

She did not want to leave him. She was so devastated. She wanted to cuddle in his arms and not let go. She yearned for him so much but she had made up her mind. She had become career-oriented—a career woman with no place for emotional attachments.

"Damn!" she said as he let her go.

"Ciao bella," he said and walked away blowing her a kiss.

Mina was devastated, but it was her choice. She had no one else to blame. She went to bed and had an agitated night with nightmares galore.

Shoukry did not call the next day. The goodbye was final, she realized. Would she regret her decision once she was in New York?

The evening before her departure was a sad one. The family was glum during their last dinner together. Even the cats were sad. They sat at each corner of the dining room just looking at the family.

The next day her family accompanied her to the airport. Everybody was crying.

"I'm not disappearing from the universe," she said jokingly and she burst into tears. "Just make plans to join me in Manhattan," she said, trying to wipe away the tears with her fist.

"You're sure you want to give Shoukry up?" asked her sister. "You seemed so happy with him. There was a special glow on your face."

"Yup, I have to give him up although I don't want to. I may be the world's greatest fool."

BEIRUT

The reason for Mina's stopover in Beirut was to see her sister and brother. She stayed with her sister who had more room and, in any case, she could not stand her brother's wife so staying with him was out of the question. She had a few days of easy living, enjoying what Beirut had to offer.

Mina's favorite place was the Hotel Saint Georges which was right on the beach. It also had a swimming pool. Its bar was rumored to host some interesting characters, like a nest of spies and she found herself surrounded by an intriguing atmosphere. She met Kim Philby, a senior MI-6 official, at the Bar. She later found out that he was a spy and that he escaped to Moscow. What a story that was. Like a movie.

She also liked going to the nightclubs on the Rue Phenicie, especially the Cave du Roi, with its foreign bands playing all the latest dance tunes. She was grateful to her brother Ted who provided a few escorts for her. They were just ordinary guys but they would do for a few nights on the town. Although they were eager to have romantic relationships, Mina was not into it all. She just did not want to start anything to do with a Middle Eastern man. She still had Shoukry on her mind and he would always stay there. Only in her mind.

As for restaurants, they were abundant on Hamra Street, her favorite being the Grenier des Artistes. She did not know why they called it that. There were no artists in sight.

"Why don't you find a job and stay in Beirut," asked her sister. Her brother also encouraged her to do so.

"At least, you won't be alone," he said. "And then, we can bring Vera and our parents over."

"I am tempted but I have decided to go to Manhattan to pursue my career as a fashion designer and I also have to get a divorce, eventually."

"You can always get a divorce here in Lebanon, you know, and you can still design clothes here," continued her sister.

"No, I want to have a real designing career and it is in Manhattan that I can do so. In Lebanon, I would be a seamstress, not a designer. There is always Paris, but getting residency there is difficult, almost impossible, so forget it. Unless I married a Frenchman, of course. So, no, I am returning to New York. I have to try it there."

That was her final decision. She had a few days of bliss in Beirut. She loved the Middle Eastern style of living— *dolce fare niente* but her passion for fashion design came first in her life. She was gung-ho about it. *The Dolce Vita can only last a few years,* she thought.

MANHATTAN

Mina flew to New York with Middle Eastern Airlines. The plane was not full and she could lie down on three seats and fell asleep. Robert came to pick her up from the airport and he hugged her tight.

"I've missed you so much, babe," he said.

"Me too," was her weak reply. *How was she going to tell him that he was no longer in the picture of her future life?*

He drove her home and she did not feel like talking in the car. Although she had slept on the plane, she was tired and wanted to sleep to forget. He wanted to take her out to dinner that night but she refused telling him that she was too tired physically and emotionally. Robert then started to kiss her passionately at her doorstep but she was rather cool. He did not seem to notice it. They set up a date for the next day.

I do love Robert, I love him with another type of love, she told herself. *I only really love Shoukry, or better still, I lust for Shoukry.*

She had to concentrate on her career now. She tried to banish the romantic feelings that were trying to manoeuvre themselves in her overcrowded brain.

She met Robert for dinner the next day and the atmosphere was rather tense. She felt uncomfortable and incredibly guilty for having encouraged him in the first place. She ignored his remarks of moving in together. He was a sweet guy and very earnest but Shoukry was spicy. And Mina liked spice and a little mystery. Was she going to compare every man she met with Shoukry now? That would not do. She had a photo of them together at the Sporting Club pool and, whenever she was alone, she kept taking it out of her wallet and gazing at it longingly.

Robert still remained in the picture. She had not had the courage to let him go. She was waiting for the right time. To tell him what exactly? *You know, Robert, I met a guy in Cairo and I fell in love with him so I think I can't continue being with you like before.* It sounded so silly and she would hurt his feelings. He did not deserve that. So, she continued to have sex with him but it was mindless. She was not into it like before.

One day, while they were having dinner, he told her that he was being transferred to Chicago.

"Let's get married and we'll move there," he said taking her hands in his and kissing the tips of her fingers.

"What? I can't possibly do that. What about my career and my sister? She is coming over soon, you know."

"Well, your sister can also join us and get a job in Chicago and you can get a designing career there too."

"No, Robert, I don't feel like getting married, not just yet. In any case, I'm not even divorced."

"You keep saying that. That seems to be your crutch and excuse. All can be arranged rather quickly with the right lawyer."

"No, sorry, I am not moving from New York now. I just got back."

"Please think about it. Otherwise we'd have to take trips to see each other, and that is not very satisfactory. I am very much in love with you and would like to share a life with you."

"Oh Robert. I just can't, not just yet."

He drove her home after dinner and she did not ask him to come in for a nightcap like she usually did. They kissed at her doorstep and called it a night.

Vako, Rifaat and Robert. All three were nice guys and they would make good dependable husbands, but she was not in love with any of them. She was looking for something else, someone much more exciting. Someone who would carry her to the heights of passion and bliss. And, she had found that someone— Shoukry. But, alas, he was in Egypt—a country where she did not want to live in.

FASHION DESIGN

Now that Mina was free from Gary and his objections, she applied for a modeling job in Manhattan and worked as a temp for a modeling agency for photo shoots. She just made it, being 5' 7". Her long flowing honey-colored blond hair did the trick. She was mostly hired for photo shoots. After a couple of weeks into this job, she heard that a design house called Charles La Bianca needed some models for their new line. She was assigned to them for a few shoots and she enjoyed the job. She had not yet given notice to the U.N. but had called in to say she was sick—with a phony certificate, of course. All she had to do was tell the doctor she was having panic attacks. That was true in a way in her unsettled, turbulent life.

One day, while having coffee with one of the male assistant managers of the design house, she talked to him about having designed some clothes.

"Would you like to see some of them?" she asked him.

"You know how to design clothes?" asked James, Charles' right-hand man.

"Indeed, I do, I was doing that in Beirut," she lied.

"Show them to me, I'm interested," replied James.

Mina was elated. She went home that evening and got all her designs in a portfolio, ready for the next day. She could hardly sleep at night. "What if he does not like them?" "What if he laughs at me?" Her brain was brimming with negative vibes. She brushed them away with positive affirmations. "He will like them," and, "he will agree to hire me as a designer." At about 3 am she finally fell asleep, after eating a cheese snack. Eating cheese just before going to bed always put Mina to sleep. She was not worried about putting on a few pounds. She was so skinny.

She dreamt and dreamt, all incredible stuff. Running down corridors, plunging into a stormy ocean, floating on air, hitting at closed doors.

She woke up with a start. It was 7 am. Time to get ready for work.

She went in early and waited for James' arrival. She entered his office gingerly.

"Is this a good time to show you my designs?" she asked.

"Sure, have a seat."

Mina sat down and opened her portfolio and laid it on his cluttered desk. James looked at them, and lingered on some.

"I like them," he said. "You have a lot of potential. Would you like to work for us as a designer with minimum wage until we see whether your designs will be selling?"

"Of course," said Mina enthusiastically, not even asking what minimum wage was and she thanked him. She went back to her cubicle and got ready for the runway shows of that day.

It was decided that she start in two weeks. She gave a two-week notice to the U.N. and she was ready for her first designing job. She was over-joyous.

Mina was doing well at Charles LaBlanca. Her salary was increased after a couple of months and she was happy. She had finally made it in Manhattan. Her dream had come true.

Calamity befell Charles LaBlanca soon afterwards. He died in a car accident and the design house was closed. Mina was left without a job. She did not give up hope though and started applying at other design houses. She did not even dare think what would ensue if she never found another designing job. After all, she had had only about two months' experience. Back to the U.N.? Definitely not.

Mina started looking at ads in Women's Wear Daily. All of the ads required experienced designers. She found a position at Saks Fifth Avenue. They had a design department on the top floor. She was hired. She did not like the job at all. The supervisor was a Belgian finicky middle-aged woman who always found fault in whatever she did. She kept pulling the fabric of her model this way and that, trying to get a better fit. There was no better fit, but this woman did not want to admit that a twenty-six-year old new girl would manage to do everything right at the first go. Mina thought the woman was definitely anal but she kept her mouth shut in order to keep the job until she found a better one.

After a few months, she had had enough of the rigidity of the woman and she applied at another job, then another.

She changed jobs quite frequently because she could not find a place where she felt she belonged. Some of them were seedy places, totally unorganized. Others did not have the desired ambiance of sophistication and glamor that she was looking for. What glamor? Some were almost like sweat shops. She did make quite good money but that was not enough for her. She needed more out of the job itself and she needed recognition.

"What is so great in making money if you don't have time to enjoy it?" she complained to one of her friends at the U.N.

"That's why I'm keeping my job here," said Claire. "I get all the time off I need. Of course, I don't have the talent you have, so I'm stuck here."

"I really dislike the N.Y. money-hungry atmosphere, where everything is measured with how much money you earn. I shouldn't really complain, though. I wanted to design clothes and I'm doing just that. But, there's something missing."

"Maybe you want too much out of life," Claire said.

"No. I just want a satisfactory job and an exciting man."

"That's already too much."

VERA

Mina was feeling lonely in New York not having her family with her. The next thing she did was ask her sister to join her. Vera had to enroll in a college to be able to get a student visa. There was no other way she could come to the U.S. and stay for a lengthy period. She managed to do this with some *piston* (pulling strings) from influential people she knew through the Philippine Ambassador and NAMRU (Naval Medical Research Unit), her most recent job. She enrolled for a degree in interior design. She was very good at that. She was the one always putting order in their apartment and introducing new finds.

It was so exciting to meet Vera at New York Harbor. She had chosen to come by ship rather than by plane because of all the stuff she was bringing with her.

Vera had not changed much. She looked beautiful and quite cheerful.

"So, how are things back home?" Mina asked, after hugging her sister. "Pa, Ma and the cats?"

"Pa has the same darn problem of not making enough money. He spends his hard-earned money indiscriminately. Well, now he will have to provide for Ma. I am no longer there to chip in. He is planning on sending the cats over by plane as soon as we get an apartment."

"And you, Vera, did you leave any boyfriends behind?"

"Nah, one maybe, my boss at NAMRU. I love him but am not in love with him. He is a great guy and, if I were not coming to New York, I would have probably married him."

"Who is he? Tell me all about him, I'm dying to know. When I was in Cairo visiting, you had a couple of guys who did not seem to appeal that much to you. You were just flirting with them. And there was always Fouad in the background."

"Fouad is definitely out of the picture. He was too bossy and wanted to control my every move. My boss at NAMRU is twenty years older than me, divorced and an interesting man. He is famous in his field. He is an entomologist and is Extremely intelligent but nothing to look at. He loves living in Egypt. I'll tell you all about him at dinner."

Mina took Vera to Mrs. Pastore's where she rented another room. After Vera got installed in her room with the trunks, which took a lot of space, they sat down at dinner. Mina had prepared something simple. *Macaronis au four avec fromage* (oven baked macaroni with cheese), one of their favorite dishes. Their renting rooms was a temporary arrangement until such time as Vera found a job and they could rent an apartment.

"You can't imagine what I found in one of the drawers of my cabin on the boat," Vera said when they were seated at dinner.

"What?"

"As I opened a drawer to put some clothes in, lying in the middle of the drawer was a dildo."

"A dildo? Are you kidding me? I've never seen one," Mina said.

"Yup, a dildo attached to a belt. I picked it up with some toilet paper and threw it out of the porthole."

They then laughed their heads off.

Mrs. Pastore allowed them the run of her apartment and they received their friends in the living room. All in all, it was a very comfortable arrangement.

Within a week Vera found a job at the Rockefeller Foundation. They were quite impressed with her references from NAMRU and the Philippine Embassy. So, the sisters gave notice to Mrs. Pastore and moved into a one-bedroom apartment together. They shared the same bedroom as they had done in Cairo when they were teenagers. The cats came over by plane a week later, slightly disoriented. The sisters were so happy to have the two cats once again. They considered them as their children.

Bringing their parents over to the States was going to be a difficult undertaking. They racked their brains to find a solution. They thought of taking a lawyer but then they discarded that idea because they knew American lawyers were exorbitantly expensive.

Mina and Vera discovered Manhattan together. They were inseparable. One was blond and the other auburn colored and they attracted a slew of men. They had quite a few dates and went to the movies, restaurants and dancing. *None of them match Shoukry,* Mina always thought.

Vera sometimes caught her in a pensive mood.

"Are you thinking of Shoukry?" she asked several times.

"Yeah, I can't help it. Don't know if I did the right thing. My designing jobs are not fulfilling. I thought I would do better by now but it is a cutthroat industry and I am tired of struggling to get ahead. I always thought of a glamorous life when I thought of fashion design but it is not so. They are mostly like sweat shops. Only the reception area gives a hint of glamor."

"So, what are your plans now?"

"I don't know. I am so screwed up."

The sisters attended a few parties together but they were disappointed because the men invariably got drunk and became obnoxious. They kept rubbing themselves against the women while dancing. This was not their scene. They were used to the parties in Cairo where there were furtive glances and a lot of flirting.

A new life started for both of them now and they had to make concrete plans.

After much pondering, Mina thought she would start her own designing business. She would make up the models and sell them to dress manufacturers. She wanted to be her own boss while waiting to become famous. She did not give up her steady employment however. With Vera's help, she worked on her own designing business in the evenings.

A few months into yet another job with a cocktail dress manufacturer, Mina started getting itchy. She saw a documentary film about Switzerland and she suddenly thought of leaving New York behind and exploring Europe.

"You are so unstable," Vera chided her when Mina expressed her desire.

"I'm still young, what's wrong with my idea?"

"I thought you were planning on having the family reunited in the States, that's what's wrong," retorted Vera.

"So, if not the States, maybe we could reunite in Europe."

"Is this what your life is going to be, a roller coaster? Maybe this, maybe that?"

"Yes, until I find what I'm looking for."

"And, do you know what that is?"

"Not yet, but I'll know it when it appears in my horizon."

"And, we will be following you like sheep, I suppose."

MINA

Mina had two jobs now and she was also painting on the side. It was a little too much. It did not leave much time for a social life. She knew that she would not be making any money being an artist unless she became famous. And, becoming famous was a long process. Someone had told her that in order to become famous you had to create a scandal. That was beyond her reach, so she decided to continue working as a fashion designer and doing her own designing and painting on the side until such time as a gallery would take her on. The problem was that fashion designing was a time-consuming job and she only had the weekends to make the round of galleries to find a match for her type of art.

After a couple of days of thinking and dreaming about Europe, Mina decided she was definitely going to Europe to investigate life over there. The documentary was compelling and Mina was convinced that was the place for her. People had extensive summer vacations, ample sick leave and sometimes two hours off for lunch—well some of them did. Forget about Manhattan and designing and smelly diners and fast food and groping young men. Did she say forget designing? Then why did she leave Shoukry?

She did admit to herself that her idea of going to Europe was challenging and she was quite apprehensive about this venture—handling completely new challenges in a foreign atmosphere where she knew no one. She forced herself to think positively. Was she not the eternal optimist?

She saw Robert one more time and told him about her plans.

"What? Is this new? When did you make these plans? You just came back from Egypt a few months ago. Have you thought about my offer of coming to Chicago with me? Have you talked to your sister?"

All these questions from Robert exasperated her.

"My idea of going to Europe has been on the back burner for quite some time now. I have to try it, Robert. I just can't settle down, not yet."

And that was that. Robert was crestfallen. Mina was glad he was going away. It solved her problem of breaking up with him. Distance was going to do it. He was becoming too sticky and Mina did not appreciate that. She wanted to be free of any commitments.

As time went by and her dissatisfaction with work set in deeper and deeper, Mina got more and more convinced that by going to Europe, her life would change drastically to the better, although she was a little apprehensive at being capable of handling new challenges in the unknown world of Europe. She had to make it, though. She had to follow her dreams however far-fetched they were. She acknowledged to herself that she was somewhat flighty and irresponsible. But then nothing ventured, nothing gained. That was her motto.

She wanted to investigate life in different surroundings, meet new people, different people, and start afresh with no appendages. Well, actually the appendages were her sister and her parents but these were really her backups—people who sustained her and did not make her feel alone in the world. She could always rely on them for their emotional support and unconditional love. Especially, her mother who was the backbone of the family. She was never a burden. She was a real doting mother, doing the shopping, cooking and whatever else that was needed. Not only was she self-sufficient, but she also helped the sisters in their day to day work and she had her own business also.

They had it so good in Cairo before the Revolution.

Thinking back on her life now, she could not imagine how she could be so impulsive. She had only $ 200 in her bank account, no health insurance, no husband and yet she embarked on this adventure of unchartered territories at full speed.

Her plan was to work for an international organization either in Geneva, Paris or Rome. There were several in Geneva. One in Paris—UNESCO, the United Nations Educational and Scientific Organization, and one in Rome—FAO, the Food and Agricultural Organization. That was the only way to get residence in a European country by working for an organization affiliated to the United Nations. She decided she would first try Geneva since there were many more organizations there. And then make her way down to Italy to apply at FAO and, if by any chance none worked out, to go to Paris as a last resort.

A friend of hers from the United Nations, Diane, expressed the desire to accompany her on her trip. She had never been to Europe and Mina liked the idea of going with another girl. Mina had been to Europe once but had not really seen much. A stop-over in Paris on her way to Cairo. She thought she was travel savvy and could handle a trip on her own, and also act as a guide to her naive companion. Diane was pretty and was lots of fun to be with as a traveling companion but she had never been anywhere except to Puerto Rico for an abortion.

Mina pondered on their trip for a few days and came up with a somewhat feasible plan. They would buy chartered tickets and spend three weeks in Europe. Their destinations would be Switzerland and Italy. They bought charter flight tickets from New York to Brussels (the cheapest ones they could find) and with the book "Europe on Five Dollars a Day," safely tucked away in Mina's carry-on like it was the Bible, off they flew, ready for their European adventure.

June 1963 was the beginning of Mina's carefree life. What bliss! She had not really been free since she was sixteen, when she met Gary. She had had a six-month separation from him during the marriage but that had not been real freedom. He was always in the background. After a few months of being separated, Gary had suggested that they get back together and she had agreed. She knew him and all his faults and she had no other man on the horizon—no doable man, that is. They had more flaws than Gary. She felt safe with Gary. She was used to him.

Now that she was finally officially separated from him, she just wanted to get away. Away from the U.S. and all the memories of married life. She felt that if she stayed put in N.Y., she would always have guilty feelings towards a husband who was not such a bad guy, after all. She had just fallen out of love, that's all. She did not think it was a good idea to continue cohabitating with a man she did not really look up to or love him anymore. Liking a guy was not enough. She was too young for that. She did not wish to settle for second best. She wanted it all. She expected much more from a relationship. She wanted the passion she had with Gary at the beginning. Only Shoukry came close to her having that feeling. But then, she had not tried him in bed. She regretted that. None of the other guys she had met were even close to that kind of passion. Perhaps Robert, a little. But that meant going to Chicago with him. And she did not fancy that in the least.

Mina had a long talk with Vera.

"I am going to try and find a job with an international organization in Europe. That is the only way to get residence over there. It will hopefully be in Geneva and then, once I am settled, I'll call you over."

"Have you really thought this out? Do you really want to leave the designing business? That's what you wanted to be in since you were a teenager."

"No, I don't wish to continue in designing. It's a cut-throat business and I don't have the stamina for it. I would like to have an easy life. I would much rather have an office job in Europe and be an artist on the side. That would be more satisfactory to me."

"But, you left Shoukry because you wanted to be a designer."

"Don't remind me of that. Deep down, I think I regret it but I can do nothing about it now. I can't go back to Egypt."

"Don't forget our parents. We have to be reunited and it is easier to bring them over to the U.S. From what I hear, Switzerland has no immigration policy at all."

"Don't worry, if things work out well in Europe, we'll find a way. There is always a way. And if we don't manage to bring them, then I'll come back and we'll go to California and try our luck over there. At least the weather is better than in New York. And then we'll call our parents over. Just don't get involved with anyone seriously over here. That would create further complications."

"No worries about that. All I meet are undesirable characters. Although I did meet a guy I like, Gerald. He is a co-worker. I told you about him but I'm not very involved with him yet."

EUROPE

Mina hated being separated from Vera and the cats but she had to do it. Vera accompanied Mina and Diane to the airport and they were off.

They landed in Brussels with too many suitcases and the travel book 'Europe on $ 5.00 a day'. They were unable to sleep on the plane. It was too cramped and noisy and the food was lousy.

It was raining hard when they landed in Brussels. Everything was gray and dull. They took a taxi and told the driver to take them to an inexpensive hotel near the train station. As they planned to take the train next day to Geneva, they did not wish to be too far away. They found a miserable hotel room for $ 8.- a night.

Their room was on the top floor, a kind of *mansarde,* (attic).

They put down their suitcases and prepared to take a snooze before going out to eat a bite. When they returned, it was raining again.

"My God, the roof is leaking," said Diane.

"It is too late to change rooms now, we are dead tired. We'll put a waste paper bucket under the leak," Mina said. All they wanted to do was sleep after the long flight.

They were not interested in visiting Brussels when they woke up in the morning, although the city had interesting museums. But this was not a pleasure trip. It was gray and gloomy and it was still raining—a feature which is prevalent in Northern Europe in springtime, Mina later found out. They just walked around town a little to get an idea of Brussels. Mina had only three weeks to look for a job and also have some fun on the side while in Europe. And, Brussels was not one of the fun cities on her agenda. In case she did not find a job with a U.N. agency, she had decided to return to New York and from there go on to California with Vera, but not to hook up with Vako who was still eager to get married to her. He wrote to her often proclaiming his undying love for her. At least there would be someone she knew who could be of help in settling down in California.

In the evening Mina and Diane took the overnight train to Geneva—second class—a huge mistake, but they could not afford otherwise. From that day on, Mina swore to always travel first class if she had the money. And she was adamant she was going to make her own money or marry money, whichever came first.

There were six bunks in the compartment. Mina and Diane took the two top bunks. A woman was washing her husband's feet before he got tucked in for the night. A baby was yelling and had to be calmed down. Some old guy was snoring to his heart's content. Mina and Diane tried to sleep but could not. They were extremely uncomfortable.

They finally arrived in Geneva early in the morning at around 5 am. As it was too early to look for a hotel, the information kiosk not being open until 8 am, they slept on the station benches with their suitcases scattered all around them. Good thing the police did not shoo them away. Swiss police are known to work strictly by the rules. Sleeping on a bench meant being homeless and that was not tolerated.

When the kiosk opened at 8 am sharp, they were the first in line. The Swiss work like clockwork, the girls discovered later on. Even the trains run on time. If the departure time is at 8.15, the train moved at 8.15, not a minute before or after. They asked for a cheap hotel and were directed to one in Plainpalais, a lower middle-class section of Geneva. They took a taxi and found a room for $ 10 a night.

"That Five Dollar a Day in Europe book is a misnomer," Mina said to Diane. "Maybe it refers to the last century."

They had no other choice so they accepted to take it. The reason Mina was in Geneva was to look for a job and not to loll around in a luxurious hotel room. She vowed that would come later on in her life. Diane was just being the tourist and following her.

On the first day, they unpacked and rested after their exhausting and uncomfortable train journey. They went for a walk around the neighborhood but there was really not much to see. They ate in an inexpensive restaurant a block away from the hotel and the food was rather good. It was *raclette*—Swiss cheese grilled in little containers and accompanied by boiled potatoes.

The next day they got up early, went to the corner cafe to have the usual French type breakfast—a croissant and a coffee. They then walked to the center of town to look around and familiarize themselves. Mina loved what she saw. People seemed so relaxed. Lake Geneva was right there in the middle of town with its *Jet d'Eau* (Jet Water Fountain) majestically rising out of the water toward the sky. Actually, the name of the lake was Lac Leman but the Genevese liked to call it Lake Geneva, Mina found out. It was June and the weather was superb, balmy and sunny. Mina thought she would love to live and work in this town. It looked so peaceful after the hustle and bustle of Manhattan. It was a walking town and they explored the center by foot. They went up to the old town and looked in the quaint galleries and boutiques. They also went to Promenade des Bastions, and walked around that area, looking at the majestic wall of the Reformation. Finally, they had a lunch of *steak et frites* (steak and French fries) in a café overlooking the lake. It was so relaxing. They had the *"Plat du jour"*, (the plate of the day) so it was not too expensive. Mina learned that lunching on *plat du jour* was the thing to do in Geneva. They never dined in a restaurant in the evening. Prices were too high. So, they bought some bread and cold deli slices to make sandwiches for their dinners.

Mina then pondered on her next move.

She asked Diane to give her dictation so that she could time herself on her speed. She used to be very fast but she had not held a secretarial job since she left the U.N. Much to her surprise, she had not lost her touch and had not forgotten her shorthand. But would she be quick on the typewriter? Of course, she would be, she had been typing away like mad at the U.N. in New York. On an electric typewriter, though.

She called three organizations and set up appointments for the next day. One was the International Economic Organization (IEO). It was housed in a huge, austere, gray, ugly building in a beautiful park with gigantic oak trees, overlooking the lake. The next one was the World Health Organization, also with its own park but a little away from the lake; and the third one, the International Communications Union for which she did not care so much. It was a rectangular ugly building close to the U.N.

The next morning, Mina was all set to go.

"I'm going to make the rounds of the international organizations," she told Diane. You can go sightseeing by yourself. Just stay around the lake and you'll not get lost and I'll meet you at the hotel to have sandwiches for our evening meal. I'll stop by a deli and bring something with me."

She put on a demure, secretarial type attire and she was ready make her rounds.

Diane did not know a word of French but Mina was sure she would manage. Geneva was a small town and most people could understand English.

First, Mina went to the IEO. She liked their mission because it was all about economics. She was very much interested in that subject, then.

"We only hire English-speaking secretaries from England," said the Personnel Manager. "The reason being that we pay for home leave every two years and also a repatriation grant to England. The trip to the U.S. is too costly to apply that practice." Mina's face fell but she was quick with a response.

"I am from London; I live there with my mother who is British," she lied. Her mother was in fact British by birth from her father's side and had a British passport but she had never lived in England. Mina had not even been to England and had an Iranian passport at the time. She could have gotten a British one if she had lived in England for a year, she had been told. But who wanted to live in gray, gloomy England. She had had her fill of the snobby British when she was working for the ten British Board of Directors at Eastern Tobacco Company in Cairo. Their hoity toity attitude towards anyone not British got on her nerves.

Mina took an IQ test and a shorthand and typing test and was told that she would be informed of a decision soon, if she called them next week. She did not like the job offerings of the other two organizations. Nevertheless, she took the tests there also just in case the IEO would not come through.

The next day she did two other organizations: The World Meteorological one and the United Nations. The latter was very difficult to get into. It also seemed quite unorganized. Too many people working there.

Instead of waiting around for responses, Mina decided to go to Rome and try her luck with FAO. She did not particularly want to work in Rome but she had to try everywhere if she wanted to stay in Europe. Having second thoughts about Paris, she did not care to try UNESCO. Somehow the pace in Paris did not appeal to her that much. Paris was wonderful to visit but to work there would involve taking the Metro and she had her fill of the New York subway system. She wanted a laid-back atmosphere and she found Geneva to be a peaceful place and the perfect fit for her.

"Hey Diane, we're going to Rome tomorrow," she said when she returned to the hotel. She was the decision-maker and Diane just followed her. They both wanted to see Rome. Mina had never been there. After seeing the movie La Dolce Vita with Anita Ekberg, Mina had a fascination towards that city. She wanted to experience old world glamor, charm and the decadent atmosphere, just for fun.

They took the train again with all their suitcases. Mina travelled very heavy in those days. She packed clothes for every occasion, with shoes and bags to match. It was so cumbersome, but she paid a lot of attention to clothes, then. The sophisticated life in Egypt and the glamor of Fifth Avenue had left an indelible mark on her. She was not practical. She was young and fashion conscious. Everything had to match, even the color of her earrings. Big fan of earrings, she was. She did not have pierced ears though. Somehow, after seeing *Yeretsguin*, the wife of their priest in Cairo, who had elongated earlobes because she wore heavy dangling earrings during her youth, she did not want to follow suit. She liked to keep her ears small and dainty.

They had a fitful train journey from Geneva to Rome, second class again but it was daytime so it was not so bad, except that the Italians were eating salami sandwiches and the whole cabin reeked of salami.

Mina and Diane had not taken anything to eat with them. They bought a couple of sandwiches from a vendor on the train and drank coca cola. After everyone had their meal, the compartment looked like one big messy picnic area.

The scenery was extremely interesting and picturesque on the way down south. They passed many Swiss vineyards as the train rambled along Lake Leman between Lausanne and Montreux. It then went through the Valais region of Switzerland where they could see waterfalls and several castles; and finally, through the Simplon tunnel of the majestic Alps. The scenery then changed and they were aghast at the picturesque Italian countryside while passing through numerous charming small towns as well as cities like Bologna and Florence. Mina promised herself that one day, when she would make it in Europe, she would take extended trips to Italy and discover all the interesting towns.

ROME

Mina and Diane finally arrived in Rome. The train station was like a war zone. The weather was scorching hot, dusty and smelly with people and food. What chaos. Just like the Cairo train station. Everyone was screaming with offers of transportation and rooming deals. Mina had read in the famous book "Europe on $ 5 a day" that this train station was one of the largest in Europe. It was easy to get lost in it and get disoriented. Mina advised Diane to keep close to her. They looked around and could not decide with which screamer to go. They finally chose an older guy, who looked quite respectable, and asked him to take them to a cheap hotel. They were hell-bent to find the $ 5 a day deal this author was talking about.

Their driver told them he would take them to a room in an apartment building which would be less expensive than a hotel room. Mina spoke Italian fluently and agreed. He accompanied them in the taxi and they drove to the apartment building. The woman who owned the apartment happened to be downstairs on the sidewalk. Mina did not like the looks of her. She was bottle-blonde, with squinty green eyes and looked like a shrew. After the regular salutations, the shrew took them upstairs to the fourth floor. No elevator. Mina wanted to check out the room first before moving in, so they left their suitcases downstairs with their guide. Mina tried the beds; they sunk in. She tried the windows they worked. She trie the faucet in the sink. No water. She then spoke to the shrew.

"*Non c'e aqua,*" she said.

"*Aqua arriva domani,*" the woman retorted with her hands on her hips, ready for battle.

The water would be coming the next day, she assured them. Too late; no way would they stay without water for a whole day. They were sweaty and tired and wanted to use the shower immediately.

"*Domani e troppo tardi,*" Mina told the shrew with the overly made-up face and told Diane to follow her downstairs. They would look for another place. The woman screamed for her money and threatened to call the police. In order to avoid trouble and waste of time, Mina took a 5000-lira bill, tore it in half and threw it at her face. 5000-lira was not much in the 1960s.

The woman shouted obscenities, and picked up the torn bill.

Mina then told their guide to take them to a cheap hotel, not a room.

They landed at the Piazza della Rotonda, where the Pantheon is located and they rented a room in the Pantheon Hotel. It was a lousy room with old-fashioned furniture that was almost falling apart and the mattresses of the twin beds sunk in. It cost about $ 8 a night. Mina threw the $5 a day book across the room. She was raving mad. They were being duped by this author who cashed in royalties, selling his outdated guide book.

The hotel was noisy— noise from outside—the enervating noise of Vespas. Vroom, vroom. The name Vespa means wasp in Italian. A Vespa is the Italian luxury brand of a scooter. They also had them in Cairo. Everyone in Rome seemed to have a Vespa, and their racket was extremely annoying. As the weather was hot and as there was no air-conditioning in the hotel, they had to keep windows open. Cars and Vespas went around non-top in a circle in the piazza. It seemed as though Rome never slept. They would use ear plugs to be able to sleep at nights. They were eager to have fun in this city that never slept.

When Mina took a shower in the communal bathroom, she noticed there was a hole in the door at about eye level. She was convinced the manager would be peeking. He did not appear too kosher to her when they checked in. He looked like a sleaze and kept repeating how nice the *Americana signorine* were, so *bella, bellissima*. Mina covered the hole with some cotton wool and told Diane about it.

They were now ready for their adventure in Rome.

They had been informed by friends back home, that the thing to do was to walk on the Via Veneto to see and be seen. That's where all the excitement was. A street full of cafes and restaurants. They got all dolled up and started off from the hotel and, as soon as they reached the Via Veneto, a slew of guys kept following them inviting them to go to restaurants and night clubs. Some stopped their cars—Maseratis, Lamborghinis and Alpha Romeos— and asked them to hop in. It was hilarious. Mina and Diane loved all the attention they were getting and laughed their heads off. Mina had heard about the exuberance of Italian men but she did not know the extent of their fervor.

One guy even stepped out of his car, laid down his expensive navy-blue vest on the sidewalk and asked them to walk on it because he considered them to be *principesse*. Mina's Italian served her well. She could talk back. They finally accepted the invitation of two decent looking guys in suits and went to a night club. Men were not in jeans and T-shirts in those days and accepting dates from strangers was okay. The rape scene was not in vogue yet.

The next day, Mina went to FAO for the test. She did extremely well and was immediately offered a job. She told the Personnel Manager that she would think about it for a day or two. She was eager to hear from the IEO first. She preferred to live in Geneva. She went to a store, where she could place international telephone calls, and called the IEO. She was told that her tests were excellent and she was offered a six-month probationary contract. Yep, she had made it. Subsequently, she refused the FAO offer.

Mina felt proud. She had landed a job with the IEO and she was going to live in Geneva.

And then she thought of Shoukry. And the reason she had left him. Was it worth it? Here she was in Europe with yet another secretarial job. All the career talk she had with Shoukry went down the drain. All bullshit. She could not write to him and lose face. For all she knew he may already be married.

The next morning, they did some sightseeing. They went to the Fontana di Trevi where they threw some coins and made a wish. Mina wished for a better life in Geneva while Diane told her she wished to meet a sexy Italian guy.

After coming from the U.S. where everything was new, it was such a pleasure for Mina to see some old-world sites, cobbled streets, quaint boutiques and low buildings. She made the round of some boutiques to look for bargains and finally settled for a hand-knitted sweater, which was quite expensive but Mina fell in love with it. The shop was a small 12 x 12 right on the street, where two ladies sat, knitting all day long. They had a few models of sweaters on hangers against the walls. They made one-of-a-kind models. Mina fell in love with the sweater she chose. It was tan color that went with her complexion and had collaged pieces of decorated leather on it. She also bought leather gloves. Gloves were very much in vogue in the 1960's. She never ventured out without gloves in the fall or winter. And, of course, she also bought more earrings. She had so many but she could not resist to buy more whenever the occasion arose. She could almost open her own shop by now.

In the evening, they went to the Via Veneto again and they accepted the invitation of two decent-looking guys to have dinner with them. The food was good and they stuffed themselves with spaghetti and meat balls, drank some wine and finally went to a night club to dance. Neither Diane nor Mina were wine drinkers or smokers. The guys smoked non-stop. These were the cha cha cha and the Italian soulful crooner days. The bands were excellent but the atmosphere was too smoky for Mina. Her eyes watered and her mascara started to run. She kept running to the restroom to fix her eyes. The guys wondered whether she was sick or something. While dancing, Mina avoided the advances of her partner and kept a safe distance from the lower part of his body. She had been trained to do this in Egypt. Guys always tried to rub themselves against the girls. They all seemed to have hard-ons. She was never in the mood to feel their peckers.

The guys wanted to meet them the next day but they refused because they did not find them particularly enticing to be with. They wanted to meet new fellows.

The following morning, they did more sightseeing. They went to the Colosseum. Mina tried to picture how it was during its heydays. It must have been a regular slaughter house. The stench must have been abominable and she did not like the vision that was opening up in front of her eyes. Man against beast. Too horrific. And, gore-hungry people watching and applauding the winner. *What kind of people were they?* They also went to the Spanish steps to see the Vittorio Emanuele monument. There were a lot of tourists taking pictures.

Their evenings were spent on the Via Veneto where all the action was. There was such a diverse choice of men. Some good looking and some God-awful. On their third night out, two German guys came up to them and asked if they could sit with them at the cafe. Mina looked at Diane and they nodded. They looked okay, quite respectable. They introduced themselves as Kurt and Helmut. Their English was not that good. Helmut happened to be the owner of a resort hotel in Tropea, a seaside beach town in the South of Italy. He showed Mina photos of his sprawling hotel and invited her down there for a vacation. She laughed him off. She did not like him that much. He had a peculiar odor which was unpleasant. They had dinner at the cafe. In the taxi, taking them back to the hotel, Helmut tried to kiss Mina but she turned her face away. His odor was quite unpleasant. It was not because he was not clean, it was just his body odor.

Diane seemed to be thrilled with Kurt. Actually, Diane was thrilled with everything that was Italian or with anyone who lived in Italy, even if the guy looked like a critter. She loved the attention she was getting. So was Mina, but she was more discerning.

"Why don't you want to be kissed?" Helmut asked her in broken English.

"I don't know you," she said. Stupid answer. Mina thought that sometimes it is exciting to be kissed by a stranger but not by Helmut.

"I hope you'll get to know me."

She just smiled and did not reply. They were dropped off at their hotel and told them they would be leaving Rome soon. Helmut was disappointed.

That was the end of him and his friend.

"They were not so bad," Diane said, once they were back in their hotel room.

"Nah, forget it, I just did not like his body odor. It is so much nicer being chased by charming Italian guys than by foul-smelling Krauts."

They were having the time of their lives. Those were the years. The guys chased girls in the 1960s. They were so many of them, for the picking. Another reason was that Italian girls were not permitted by their families to date guys, then. The girls were more liberated in the north of Italy, Mina was told. But in the south, girls dated guys clandestinely just like in Egypt. So, the guys chased the tourists who were more attainable.

Their next night in Rome was not so productive, men-wise. They were approached by several Italian guys but none of them was appealing so they decided to call it a night. While they were walking back to their hotel, they heard someone calling them from behind.

"Do you girls need any help?" the person asked.

"Oh my God, an American," Mina uttered.

They were not in Rome to meet Americans. They were in Rome to meet Italians. They could have all the Americans they wanted back in New York.

He seemed quite a decent chap, tall, dark and good-looking. They spoke with him and accepted his invitation to take them to the beach the next day. He came by with a pale green Topolino. After having ridden in posh cars around Rome, they were downgraded to the smallest car on the planet. His name was Don and he was from Rhode Island and had his own business—a textile yarn business—in the South of Rome, owned by his family. He happened to be younger than Mina. In those days, she preferred older guys so she did not pay much attention to him. She tried to pass him off to Dianne but he did not seem to be interested in her.

They saw Don again the following day to go to the beach. He was cute and accommodating. They exchanged addresses. Mina's address was the American Express in Geneva. She did not think she would ever see him again.

On their last evening, while on the Via Veneto again, two Italian guys approached them. They looked decent enough and the girls accepted to go dinner and dancing with them. They went to a sort of cave where it was so dark and Mina kept straining her eyes to look at her companion more closely. Diane fell in love with Sergio, one of the guys. The name of Mina's date was Guido. Nothing special, she thought, just an ordinary looking guy trying to make out with a foreign girl and Mina was not interested to take up with him. After having danced all evening, she said she was tired and was dropped off at the hotel while Diane took off with Sergio. Mina was surprised at Diane's decision.

The following day, Diane came back to the hotel and packed up her stuff.

"Mina, I have decided to stay on in Rome with Sergio. I will not go back with you to Geneva," she announced resolutely.

"Don't be daft, he's just a fling."

"But, he said he loves me."

"And you believed him!"

"He has a nice one-bedroom apartment where he asked me to move in. He lives with his mother in another apartment so he will come and visit me in his bachelor pad."

"Ha, ha, Diane you're such a dope. Most Italian bachelors live with their mothers because they are fed and taken care of. These flats are *garçonnières* where they take prostitutes, just like in Egypt and in other Mediterranean countries. Don't be fooled by him. Italian guys are smooth operators."

"I love him too, he is so cute, and the sex is great."

"You are so stupid, I can't believe what I'm hearing. You don't even speak Italian and he barely expresses himself in English. It's all about sex. He has found a free sex partner. Well, I'm going to Geneva tomorrow and I strongly suggest you come with me."

"No, I think I'll stay with Sergio."

"Don't come back and cry on my shoulder when the shit hits the fan, because it will, I assure you."

"He is such a darling when he tells me Italian love words," Diane kept repeating with a love-sick look on her face.

"You don't even know what he is saying. For all you know he is telling you porno stuff, and you go on smiling like a dope. Are you so sex-starved?"

"I don't think he is being deceitful with me."

Mina gave up dissuading Diane to commit the folly of staying behind with Sergio. She was just one other naive American girl in love with Italy and Italian men.

Diane bade her friend goodbye and left the hotel. Sergio had come to accompany her and was waiting downstairs with his car.

Mina had accomplished what she had to do in Rome. Now it was time to tackle Geneva and her new job offer at the IEO.

GENEVA

The train ride back to Geneva was uneventful. First thing Mina did, when she arrived at the train station, was send a cable to Vera reassuring her that everything was okay, that she had found a job. Then she went to check in at the same hotel. The view from the hotel was nothing to look at, just a large unkempt square where a lot of vendors displayed their goods. She was told it was the Flea Market of Geneva on certain days. Just as she was going to go to bed at night, she saw a huge brown cockroach on the wall next to the bed. She could not catch and kill it because she had a horror of crunching any living thing. She could not stand the sensation or the feeling under her shoe. She tried to sleep but could not do so with the insect roaming around on the wall.

She called down to reception and asked to change rooms. It was midnight. They assigned her another room. Mina left the light on in the first room so that the cockroach would disappear in some dark hole when she got back in the morning. In the morning she went down to Reception and informed them that she would be moving out that day. They were not too happy about it, especially her having kept the lights on in the first room, that electricity was expensive, etc. She packed up her bags and asked a taxi driver to take her to another hotel. This one was slightly more expensive but it was worthwhile as it was centrally located, right at the railroad station.

The first thing she did on the Monday morning was call the IEO. She was asked to come for an interview with the Personnel Manager. Again, she dressed up in a demure secretarial outfit and went for the interview. The position she was offered was not a good one. She was told that all new secretaries start in the Typing Pool at the lowest level, G.3. (G meaning General Service Category). Her previous experience in top-level jobs in Cairo and New York were disregarded. Mina thought that was stupid and she discussed the matter thoroughly. After all, she had been secretary to the President of Barclays Bank in Cairo and she had also worked at the U.N. in New York. She did not think she should be downgraded and be a newbie like some English country girl fresh out of a village in England. After her insistence, a position was found for her at the Annex for Tripartite Studies (ATS)—a Department of the IEO. She was to be one of four secretaries in a small villa which housed this department and was on the same grounds as the main building situated on Lake Geneva. The building of the IEO itself was austere and gray, but the Annex was an old-style, turn-of-the-century villa. A family must have lived there at some point, because it had a bathroom with a bath and a kitchen.

She was taken there to be introduced to the Director of the Annex. Mina admired the view from the villa. It was spectacular. It overlooked Lake Geneva and a large luscious park with huge shady oak trees. She could hear the birds chirping. There was no traffic noise. None of the N.Y. Seventh Avenue frenetic goings and comings. She could not be happier in her new surroundings.

"A young lady from Egypt has joined us," the Philippine Assistant Director of the Annex said, introducing her to the other secretaries. Mina was surprised he did not say a young lady from New York. The three other secretaries were English and turned out to be loads of fun. They readily adopted her. She was a curiosity. A girl from Egypt who was coming from New York. The only non-English secretary in the IEO who could work in English and French.

She was disappointed at the pay she was offered, only 1,000 Swiss francs a month. A quarter of what she was getting in New York. The girls assured her that this was good pay because a secretary outside the U.N. system in Geneva got only 750 francs a month. And, they also assured her, the money would go a long way. She believed them.

She started work the very next day. She was bombarded by umpteen questions. Where was she coming from exactly? Why Geneva? How was Egypt? How was New York? Mina found the girls to be a congenial group. They accepted the pretty foreigner from all these far-off lands. Mina's background seemed to fascinate them as they came from small villages in England and had not seen much of the world yet. They advised her on how to get lodgings. That was the most difficult part. Mina had to hurry and find an apartment so that she could bring Vera and the cats over from New York. Vera had never lived alone in her life and she was getting impatient to join her.

Mina's new life was in Geneva now. She had to make herself comfortable and assimilate. Her French was top notch so she was very at ease in her dealings with the local population. She gave thanks to her upbringing, learning four languages in Armenian elementary school in Egypt. What a cosmopolitan country that was.

And then again, she thought about Shoukry. She missed him. She missed his lips and his warm hands all over her body. Sometimes she thought she was stupid for not having given in to him. He was always in her thoughts.

To start with, Mina had to leave the hotel. It was getting to be expensive. She went to the notice board of the IEO to find out whether anyone was renting a furnished room. She needed one immediately. She found a room with an older English-speaking Swiss-German woman. It was not too far from work. It was within walking distance. It would take her about a half hour. It was rather expensive though, 300 Swiss francs a month. She was told by the girls that people usually paid between 150 to 200 francs for a room. But these had no privileges. The Geneva housing market was renowned for being extremely tight, *like a virgin's twat*, Mina thought and laughed to herself. She did accept the 300 francs room because she would have access to the kitchen and could take one shower a day. All the other rentals gave no kitchen privileges and allowed only one shower a week. The Swiss had clean houses but personal hygiene did not seem to be a priority. She guessed they consumed a lot of deodorant.

The landlady had a married daughter who worked in an international organization and lived apart.

"You know," the daughter told her when she moved in, "guys are scarce in this town, a man can have a girl for a cup of coffee, so don't build up your hopes."

She visited an old friend of her mother from Cairo who was divorced from a Swiss man and lived in Geneva. The apartment was dingy and smelled badly. It smelled old. Mina hated the smell of old furniture and old people. The latter had a distinctive odor. This woman reiterated that Mina would not find an apartment, nor a man in this town. She, herself, was looking for a man. *Did she not see the way she looked? All wrinkled and endowed with a voluminous bottom?* She never saw the woman again during the years she was in Geneva. She always kept away from pessimistic people. They did nothing for her morale, she being the perpetual optimist.

Mina loved challenges and she proved both of these women wrong.

The room was a temporary arrangement. She had to rent an apartment fast to bring her sister and the cats over.

Mina did not have to use the kitchen much in her new lodging, because she had dinner dates every evening of the week except for one evening when she stayed home to wash her hair, do her nails and attend to other girl stuff. This was always on a Monday. Mondays were not active days in town.

Mina adored Geneva, the laid-back atmosphere, and the relaxed pace of the people in the streets. She liked the sidewalk cafes, people having their coffees without the hustle and bustle of New York and without hurrying back to work, carrying paper coffee cups.

The office work was tedious and boring but the people were rather interesting. Besides the English girls, the other staff members were from all over the globe. All the men were in the Professional grading system, starting from P.1 while all the girls were in the General Category System starting from G.3. The messengers were G.1s. Besides the Philippine Assistant Director, there was a Frenchman, a Czech, an Argentinian, an Egyptian, a Chilean and a Cuban. She liked talking to people from diverse countries, especially the Egyptian and Argentinian guys who shared an office together and cracked jokes all the time. It was a hum drum job in pleasant surroundings providing her with a decent livelihood. *What on earth was interesting in typing documents having to do with economic laws in different countries?* She asked herself. It was boring personified. She also realized that the guys, who were giving her dictation, wanted to fill their time and produce as much paper work as possible by writing insipid memos to other departments with umpteen copies: One for the file, one for Registry, one for the Director, and on and on. To erase a mistake, it was hell, flipping through all the carbon copies. Once the correspondence was filed in the proper file, presumably, it was forgotten. Nobody referred to it ever again. Nobody could find it again. The files had such strange titles, no wonder the memos could not be found.

And then again, she thought of Shoukry. She was obsessed by him and missed him terribly. She had left him because she had wanted a fashion design career in the U.S. And now, she was in Geneva seated behind a typewriter, for God's sake. *What was she doing here?* She thought of the life she would have had, had she accepted his marriage proposal. A life with servants, an active social life and passion with the man she loved. She had given all that up for a designing career which had vamoosed. Was she regretting it? Of course, she was but there was no going back. In her last letter, her mom had written that she had seen Shoukry with a woman, at the Normandy cinema.

"I don't want to break your heart dear, but we saw Shoukry at the movies the other day and he was seated with an attractive woman. They did not seem to be lovey-dovey. He did not have his arm around her. Not that you can put your arm around the opposite sex in Cairo. As you know there is the morality code and it is strictly forbidden. They seemed to be chummy-chummy, though. He did not see us."

Mina's heart gave a wild pang when she pictured this scenario and she was insanely jealous. She wanted to punch the woman and grab Shoukry away from her. She realized that she would have to punch lots of women.

"*You, silly girl,*" she told herself, "*of course Shoukry would have girlfriends after I left. He is not going to sit home, be a monk and lament my departure.*"

She thought of calling him. To do this, she had to go down to the train station where she would be able to place an international call.

"*I don't have the guts to do that. What would I tell him? Hi Shoukry, guess what, I am in Geneva working as a secretary. I think I regret my decision of going back to the States, but I am not quite sure yet. Perhaps I should have accepted your proposal, after all.*"

That would sound so idiotic and she would lose face. So, she banished the thought of calling him and had a miserable night at home. It was one of her stay-at-home nights.

Geneva was certainly a desirable town to live in, a walking town. It was a small town but not a friendly one. There was the lake for swimming in the summer and the mountains for skiing in the winter.

Mina was eager to learn how to ski. She had to find someone to initiate her and teach her the ropes.

Mina had her own small office at the Villa. It had a window, not like the U.N. offices in New York. She sat facing the window to look out on the magnificent landscape—the grassy lawn, the trees and the shimmering lake. It was all so peaceful. She had her back to the door unlike most people who faced the door. At lunchtime, Mina would walk out of the villa and sit under a big old oak tree facing the lake. She taught herself Italian and Spanish while having a sandwich on the grass. There was none of the frenetic pace of New York, having a hamburger in a jiffy, in a greasy diner where one had to leave as soon as one had eaten to make room for the line-up of people waiting at the door. Mina and Vera sometimes had to order more stuff just so they could stay longer in the diner.

Mina was earning less money than in Manhattan but she had a better quality of life. She had more time. That was important to her. Of course, she did not have Shoukry. Always Shoukry. She yearned for him every day.

She liked everything about Geneva. It was small enough that she could walk almost everywhere. The Swiss were not an overly friendly people, though. They did not like foreigners. Some of them were xenophobes. They envied the salaries and the time off of the employees of the U.N. system. They were not as well paid and only had two or three-week vacation time a year, whereas the staff of the U.N. organizations had a six-week vacation time a year. There were about fifteen international organizations, not counting the NGOs.

Mina congratulated herself to have made the move from New York to Geneva. She felt exhilarated. The proximity of Lake Geneva was a great plus. It had a beach with a swimming pool. The high-water jet on the lake in the summer was one of the most photographed sites. The lake divided the left and right banks of the town. The right bank was known to house the wealthy whereas the right one, the middle class and the internationals.

The people in Geneva were generally well dressed, especially on Rue du Rhone, the street where all the expensive brand-name boutiques were located. Mina liked walking up and down that street, window-shopping. They all displayed fabulous clothes, which she could not afford, in their windows. She particularly liked the color of stockings she saw on the women. They all looked as though they had tanned legs. She found out the color was called *saskia* and she bought several pairs of that color the next day.

The most crucial problem for her now was to find an apartment.

THE APARTMENT

"Apartments are extremely hard to find," she was told over and over by everyone. "You have to be lucky. It is almost impossible to get one. There is a housing shortage in this town and management companies of rental properties give priority to the Swiss." How was Mina going to manipulate the system? She was also told that it was easier to find an apartment in a new building being constructed than in an old one. People in the older buildings never moved out or, if they did, there was a long waitlist of Swiss people who were given priority. Rents in the older buildings were relatively low whereas in the new buildings, they tended to be twice the amount and most Swiss could not afford it.

Mina thought that, with two salaries, she and her sister could afford an apartment in a new building.

She consulted the yellow pages for rental agencies. She called all of them and found out that, in fact, the Swiss were reluctant to rent to foreigners. The apartment shortage was humongous. There seemed to be nothing available, or they were too expensive for her budget. Some of the rental agents were even impolite, while others wished her luck in such a tight situation. Mina did not despair, however. There had to be at least one available apartment in the whole of Geneva within her budget, for God's sake! She finally found one in an older building, by sheer luck, but when she went to look at the location, she immediately gave up the thought of renting it. It was on a busy street going uphill, where traffic noise was horrendous, specially the noise of the buses stopping and starting up. She was almost in despair when, just by sheer luck, she found a small new building which was going to be ready for rental in a couple of months. It was in a good location, on the right bank, convenient for work, a supermarket and bus stops.

Mina went and had a look at the building and decided to rent a first-floor apartment at the back of the building, overlooking a small park. Not the ground floor. In Europe, first floor is above the ground floor. She rushed to the Management Office downtown and faced a Swiss, dour, old-maidish type of woman. *Uh, uh,* she said to herself. *I can tell she does not like me.* Mina tried to be as humble as possible which was so unlike her. She was usually assertive. A friend of hers had once told her that when she enters a room, she acts as though she owns it.

Together with the agent, she visited the available apartment. Two bedrooms, a small narrow, miserly kitchen and an old-fashioned bathroom and a separate toilet. It had a balcony overlooking the park. That, she liked. She also liked the fact of it being on the first floor. She was thinking of the cats who were prone to falling off the balcony when they chased each other. The railing was in slippery metal and she was sure they would fall while jumping around to play. The first floor was fine with her. If the cats fell, they could not hurt themselves.

Mina had finally found her apartment.

When Mina went back to the agency to sign the contract, she was asked to fill out four pages of information—one question was about her job situation. She only had a six-month contract which was the probationary period for the IEO. The agent told her that the policy of the company was to rent apartments to people with steady jobs. Unfortunately, she did not belong in that category.

In Switzerland, apartment rental agencies cannot terminate a rental agreement as easily as in the U.S. There were strict laws protecting the renters. Mina would be at risk of not having a job after her probation was over, occupying an apartment and not being able to pay the rent. She kept telling the agent that this was only the probationary period and that the actual contract would come later on. No deal. Mina was desperate. She went crying to her boss, a fatherly professor from Ann Arbor Michigan. He immediately got on the phone to the Personnel Department of the IEO and informed the Manager that he intended to keep his secretary beyond the probationary period and asked him to call the rental agency and vouch for her forthcoming permanent contract. The Personnel Manager agreed although he had never been asked to do this before. Permanent contract meant that the person could never be fired unless he or she killed someone.

The agency finally agreed and Mina had her apartment at long last. It would not be ready until sometime in the middle of September. It had the bare minimum. White walls, a toilet without a sink, a bathroom with bath, bidet and sink. You had to come out of the toilet and go to the bathroom to wash your hands. Mina was surprised. Have a bidet in a bathroom but no sink in the toilet. You'd think a bidet was the most essential item to have. There was also an unfurnished kitchen except for some miserly-looking white cabinets on top of the sink. No fridge, no stove, no nothing. The master bedroom had a built-in cupboard that was only 4 ft. large. One side (2 ft.) for hanging clothes and the other side (2 ft. also) with shelves. The floors were not done. They were bare, unfinished parquet. It was the job of the renter to sand and polish the parquet. This meant that Mina would have to fork out quite a bit of money to finish the apartment to make it habitable. *Darn, why is Switzerland so behind in the housing business? Are they still living the WWII years?* Mina asked herself but she resigned to do the necessary. *Is this the life I am looking for? Just to be in Europe, I have to work my ass off and put up with gross inconveniences?* Well, she had chosen it, so she gave herself a mental boost to carry on.

Mina now was ready to receive her sister. She cabled Vera to sell everything in New York, pack her bags and come over by boat, so that she would be able to bring all the suitcases full of stuff, her paintings and also the cats. She then wrote her an express letter with precise instructions of what to do with their belongings. What to sell and what to bring over. It was a colossal task but Mina knew that Vera could handle it, maybe with a friend or two.

"Vera" she wrote, "don't worry, when you come here, you'll soon find a job with an international organization and you can have a lot of dates here, contrary to what people are saying. So, come over as quickly as you can. And also, withdraw some funds from Citibank." They had a joint account.

Vera was extremely capable of coping all by herself and selling the furniture. She sold it mostly to the people in the building. It took about a month. She also gave notice at her workplace. She liked her office work actually because she had met quite a few interesting people and a man who became her lover. He was on the verge of divorcing his wife of four years. Vera had left one lover behind back in Egypt when she moved and now this was the second one. A good thing she was not that attached to them.

Everything that had to go to Geneva was packed in the two huge shipping trunks—from their parents' days when they went to Europe on extended stays of more than six months—and big suitcases. As for Mina's paintings, she had them shipped with a shipping agency. Vera was going to come by boat to Nice and then by train to Geneva with the two cats.

One of the people Mina contacted upon arrival in Geneva was the Armenian guy Hagop, who was Vako's friend from Cairo. He worked in a travel agency. He was a friendly guy and volunteered to help her get what she needed for the apartment. He also showed her around a couple of times. Mina felt he was like a brother to her. She never had one. At least she had one friend in a strange town. Hagop, however, had other designs. She could feel he was attracted to her and wanted to monopolize her as his girlfriend but Mina had no such intentions whatsoever. He did not appeal to her as a sexual partner. No vibes were emanating from him and she did not encourage his advances. She enjoyed his company as they had a lot to talk about.

ADAM

Mina achieved a lot in a short time and she was mentally exhausted. She had a job, she had an apartment and all she needed now, was a boyfriend.

After signing the contract, she did not feel like cooking dinner that night so she went to the Movenpick restaurant to eat a proper meal. She was told that the best place for singles was to eat at that restaurant, right smack in the middle of town, on the fashionable Rue du Rhone. It was an informal place. The basement hosted a formal restaurant with tablecloths and was more expensive. The ground floor was casual. It had a bar and tables lined up against the walls for singles and also around the restaurant for foursomes. People often shared tables sometimes if there was no available space. It was a busy place with a friendly atmosphere and good food at reasonable prices.

Mina sat at an outside table, on the sidewalk, against the wall. Seated at the next table was a nondescript kind of guy with black horn-rimmed glasses writing symbols in a notebook. He seemed very preoccupied but, nevertheless, he looked up from his notes and their eyes locked.

He smiled. She smiled back.

He started a conversation in French. Mina could immediately tell he was American.

"You're American, right?" she asked.

"Yeah, I guess my accent gave me away. Where are you from? You're certainly not Swiss. I am Adam," he said and extended his hand.

"I'm Mina."

Here she had to go into her spiel about being born in Egypt but not being Egyptian; an Armenian, living in New York with an Iranian passport and then finally coming to Geneva to explore Europe and choose a permanent place to live. Every time someone asked where she was from, it was the same old story. They did not ask what ethnic origin she was but where she was from. She could have been from upper Mongolia but not Mongolian, for God's sake! *Just ask me who I am or what my origins are, not that I am so very proud of my origins, but still,* Mina told herself. Afterwards, when she was older, she was proud to say she was Armenian. In those days, not many people knew about Armenia and Armenians. Actually, when she said she was from Egypt, people's interest lit up. She found Americans more ignorant than Europeans. They always thought of Egypt as being built on sand and all it was famous for were the Sphinx, the Pyramids and camels. Often, she had to educate them and describe the cosmopolitan life people enjoyed in Egypt—all the glamour and sophistication. She missed that.

Adam was a Jewish scientist from New York working at CERN (European Organization for Nuclear Research) on a summer contract. There were so many of these international outfits in Geneva. They sprouted everywhere, like weeds. And the employees were usually foreigners who could not work in the Swiss sector. Their residence visas depended on their jobs. Just like Mina's. If she quit her job, her residence papers would be taken away and she would also lose her apartment. Her job was her passport to her new life.

Adam and Mina became quite friendly during dinner and he invited her out the next day, which was a Saturday, to go to Annecy, a charming picturesque French resort town with its own lake, about forty-five minutes away from Geneva. He told her that Annecy was an Alpine town called "Venice of the Alps" because of the rivers and canals that pass through its old town. The lake was renowned for being clean and swimmable. He took her to the Pere Bise Restaurant, which was in the Guide Michelin and expensive, of course. This Guide was Adam's Bible. He liked to eat well and in renowned restaurants. It suited her fine. He was an out-of-the-ordinary kind of guy with an ironic sense of humor.

She rather liked that about him. He criticized the French. He criticized the Swiss. He criticized the Americans. In fact, he found fault with everything and everyone. He always ate out and liked female company. He was not easy to get along with because he had his own set ways and was extremely self-centered. It was always about what *he* wanted to do. She went along with it because he was an interesting companion and paid for the meals and also, he took her to places she would never have been able to go, all alone. She never interfered with his plans nor did she make any demands on him. He told her that he did not care for American girls because they were too sticky and marriage was always on their minds.

"And especially Jewish girls," he said, "they think they are princesses."

She was astonished at his remarks about Jewish girls. Mina, herself, would never criticize Armenians to foreign people. Well, he was safe with her; she had no marriage designs on him. He was just an interesting companion.

"There are two Pere Bise Restaurants," he said, "one owned by the father and the other, by his son. The father's, which is this one, is more expensive than the other. Next week I'll take you to the son's."

They ate a seven-course meal. Mina had never seen so much food being served in a restaurant before. It seems the son's restaurant served only a five-course meal. She could not eat all of it as she had a bird's stomach and she thought it a pity that there was no take-out and the delicious food was going to waste.

"Can I ask that the extra food be put in a box to feed my cat maybe?" she asked Adam.

"No, no. It is not done in Europe. Forget it. People would think you were a peasant."

After lunch, they walked around the medieval area in the old town where there happened to be a street market. Mina bought a few trinkets as souvenirs. They also visited St. Peter's Cathedral.

Adam ate out every day and almost every evening he invited her to go to dinner with him after work. He liked her company, she guessed, and she more or less liked his. He was not good-looking by any means but he was brainy and well-travelled and an extremely interesting man.

He had rented a furnished studio for the months he was working in Geneva and took her there after several outings. And then it happened. Not satisfactory, according to her limited sexual experience. He was not a good kisser. His lips were shapeless and too lax and his hands were too small and weak. Mina preferred strong hands. She just liked his sharp mind and his caustic sense of humor. Very New York. They became an item around Geneva, much to the chagrin of Hagop.

As he was an avid mountain climber, Adam took her one day to Chamonix in France. Mina did not like that mountain resort town at all. The people were all sporty and talked about nothing else but mountain climbing in the summer. She supposed they would talk about skiing in the winter months. Mina was more of an *apres-ski* (after-ski) type.

Sometimes she went to the movies with Hagop. Adam began asking her questions about the evenings she was not with him. She told him the truth, that she was seeing one other guy, but platonically. At one time, they were all seated in a group at the Tennis Club where Adam played tennis, including Hagop, and the two guys looked daggers at each other. Mina was amused. *How silly men can be,* she thought.

Adam and Mina never talked about religion. She was not that interested in religion anyway. One day he told her that his father was a rabbi and worked for the Jewish Defamation League or something like that. He was rather hesitant to tell her that. He waited for her reaction but she did not have any. He was not a rabbi himself, so she couldn't care less what his father was. Adam was an agnostic or an atheist and as long as he did not brainwash her about religion or Middle Eastern politics, she was okay with him.

Then the summer ended and he had to return to New York.

"Come to New York with me," he said "and we'll get married."

Mina was surprised at this suggestion. She looked at him to see whether he was joking. Not at all. He was serious. She did not see it coming at all. She had thought he was the eternal bachelor type and so engrossed in his work. They had never talked about love and marriage.

She was in no way eager to go back to New York where she had just escaped from, and did not have any intentions of marrying Adam in any case. She had just gotten out of a marriage and she was not even divorced yet. She wanted to have fun before embarking on another serious relationship if she ever did meet the right guy for it. And, Adam was not the right guy for her.

She was looking for another Shoukry.

"You can't be serious, Adam. I can't possibly make any wedding plans. I'm not yet divorced."

"Well, think about it, and get a divorce for God's sake!" he said.

"We'll see, it's not as easy as you think. My husband is in New York and I'm here."

"That's why you have to come with me to New York and get the divorce there. That would be much easier than getting a transcontinental divorce and it will make your life simpler."

"You are forgetting the fact that I just rented an apartment here and my sister Vera is coming over with the cats," she reminded him.

"Well, tell her not to come."

"Don't be illogical. I can't possibly do that, and I like living here. You forget that I ran away from New York to explore Europe."

"You can always come back to Geneva with me in the summers. I intend to get summer contracts with CERN in the years to come."

"No, Adam. I can't possibly return to Manhattan. I really don't like that city. It is too aggressive and you need a lot of money to enjoy all that it has to offer. Being small fry in Manhattan is just not my thing."

"Oh, come on, we'll have fun." Adam persisted.

"Marrige is not all fun, you know. I have been through one and I know what it's like."

"Whatever you say. If you change your mind, just holler."

There was nothing more to say and Adam left for New York. They promised they would write and they did. The letters were flippant, one-pagers, back and forth. He always asked her about her sex life in a joking sort of way and wrote about his own. He was seeing other girls. Of course, he would. She found it strange that he would talk about them with her. She was not in the least bit jealous. Maybe he thought she would be and would hustle over and go to New York to get married.

THE OFFICE

Something had to be done about her manual typewriter. Mina was not used to typing on a manual. It was curbing her typing speed. She was also getting a neckache and pounding on the keyboard was ruining her well-manicured nails. She put in a request, through some bureaucratic channels, for an electric one and, much to her surprise, she was provided with one. Taking courage, she then she asked for a proper typewriter desk as the desk she was using was too high and her sitting position gave her a backache. She had seen photos in a magazine of the right sitting position for typing and she showed the powers to be the image in question. She won this round also. She was given a desk with an attached, lower side table for the typewriter. She wondered how come the other girls had not thought of these important things. Well, they were country girls from England and were so happy to have this "high-paying job" (for them it was) that it didn't dawn on them to complain. In England where they came from—not from London—salaries were very low. The girls were surprised at her cheekiness.

Mina liked the Scottish secretary at the Office. Carol, that was her name, had a great sense of humor and had an Italian boyfriend with whom she could not get married because he had an older sister and the mother kept reminding her son that the Italian custom was for the older sister to get married first. Carol always showed off the gifts her boyfriend gave her. They did not live together. He lived with his mother and sister—Mediterranean style.

"Men should give you gifts if you have a relationship with them and they can't marry you for one reason or the other," Carol told Mina. "I see him almost every day but we're not married and it is his fault for obeying his mother and following that stupid Italian custom."

"What about children?" Mina inquired.

"Bah, who knows what will happen in the future. I'm still young. I don't like them anyway. They are bothersome. Also, I'd like to keep on working. I like it here. Italo (that was his name) does not make oodles of money for me to stay home and look after children."

Mina was surprised at this 'gifts from men' business. She had never asked for gifts from any man. They were just given to her, mostly by her husband before and after they got married. She found this a little strange. But this was Europe and things were different, she guessed. She was not sure she would ever be able to ask for gifts. She was not brought up that way. She did not think it was classy.

The other two secretaries were married and they had nothing to contribute to this conversation. Also, Mina was not interested in married life and stories of children.

VERA'S ARRIVAL

A month earlier, Mina had dreamt that their cat Mickey, the Siamese, had fallen out of the window of their New Jersey apartment and died. She woke up in a sweat with her heart beating erratically and could not wait to go down to the train station to call Vera. In the 1960s, long distance calls from Switzerland could only be made from the train station phone booths if one did not have a phone and an international plan. She rushed down to the station before going to the office and she was finally connected after a wait of fifteen minutes.

"How are the cats?" she blurted out without saying hello first.

"They're fine," Vera said. "Is this why you're calling?"

Mina told her of her dream and how scared she was that something had happened to Mickey.

"My dreams always come true," she continued. "Will write you an express letter to tell you what you have to do before coming over and what to bring with you."

The call was quite expensive and she had not yet cashed her first month's salary so she kept it short. Her dream had not come true this time. *Thank God* she told herself and made the sign of the cross. She was doing this quite a bit lately. Her mother had taught her to give thanks to God when something good happened to her. She did it once for finding a job, then for finding an apartment and now for the cat.

Mina was thrilled that everything was falling into place. She had found a job and had also solved the problem of the apartment. She now waited impatiently for Vera's arrival. She wondered how Vera would manage all alone with all that luggage and the cats. She supposed someone would help her out. She felt a little guilty for not being there to help her. About a month later, Vera arrived by train to Geneva on a sunny Saturday afternoon. She had taken the boat from New York over to Nice, France, and from there, the train to Geneva. Mina was so excited that she could not sleep the night before.

When she went to meet her at the train station, Vera disembarked with only one cat cage. After hugging and kissing a couple of minutes with happy tears welling up in her eyes, Mina asked whether the two cats were in the same cage.

"Our Mickey died," said Vera with a sad face.

"What? How? Why didn't you tell me on the phone?"

"I didn't want to cause you any undue heartache," Vera said. "I preferred to tell you face to face."

Mickey had died of kidney failure and was buried with the help of the janitor of the building in the spot where Mina saw him fall in her dream. The day she called was the day they buried him. She was so devastated. She could not hold back her tears. She regretted the fact that she had not been with him on his last days. She realized then that she must be psychic. Many other occurrences in dreams had come true before. Before they got all the luggage in a cab, she opened the cage to hug Timmy, the Maine coon cat.

Gary had given Mickey to her in Egypt. The second cat, Timmy, was also given to her by him in New York. Timmy had cured her of a deep depression caused by the distance of her family. She had not reverted to tranquilizers. Timmy had done a good job by sleeping on her bed, or sitting on her lap when she was moping. He gave her a lot of comfort. She thought cats were psychic too.

Mina gave up her room at the end of August, before Vera's arrival and sublet a small furnished apartment for two weeks from one of the girls in the IEO, until their own apartment would be ready around the middle of September. The sublet was a miserable place. No space in the cupboards to put any of their clothes, so they strung a rope across the living room and hung them there. They were not going to be receiving any guests anyway. They were really cramped in there but, as it was temporary, they did not mind it. They shared the queen size bed. Mina continued going to work and Vera started looking for a job by making the rounds of international organizations.

"You're sure you want to be in Geneva?" Vera asked. "Housing seems to be a big problem and apartments are so small."

"Yes, I'm sure. You'll love it. We have to make some sacrifices."

Mina was optimistic about making their home in Switzerland. They would eventually bring their parents over and finally they would all be reunited except for the older brother and sister who were happy in Lebanon and did not want to move.

They moved into their new apartment in the middle of September. They had to do something about the parquet. They had very little money at their disposal until Vera would find a job so they did everything themselves. They sanded the parquet and polished it, on their knees. The smell was abominable and they wore masks. They congratulated themselves for doing a good job.

Mina was so grateful to have found an apartment and on the first floor so that Timmy would not get hurt if he fell from the balcony. He had fallen once from their third- floor apartment in Cairo. It was lucky he was alive.

Hagop was very helpful and took them to the Flea Market. They bought a gas stove with four burners and a small oven, a tiny fridge, a small Formica kitchen table with three chairs, a huge brown cupboard and three bed frames. They bought new mattresses and pillows from the cheapest store in town. They would certainly not buy mattresses from the flea market. They would probably be encrusted with fleas.

After buying some casseroles and dishes from Uniprix, the least expensive department store in town, they were now settled in their new abode. Things were done slowly in Switzerland. The telephone installation took about a month.

Vera found a job with WMO (the World Meteorological Organization) three weeks after her arrival and they were thus reassured of having enough income between the two of them to keep a household going smoothly. They were now ready for their mother to come over. It was easy for her because she was British and the British were allowed to leave Egypt and go to abroad on vacation. She obtained a tourist visa for six months. Their mother was of great help. She did the shopping, cooking and most of the household chores. They also could afford to hire an Italian neighbor who happened to be a cleaning lady. She became a great friend to their mother and, while doing most of the talking in half-French, half-Italian, she did the job. Luckily, she was paid by the job and not by the hour.

In order for their mother to stay permanently in Geneva, she became Mina's dependent at the IOE. Children, spouses and parents could be classified as dependents of employees of international organizations if they did not work. She was therefore granted a Swiss residence permit attached to that of Mina's. She was also on her medical insurance plan.

"When you're young you can put up with inconveniences," said their mother when she arrived. "I feel very cramped in here after living in our ten-room apartment in Heliopolis. The more you get used to luxury, the more you're unhappy when confronted with bare basics, especially when you get older. Well, I can do with the sacrifice just to be with you girls, though I don't know where we'll put your father if and when he gets here."

"We'll get another apartment," declared Mina. She was being optimistic again.

Vera and Mina shared the larger bedroom. Besides the built-in cupboard, they also had one dresser with two large drawers and two smaller ones, which Mina had bought off from one of her colleagues. Only one single bed could fit in their mother's bedroom. They bought a dresser and one large stand-alone cupboard from the Flea Market. This was shared with their mother. They had all these beautiful clothes from Egypt and the U.S. and did not know where to put them. They bought another cupboard and put it in the living room. The apartment was too small for them but they accepted the inconveniences, just to be in Geneva.

To house their shoes, they put up a tall shelf in the toilet which had a lot of space as it had no sink. They covered it with a colorful cloth to make it look appealing. They also put the cat's litter box there.

The kitchen was hardly large enough but they did manage to squeeze in the small table and the three chairs. The kitchen did not have built-in cupboards. They therefore had to buy a cheap rickety white cabinet from the Flea Market to house the casseroles, frying pans, dishes and the cutlery. It was a far cry from an American kitchen. They also bought a sofa for the living room from the Flea Market, and they covered it with a decorative cloth brought over from Egypt. Mina concocted a work table for herself with a door and four legs. That's where she did her art work, which was mostly sketching. She installed that in the living room. They did not mind the haphazardly furnished apartment as they looked forward to an adventurous life in Europe.

They had a balcony overlooking a small park so it was quiet at nights. They were thankful for that and in summer they had their dinners there.

They were more or less settled in their new apartment but there were still things to do to make it cozier. With her next pay-check, Mina decided to buy a couple of rugs. Timmy had already made himself comfortable in a corner of the couch in the living room where the sun warmed him up. He was a happy cat and this made them happy also. They had heard that cats do not like changing living environments and that they would often get depressed and pass away. Not Timmy, he was the King of the apartment and dotted on by three women. It was too bad he did not have Mickey to play with.

They had no T.V. They could not afford one yet. In any case the sisters were busy going out every night. They were not T.V. fans. They mostly read in the evenings or knitted or sewed. They had a transistor radio and they heard of Kennedy's assassination. It did not really touch them because they were not really Americans. They considered themselves international and not attached to any country in particular.

BERNARD

Mina took Vera to the Movenpick one evening to show her the set up. The restaurant was completely full up. A waiter greeted them and told them he could seat them with one person occupying a table for four. It was the custom in this restaurant to share tables if there was no space available.

The waiter asked the man whether he would be willing to share the table with two young ladies. The guy looked up from his meal, smiled and agreed. They smiled back and sat opposite him.

His name was Bernard. He had an ordinary face, with carrot-color hair, and bi-focal glasses. He was extremely friendly and told the sisters about himself whereupon Mina told him a little of their story. At the end of the meal, he offered to pay their bill. They objected but he insisted and asked them out the next day to go to Geneva Beach. The beach is on the left bank. The water is a little murky except in the middle of the lake where there is a strong current. The beach itself is wide and grassy and there is an Olympic-size swimming pool, as well as ping pong tables, a basketball court and a bocce court. The sisters did not venture in the lake but used the swimming pool which was warmer and cleaner. They spent the whole day at the beach, ate sandwiches with a couple of Swiss beers— Feldschlosschen. Mina did not particularly like the taste of that beer. It was on the sour side. She preferred Stella, a Belgian origin beer they drank in Egypt, or Heineken.

Bernard then asked Mina for a date on the coming weekend. As he seemed to be a pleasant companion, she accepted. He took her to a cozy restaurant around the lake.

"I'm married but my wife left me for another man," he said to her at the end of the dinner. He showed her a photo of his wife—she was an attractive woman.

"I would take her back if she left him," he continued.

"I don't think that's a good idea," Mina said. "She must be in love with this other man. Why would she leave him to come back to you?"

"You never know." He seemed to be optimistic.

Bernard and Mina became great friends—platonic friends. Every time they saw each other, however, he kept repeating "I have a great desire to kiss you," but he never tried until one time after a movie when he tried to kiss her at her doorstep.

"I don't kiss a man who is still in love with his wife," Mina said and drew back. That was not the real reason though. He just did not attract her physically and an amorous adventure with him was out of the question. His lips looked dry and his eyes were dull and gray. And, most of all, he was kind of flabby and she did not like the color of his hair.

He was not Shoukry. He did not have impish eyes and he did not know how to flirt. Mina liked to flirt. He was not a stupid fellow, though. He understood that she was not into him. Nevertheless, he asked her out several times as he liked her company. One evening, during a dinner at the Perles du Lac restaurant on the lake, he asked whether she would like to meet someone interesting.

"Why? Who do you have in mind?" Mina asked rather perplexed.

"There is a guy working in your department at the IEO who is a French aristocrat. He is a Count. His lineage comes from the Haute Savoie region of France. He is wealthy and has a three-bedroom apartment in one of the "Bude" buildings, of which I was one of the architects. You should try to meet him and pursue him. He is a good catch.

The Bude buildings are a group of four buildings built in Geneva during the 1950s with swimming pools on the roofs. It was a new concept and the apartments were for sale, condo style. They were all sold to wealthy people. The Swiss banks did not offer large mortgages. They needed a big chunk of private capital. The location of the buildings was desirable because they were close to the international organizations and also there was a supermarket right down the block.

"Oh, Bernard, how sweet of you, but I don't pursue men. They should be pursuing me."

"Well, I mean, try and befriend him. He is a most desirable catch."

Mina was curious so, when she went to work the next day, she tried to find out who this guy was. The girls in her office told her that he was quite reclusive and was not easy to approach.

It was a friendly atmosphere at the office. The work was totally boring, though. Mina often wondered who would be excited about taking dictation from slow-speaking, "hmm-ing" and "uh-ing" guys. And then typing some incomprehensible gibberish in five copies to be put in separate files whose titles were long and meaningless. The filing system was archaic and it was housed in the main building. Most of the time, people could not locate the filed correspondence because they were misfiled. They were supposed to be according to subject matter but if the subject was vague, it was impossible to find it. The files had such complicated titles that it was impossible to do a proper filing. Mina invented her own filing. She just piled the letters and memos, that she could not find a suitable file for, on a table in her office. So, if anybody asked to see a certain letter, she just looked through this pile and there it was. Simpler than looking through several files to locate the darn thing. After about three months or so she would chuck them all out. She considered them obsolete. She did not tell anyone though. She just came up with the excuse that "it was probably misfiled." Nobody looked any further. They were unimportant, anyway.

She thought that these men, for all the bosses were men, wanted to show that they were busy and doing important stuff. According to Mina, they had paper-shuffling jobs. It was so disappointing to write about unimportant stuff. Vera told Mina that it was the same scenario at her office with all the correspondence being about the climate and the weather.

Mina worked as secretary to the Director of the Annex when his secretary was absent. He gave her a lot of work. She hardly had time to do any personal work at the office. She worked long hours from 9 to 6 pm. with one hour for lunch. She sometimes cheated and took more time for lunch to go shopping. The secretaries covered for each other.

FRIENDS

After Vera's arrival, some of their friends from New York expressed the desire to visit them. Mina had been writing such praiseful letters about the wonderful life in Geneva that they wanted to experience the same kind of European adventures. Three of them came at weekly intervals. They had a very busy household.

There was Gwen, the Australian girl who was unbearably cheeky and would show up at their house every day after work. She was a mousy girl but an experienced man-chaser. She had been married to a Hungarian guy in Montreal and then had divorced him. Whether it was by mutual consent or not, it was difficult to tell because Gwen was a born liar. Mina never found out the reason for the divorce. Gwen soon found a job in an international organization and also hooked up with her generalist doctor who happened to be married. She rented a room in the apartment of an old lady and invited her man-friend over for candlelit dinners. The guy could not very well take her around town and be seen with another woman. The evenings she was not engaged otherwise, she barged into Mina's plans for the evenings, whether going to a restaurant or a night club or just staying home and playing cards. She had the habit of ringing their doorbell right at dinner time to be invited to eat with them. This went on for a few times until their mother got fed up and told Mina to find a reason to curb her visits.

The next time she came around, Mina brazenly told her they did not have enough food for her. This was repeated a couple of times until Gwen got the hint and never came by unannounced from then on.

There was Susie from New York who was a sweet girl, also divorced and looking for a hook up. She also found a job with an international organization and stayed in a rooming house. She was in Mina's group for some of their social activities. She was rather envious of Mina and Vera who had multiple dates and she told them, "I don't understand, you treat men like dirt and yet they chase you, knowing you don't care a hoot for them."

Whereupon Mina said, "Susie, you should learn one thing. Don't ever chase a man. Never show you're eager to be with him. The more unattainable you are, the more they will chase you." Actually, this was the 1960s. Things were different then and men were certainly different in Europe.

Susie did not know how to do that. She always showed eagerness. She got discouraged with the man situation after a while, and moved back to Manhattan and went back to her hubby who adored her. Mina heard that she eventually had a kid and was happy with her life.

Last, there was Jeanne also from New York. She was a Christian Lebanese originally from Egypt. She did not have to work. She was wealthy, or rather had rich parents who kept her in style. She found a rooming house not far from the sisters' apartment and signed up for a business course at some institute of higher learning. She wanted to be in business one way or the other, whether in the States or in Europe. She eventually got bored with the course but stayed on for residency purposes. She was a fun girl and a regular in their group. She stayed in Geneva for about a year. They went everywhere together: Skiing, cafes, nightclubs, always hunting for eligible guys. Jeanne managed to find some good viable ones. She was wily and knew how to work the system. After a while she got bored that she was not finding a suitable husband, and returned to New York to live with her parents until she found an interesting job. She finally got married and settled down in Manhattan.

GENEVA

The dancing clubs in vogue then were the Club 58 and the Griffins Club. Both were private clubs with membership. However, women alone were welcomed for free. There was also the La Tour nightclub in the old town. It was a very small place but bouncing with good music.

Mina and Vera were meeting men galore all over Geneva and Mina shared her encounters with the girls at the office. It was like a TV series of episodes. Geneva was an international town and men often came on business trips and conferences. They were lonely and wanted to have female companionship for dinner and much more if they could get it. Some of the men the sisters encountered were married, on business in Geneva. The sisters only accepted lunch or dinner dates, nothing more. These men were being paid a per diem so why not have the company of a woman along. Mina and Vera seldom accepted dates alone. They made sure they were a foursome. Refusal to participate in anything more was easy that way. They were not paid escorts, after all. They sometimes took their mother along to the daytime activities and the guys did not mind it at all.

Bernard happened to be still in the picture. He kept inviting Mina for daily excursions in France and Switzerland and also to go skiing. She did not accept overnight stays. She did not need any additional problems. She considered Bernard a good friend and nothing more and she made this clear to him. He finally accepted it.

The sisters and their mom went on shopping expeditions on Saturday mornings. This was their much sought-after time of the week. They had credit cards in all the major department stores of Geneva. Their favorite shop was the Bon Genie store on Rue de la Confederation. It was a more exclusive department store. Often, Mina and Vera were all alone on the second floor of women's apparel. They would try on clothes and dance around beaming and doing model poses in front of the mirrors with two saleswomen oohing and aahing. They would then choose a bunch of clothes to take them home and try them out for three days. They would keep what they wanted and have the others sent back with a van the store provided. They had home delivery service. How they loved their shopping sprees. They felt like princesses with this special treatment. They were making good money and they could afford to splurge.

There was also other department stores like the Grand Passage, Uniprix, Comptoir des Tissus, Spengler and Aeschbach for shoes. They mostly shopped at Bon Genie, though. The choice was better and more exclusive.

After shopping they would all have lunch at the Movenpick, where they invariably met people. Their Saturdays were like social outings. They looked forward to them.

THE ACCIDENT

A few months after they had settled in, Mina had an accident at the Office. As she was walking along the length of the corridor in the main building of the IEO with a soda bottle in her hand, bought from the vending machine and going towards the ladies' resting room, not the restroom, to have her lunch, she tripped and fell. It was one of those rainy days and she could not sit under her favorite tree outside in the park. While she was trying to get up, she noticed that the bottle had broken and she was bleeding all over the floor. She rushed to the infirmary. The nurse there tried to stop the bleeding by submerging her hand in hydrogen peroxide solution.

"I can't stop the bleeding," she said. Mina almost fainted. If the nurse could not stop it, what then? Was she going to bleed to death?

"I'll have to take you over to a *permanence*," she said. A *permanence* is an urgent care center.

There are several *permanences* scattered all over Geneva. The nurse took Mina in a cab to the closest one, which was at the train station, in the middle of town. They went up the rickety steps to the second floor. There was no elevator. The doctor in charge was not there. The attending nurse told her that he was having lunch in a nearby restaurant. The nurse installed her on a cot and asked her to wait. The wait was interminable. Her hand was bandaged but she did not look at it because she abhorred the sight of blood if, by any chance, it was seeping through. Finally, the doctor came, a small, balding guy with myopic eyes and a cigarette dangling from his bluish lips.

"Let's see, what we have here," he said.

Mina extended her hand but did not look at it.

The doctor undid the bandage, cleaned up the wound, wrapped it up and said, "there you go, all fixed. Just pass by the cashier on your way out and pay."

Mina got up from the cot and looked at her hand.

He had bandaged the wrong finger, the dope. Instead of the ring finger, he had bandaged the middle one.

"But, doctor, this is not the injured finger," she said looking at him incredulously.

"Let me see," said the doctor and looked at it. "Oh, the wound was already closed, that is why I couldn't see," he muttered and proceeded to bandage the right finger this time. *Why don't you say you are incompetent, myopic and too drunk with wine to see clearly,* Mina wanted to blurt out but restrained herself.

"The ligament controlling your finger is severed," said the dopey doctor. "I can't sew it together. It's too late. The ends are far apart. You would need major surgery of the hand to sew it together." Had he been on the spot, he could have done that before the ends of the ligament spread so far apart. One end was lodged at the wrist and the other at the bottom of the injured finger.

What an incompetent doctor he is. A doctor, nevertheless. What is an urgent care center good for when the attending physician is not on the spot at all times? Mina asked herself. Well, that was one bad point for Geneva.

Mina went home and wanted to have the comforting arms of her mother around her. She wanted to be protected. She felt like a child. She wanted to get back into the womb and feel safe. *What is going to happen to my finger? Will I be able to type? Will I be able to paint? After all, this is my right hand.* All these thoughts were going through her mind as she lay in her mother's lap on the couch. Her mother stroked her head and comforted her the best way she could.

She did not go to work for a week and she started physical therapy immediately. The best therapy however was starting to type again to regain the agility of her finger. After three months of therapy, the workers' compensation insurance wanted to settle the case as soon as possible. They informed her that either she should get it operated and the surgeon would try and bring the ligament together, or, she should accept a lump sum settlement.

The value of the last phalange of the ring finger of the right hand was Swiss francs 5,000. Five times her monthly salary. She did not care for an operation because she was told by the IEO doctor that it might not be successful and her hand could be worse than it was. Therefore, she accepted the 5,000 Swiss francs and invested it at 18% in bonds. Yes, that's what bonds were paying then. Luckily, her finger healed and she did not lose her agility in typing or taking shorthand, or writing and painting or knitting. The only movement she could not do is bend back the last phalange of the ring finger. She did not care about that all that much.

NORBERT

Around this time, Mina thought of calling Norbert, the Belgian guy she had met at the U.N. in New York four years ago. She knew that he worked at the World Meteorological Organization where Vera also worked. She called him at work.

"Hey Mina, what a surprise. Are you in town?"

Mina gave him a short *compte rendu* of her situation and he invited her out to dinner. They went out a few times to lunch and dinner and sometimes dancing at La Tour nightclub. Norbert was not a good dancer. In Armenian, he would be described as *pat godrogh*. (stiff as wood). He told her that he had gotten a divorce from his Belgian wife since he saw her last. He had a child who was living with the mother in Belgium. He tried to dance cheek to cheek but Mina was in no mood for it. He did not feel cuddly.

Norbert kept calling her and inviting her out. One evening he took her to a lookout point in Cologny—the most expensive and exclusive residential suburb in Geneva— where one could see all of Geneva and the lake. The view of the lake was stupendous. He parked the car and Mina could sense that he wanted to kiss her. She was perceptive. His breathing gave him away. He was quite an okay guy and somewhat attractive but he had a peculiar smell. She kept her head turned to the right looking at the view so as not to give him the opportunity to venture a kiss. Had she turned to look at him, she was sure he would try to kiss her and then it would be awkward to refuse. When he brought her home, she subtly rejected his efforts of trying to kiss her goodnight.

His remark was, "You need an indifferent type of man."

"Why is that?" she asked.

"Because you are aloof and not easily approachable. A man does not know how to deal with you. Or, maybe, you are like this only with me. Actually, I would like to take you to Paris and have a passionate affair with you."

Mina just laughed and brushed his comment aside. *He has not even kissed me and he wants to go to Paris to have an affair with me. Did he think that the Parisian atmosphere would induce me to fall for him?*

"Oh Norbert, that's ridiculous. I am in no mood for an affair with you or anyone else. In any case, I can't take the time off from work right now." She would have taken the time off if he were the right guy.

He said nothing further and she got out of the car.

He called her up a few days later and asked her if she wanted to work as his secretary in the WMO. The post had just become vacant and she would get a higher grade than the one she had in the IEO and more pay, of course.

"I'll let you know, Norbert," she said.

Mina pondered over the idea. She felt secure at the IEO. She was used to it. The working atmosphere was pleasant and it was next to the U.N. beach. Also, she liked the English girls she worked with. But a grade higher would mean about 100 Swiss francs more a month. That was a lot of money in those days. But then she thought it would not be a good idea to work for a man who was after her *derrière*. If he got mad at her for not getting what he wanted, he would get rid of her and God knows where she would end up. Or, if they did become familiar—which was highly improbable as far as she was concerned—it would be awkward to terminate the relationship and still continue working for him.

Mina made up her mind and called him up.

"Norbert, I thought about your offer but I prefer to stay in the IEO because in six months they're giving me a higher grade anyway and I feel at home here. Thanks for thinking about me."

After that, she saw him a couple of times for lunches or dinners and everything was above board. Nothing was mentioned about Paris, or an affair and he did not try to kiss her. If he was waiting for her to make the first move, he could keep on waiting.

Vera told her that Norbert was some kind of a womanizer and to be on her guard. That was not necessary as she had not taken him on as a boyfriend. The funny thing was that about four months after the "I'd like to take you to Paris" incident, she saw him in a restaurant with a pregnant woman. Mina was with Bernard. On leaving the restaurant, Norbert passed by their table and introduced her as his wife. *What was that all about? He had invited her to go to Paris with him and now he had a pregnant wife? That goes to show you that you can't trust a man.* Mina told Bernard the story with Norbert. He chuckled.

The girls at the Office were enjoying her anecdotes. They wanted to know all the details but she was not that open with them and did not tell them everything that transpired with her men friends or her feelings towards them.

Vera was having her own escapades at the Office. Two guys were pursuing her. One was her boss and it was a difficult situation.

Their mother was amused by their stories. The sisters shared everything with her. She was their confidante. She always gave them good advice.

"Be careful girls," she would say, "just don't get into trouble."

MARCEL

The summer was lousy in Geneva and in the whole of Switzerland. It just rained and rained. Mina and Vera went away on long weekends to the mountains where it was sunny. It cost them a pretty penny but it was worth it. Most often they took their mother and the cat along.

The next fellow Mina met was also a Belgian. *What was happening? Had the Belgian male population invaded Geneva?* Mina asked herself.

It was in early October and the weather was particularly warm— they were having an Indian summer— so Mina continued to go to the U.N. beach every noon during her lunch break. Sometimes Vera came over if she could get a ride. The beach was adjacent to Mina's Office. There was no sand, it was a grassy beach with a little *buvette* (kiosk) where you could get something to drink and eat. It was quite crowded that day. While she lay down on her towel in the sun after taking a swim, a shadow materialized next to her and a voice asked in French, "may I sit down next to you?"

She looked up and saw a not too bad looking, tall guy, slightly bald, with dark sunglasses. She would have liked to have seen his eyes before replying. But no chance yet. She just shrugged and said, "you may."

A conversation ensued. His name was Marcel and he turned out to be a high-ranking official working at the U.N. He asked her out for a dinner date. They went to dinners and the movies and weekends here and there. Initially, she was attracted to him, but after a while he got to be too possessive and she wanted to distance herself from him. He wanted to see her every day but Mina was reluctant to go steady. She wanted to accept dates from other guys. She wanted to play the field, widen her horizons until she met someone she really cared for. And she meant really, really cared for. Forget about love. Mina knew she would not fall in love that easily. That consuming feeling she had with Gary when she was sixteen, and subsequently with Shoukry, could not be duplicated, she thought. So, she played the field. She was a playgirl. *After all, why are there playboys only? Why can't girls act the same way as guys do?* She did not think there was any sense going steady with a guy if he was not such a desirable specimen. For her, they were playthings—amusing ones, sometimes and at other times, bores.

Marcel took her on skiing weekends to teach her how to ski. She loved skiing. It gave her a certain freedom to be zipping down the slopes. Although Marcel was quite accommodating of her needs and tried to please her in every way, she was not really into him. He was a good kisser though. He started having serious intentions towards her and told her he was very much in love with her. He expected a response but she did not give him one.

Marcel was rather a stingy man and Mina hated that streak. He would tip very little in a restaurant and expected a lot. *Le comble* (the limit) was when he went to Berlin on business and returned with a gift for her, a scarf which was not silk but of some inferior fabric. She gave the scarf as gift to her maid. *How could he possibly be so blind as not to see that I only wear silk scarves?* She asked herself. Her mother had taught her about quality since a very young age.

"Why are you treating me so nonchalantly?" Marcel asked her one day.

"I am not yet divorced and I can't possibly make plans. I'm just not ready to have a serious relationship," she told him. She could not very well tell him that there were a lot of things about him that she disliked. First and foremost was his possessiveness. Secondly, he wanted too much sex, sometimes twice a day. He acted like he owned her.

Not being divorced was a good excuse to rebuff her suitors' advances. Marcel was crestfallen and looked at her with a hangdog expression. She felt sorry for him but she had to be honest. She didn't want to give him false hopes.

She continued seeing him upon his insistence from time to time but it was just for the occasional lunch or dinner. He was a good man but not for her. Carol from the office also agreed with her that he was not suitable for her and that she needed a much more worldly and sophisticated man.

She stopped all action in the couch department with Marcel. He finally understood her feelings and they parted rather acrimoniously.

Around this time, Bernard called her out of the blue and invited her to dinner. During the dinner, he announced solemnly that he was now divorced from his wife and that he no longer cared for her.

"I'm ready to start a serious relationship with you," he said.

Mina was rather taken aback. She had not expected this proclamation. Bernard was a sweet guy but physically not her type at all. She could not envisage going to bed with him. She told him she was involved with someone else, although she was not—not yet, and that ended the Bernard chapter for good.

Nevertheless, he came to one of her exhibitions accompanied with a woman and introduced her as his fiancé. He bought two etchings at her next show.

THE OFFICE

One of the men Mina worked for was the Director of the Annex when his secretary was away. She seemed to be sick all the time. The Director was an elderly British guy who kept a bottle of booze in the right bottom drawer of his desk. He needed it to keep him awake. Sometimes, he actually did not notice Mina's presence in his office, and he would stoop down towards the drawer, take out a bottle and have a discreet sip, or so he thought. He was a jolly fellow and he did not seem to care that alcohol was *verboten* at the Office.

Another man was the Philippine Assistant Director with a strong accent who had introduced Mina to the others by declaring with a solemn tone, "we have a young lady from Egypt who will be working for us." Sometime she had a hard time understanding his pronunciation. The letter "v" sounded like a "b" and vice versa. Mina was considered a curiosity at the Annex. Here she was, from Egypt, working in English. It should come as no surprise if they knew anything about life in Egypt, but they were not a worldly bunch of people. They did not seem to be well travelled. They ignored the fact that almost all business was conducted in English in Egypt and some in French.

The newest arrival to the existing staff was a youngish Frenchman who was rumored to be extremely intelligent. He had a bright smile showing a good set of teeth and twinkling eyes. He was a graduate of the ENA in Paris (National School of Administration) which was one of the most prestigious schools in France if not *the* most prestigious school.

He was therefore regarded with awe. He came with modern ideas of putting the Annex into shape.

In those days, secretaries called their bosses with the prefix 'Mr' but the bosses addressed secretaries by their first names. Mina thought that was ridiculous and outmoded in a democratic society. She disliked being considered an underling and was very much into women's lib. She took care of that habit in her own way.

One day, this Frenchman, whose first name was Christian, passed by her office and said, "Bonjour Mina." She immediately replied, "Bonjour Christian." Mina noticed that he was taken aback and she guessed he did not like the idea of being called by his first name by an 'underling'. Next day, when he passed by her office, he said, "Bonjour Madame Seferian," to which Mina just replied, "Bonjour." And so, it went on like that from then on. They went back to being formal. In Mina's world, everyone was equal until proven stupid.

One year into her job, the British Director retired and an Australian succeeded him. His name was Tim Drake. He was not a demonstrative fellow. He was a slim, mousy looking guy with a face hard to read. He was very anal, unlike other Australians she had met in the Main Building during coffee breaks. Australians tended to be easy-going, burly fellows who laughed quite a lot. This guy was a workaholic.

Mina worked for him and instantly took a dislike to him and the work. He dictated too much and rather slowly. She tended to doodle all around the page while waiting for the next sentence. Her doodles gave her ideas about paintings.

Another custom Mina detested was when she was taking dictation, Mr. Drake, would ask her to get coffee for him. *Who am I? His maid?* Mina asked herself and she stopped that habit in her own subtle way.

There was a messenger by the name of Pascal at the Annex who was in charge of delivering the mail from outside and took mail from out-baskets to in-baskets. He also did odd jobs like photocopying. When, at the next dictation session, Mr. Drake asked her to get his coffee, she said, "I'll ask Pascal to get you a cup." Mr. Drake got the hint and, from then on, he always asked her to ask Pascal for his daily cup of coffee. Mina had also won that round.

The other secretaries were astounded at her cheekiness.

"Good for you, Mina," they said.

SUMMER

Summer was late coming to Geneva that year. Mina did not know that the lousy spring weather drags on in Switzerland with some hot and some cold days, but mostly rainy days. She had to wear wool sweaters in the middle of summer.

The greatest news was that a new hotel was inaugurated in Geneva and it had an outdoor swimming pool with cabanas all around it. It was the Intercontinental Hotel and it was located near the U.N. Outside guests could become a member of the swimming pool facilities in the summer. Mina and Vera immediately opted for that and rented a cabana for the summer months. It was exorbitantly expensive but it was worth it. They spent weekends there and also went swimming after work or during their lunch break if they managed to get a longer one. This was *the* life. Not the one she had in New York, spending her lunch hour in some miserable burger joint on Seventh Avenue.

Another swimming pool club was inaugurated in Divonne les Bains. Divonne was a French town situated between the foot of the Jura mountains and Lake Geneva and was only twenty minutes away from Geneva. It was a small, charming, spa town and it had its own lake. It also had a thermal station where the sisters went often to keep in shape. The atmosphere at the Olympic-size swimming pool was very social. Divonne also had a casino but Mina was not into gambling at all. Nor was Vera. They had had enough of the gambling mania of their father while living in Cairo.

A third possibility was Evian les Bains. That was an older spa town in France, also with an Olympic size swimming pool but it was further away than Divonne les Bains, so the sisters did not go there that often. There was a good art gallery in the town and Mina got an exhibition offer from them. She had to smuggle her paintings camouflaged in her car because she did not want to make a list for customs and follow the legal procedure which was painstakingly complicated. She exhibited only her etchings and it was a successful show.

People were very much into etchings then. She loved the process but disliked the odor of the acid. She made it a point to go to the Centre de la Gravure in Geneva at least once a week to produce her etchings. It was quite a hassle doing that because there was no parking facility. She had to park far away and carry all her paraphernalia back and forth. She produced a multitude of etchings and sent them to London galleries and even to Hong Kong.

LOUIS

In August of that year, a couple of weeks after her dinner with Bernard, there was a cocktail in the Department. Mina attended it to see if she could meet this French aristocrat Bernard had talked about. On her way towards the bar of the lounge where the cocktail was being held, this man materialized next to her and introduced himself. Well, he was not that difficult to meet. He was tall, well built, with scarce blond hair, icy blue eyes and well-defined lips. His suit was impeccably tailored and he spoke exquisite French. He introduced himself as Louis and they conversed about this and that. The conversation was not too exhilarating. Again, Mina was asked where she was from. She had to go through the spiel but he understood immediately. In fact, he had been to Armenia. Wow! She was impressed. She had never been to Armenia and this Frenchman had. He had been to Moscow, St. Petersburg and then travelled south to visit Armenia. Mina asked him loads of questions about her country. It was during the communist regime so things were not that good then. He told her that the schooling system seemed to be excellent because there were no illiterate Armenians in the country. "One good thing about the Communist regime," he said.

He volunteered to take her home after the cocktail and she accepted. He had a convertible Mercedes sports car. She was not that impressed about cars. She had been in expensive cars in Rome so this was not new to her. He flirted with her on the ride and she flirted back. He asked her for a dinner date the following evening and took her to a restaurant she had never been: L'Auberge de Carouge, a cozy restaurant with a lot of woodwork in a quaint suburb of Geneva, where a few galleries and boutiques were located. Mina had walked around Carouge in one of her wanderings trying to find a gallery to exhibit in and had not succeeded. They all seemed to cater to well-known Swiss artists. Carouge is a Mediterranean style hamlet and is nicknamed "the Greenwich Village of Geneva." Louis told her that in the evenings, a bohemian vibe emanated with a plethora of cafes and jazz clubs. Bernard had taken her there a few times for dinner in one of the funky restaurants. She did not particularly care for jazz clubs. Jazz was not her type of music. She preferred the Latin beat.

Mina was not attracted to Louis physically, but he was extremely knowledgeable and had excellent manners. She appreciated his company. A French girlfriend in New York had once told her that she should not judge guys on looks alone but should give them a chance and that, eventually, they might grow on her.

She was right. Louis grew on her.

He had a doctorate in economics and he taught her about French literature. He also loved classical music and they went to a few open-air concerts in Parc de la Grange on the Left Bank. Mina very much enjoyed classical music. After all, she came from a background of a concert piano player aunt and a soprano cousin, so classical music was not foreign to her. They saw each other often and she noticed that he was always looking at her as though sizing her up, like one does a Louis XIV furniture, which he was in love with. *Was it because of the name Louis?* she asked herself. It was a stupid question but it did come into her mind.

"Holding hands with you gives me extreme pleasure, something I have not had for a long time," he said one day as he was driving going to dinner and holding her hand. The first time he kissed her was like one would kiss a pretty cat, a peck on the lips. The relationship navigated to the bedroom a few weeks later.

Louis had not completely furnished his apartment. It had been about four years since he had moved in but most of his stuff was still in cardboard boxes. Besides his bedroom there were two other bedrooms, in one of which there was a desk and a chair, nothing else.

The other was full of boxes, still unpacked. The living room was not furnished except for an armchair and an expensive stereo set on which he played his classical records. The kitchen had no furniture because he never ate there. He was the quintessential bachelor. The fridge was bare. Mina was not comfortable being in his home. It felt like being in an unfurnished unwelcoming flat. Louis liked walking from room to room, breathing deeply and listening to music, while she sat on the only armchair in the living room looking at this strange man.

Knowing that she was an artist with no studio, he offered her one of his bedrooms to paint in and gave her the key to his apartment. He often went to Paris on weekends for personal business and she took advantage of his absence to paint in her 'new studio.' Actually, she did some of her best paintings there—with artificial light. All man and woman configurations with arms and legs intertwined like those of an octopus.

The girls in the Office started teasing her.

"You will soon become a countess," they said.

Louis had the title of a Count and he had an impressive last name with a 'de' in the middle.

"We have not come to that stage yet, we're just friends," Mina said. Although she wished for that to happen eventually. She was unwilling to bare the details of her private life to them just yet. Mina never hatched her eggs before they were due. She thought it would bring bad luck. She was extremely superstitious. She wore a blue eye on a safety pin attached to her bra as her mother had told her it would ward off the evil eye.

"This is the first time we see him involved with someone," they said.

"It may happen sooner than you think."

Carol, the Scottish girl, was quite audacious and cheeky and asked Louis one day, in Mina's presence, when he entered her office, *"alors, Louis, on est amoureux?"* (so, Louis are we in love?). Mina was taken aback and felt cripplingly embarrassed. He blushed, poor guy. He did not deny it, which was a good sign, so to speak. Mina liked him even more after the blush. It proved he was human and sensitive.

Louis lent her his car when he was absent from Geneva. Mina did not yet have a car and she used to take the bus to and from work. He was a finicky fellow, much worried about dirt and stains at home and dents in the car and she wondered how come he trusted her with his Mercedes convertible. And, a shift car, at that. Mina was used to automatics. She guessed he was ready to cover any damage that would ensue. Ha, ha. She got used to the shift car by driving around the block a few times. When she drove up in front of the Annex with the car everyone in the building gawked at her. Their relationship was no longer a secret. Mina was greatly amused and the girls teased her even more.

Christian, the French guy from the ENA, was impressed when he saw Mina with Louis' car. The French have a peculiarity; they are extremely class conscious. Because of the fact that a non-aristocratic woman, Mina, was being courted by an aristocrat, it made her look important in their eyes. "She must have something special," is what they thought. Therefore, Christian was overly courteous with her from then on and addressed her with deference. Mina was amused and giggled to herself.

The word marriage was mentioned by Louis once or twice. But Mina was not too keen about it, because she did not love him. She liked him a lot but love him? Love was too big a word. No, she did not love him. In fact, she did not think she would ever fall in love again and experience the passion she had with Gary or with Shoukry. It was just not happening with any of her beaux. Was she being too cautious and choosy? Too demanding? Her criteria were way over the roof. She often thought she should be more accepting of flaws. After all, she had them too. But, she was looking for that something extra. She wanted to be irresistibly attracted to a man. She wanted him to be a like a magnet, drawing her to him, like Shoukry had done.

She had been with Louis for four months now and she was not yet bored. That was a good omen. She asked her mother and Vera what they thought of him and whether it would be a good idea to marry him although she did not love him. Her experience had been that, after being married with someone for a number of years, love flies out of the window. Didn't this happen with Gary who she loved passionately—puppy love—but passionate for sure. A constant yearning for someone, that's what she meant by passion. And she challenged anyone who told her the contrary about that kind of passionate love lasting forever.

Another type of comfortable love comes gradually into the picture and couples grow old together celebrating their fifty-year or seventy-year anniversary, if they were lucky. Or, they divorce and try again and again to recapture the feelings they had when they were young, naive and impressionable.

"He is a reliable, intelligent and cultured man," her mother said.

"He loves you, I can tell," Vera said. "He is also very respectful and has good manners," she added.

"But I don't really love him. He does not make my heart beat pitter patter."

"Well, wait then, don't rush it, you may meet someone else," Vera said.

Mina took their advice into consideration and mulled over the possibilities and the reasons for her hesitation. She wanted to be prepared to respond if he popped up the question or would she have to pop it up for him if she came to a decision? He seemed to be shy in expressing his feelings. She knew that a long-time bachelor feels trapped when he starts having feelings for a woman. She wondered how many relationships he had had before her. He was after all, forty years old, ten years older than she was.

Mina went on skiing weekends with Louis. One weekend he invited her to Paris. Finally. She had been waiting for that invitation. She was curious to see how he lived over there. They took the TGV, the rapid French train which only took about four hours. They travelled first class, of course. Louis had an *abonnement* (a season ticket) as he took that journey twice a month. His apartment was a one-bedroom in one of the chicest *quartiers* in Paris. It was on Avenue Montaigne opposite the Plaza Athenée Hotel. And the Dior boutique was one block away. There was a small restaurant next door where they had breakfast, the usual café crème and a buttered French baguette. Louis' brand-new fridge in the Paris apartment was also bare. He did not even have instant coffee in the kitchen. Mina's trips to Paris increased. She enjoyed going there and strutting up and down the Champs Elysees in her trendy clothes, and going to the theatre and museums with Louis. He taught her a lot about French literature and antique furniture. She was his muse.

THE MURDER

On her return from one of the trips to Paris, Mina was late coming to work on the Monday morning. While going up the stairs to her office, she saw that everyone was in the conference room with faces fit for a visit to the morgue. She sat down breathlessly in the one available chair which she pulled over to be closer to the conference table. She looked at all of the people seated around the table and she didn't know what they were talking about. They looked worried and were rather glum. They were talking about an unfortunate happening—a murder. *Who was murdered?* Mina turned to the guy sitting next to her and she whispered.

"What has happened?"

"Ricardo got killed," he whispered in her ear.

Ricardo dead? The Peruvian Librarian dead? He was a short fellow, very God-fearing and drove a white Mini sports car. He had taken her home once or twice. There were images of the Madonna all over his dashboard and the rosary hanging from the rearview mirror. He always did the sign of the cross before he got in his car. He was very religious and also gay. Not many people knew about his predilections. He was also very authoritative. When he gave her assignments, he clicked his heels like Hitler and pointed his finger at her, ordering her in a staccato manner of speech to do the job in the manner he dictated. Often, Mina disregarded him. Her opinion of short men was that they all acted like Napoleon, high and mighty to exude power and authority lest they be pushed under the carpet. She *would* have liked to push him under the carpet.

No one seemed to know the fact that Ricardo was gay until that morning. The story was that he had picked up a young man in a bar and taken him home with him. After they had done their business, Ricardo had fallen asleep. He had awakened and had seen the guy rummaging through his desk. "What are you doing?" he had asked and had lunged at him whereupon the guy had taken a knife out of his backpack and had stabbed him several times. The police had informed the IOE of the unfortunate incident. The details also came out in the newspaper when the perpetrator was caught and admitted his crime in every detail.

Mina didn't remember how they found the perpetrator. He was only seventeen years old and got a seven-year sentence and was out after five. The justice system in Switzerland is quite lax. Murder does not get life. And, this was considered a sex crime.

Mina had not liked Ricardo and had wished many times that he would disappear from her life because his assignments were rather stupid and she did not like his bossy manners. But, she certainly had not wished him dead.

Almost all the members of the Annex staff attended the funeral. He did not have a family and did not have many friends. Poor fellow—what a way to go.

LOUIS

Mina was quite curious about Louis' past love affairs, not that she was jealous. No, just curious. The occasion presented itself and she snooped. She took advantage of being alone in his apartment when he was away in Paris. She did not feel good about it but she did not feel guilty. She just had an uneasy feeling. After all, he had trusted her. But she couldn't help it. She had to find out about his past amorous life. He never talked about it, not that she did either. She also went on an inspection tour of the bedroom and the bathroom to see whether there were any telltale signs of other women having been in the apartment; like hair in the bathroom or under the bed. She was so scared that, in so doing, something bad would happen to her in retaliation. Something from God. She was God-fearing and superstitious.

Nevertheless, she had to know in order to act accordingly with him. One day, when she was alone his apartment, she went over to his desk and opened all the drawers. There were some useless papers, bills, spare keys, paper clips and cards, and then she found something worthwhile—some letters written by one particular woman by the name of Gisele. Aha, she was almost hesitant to read them, lest it would shatter her illusions of his intentions towards her. She knew men can be devious and sneaky.

By the tone of it, this woman was wailing, proclaiming her love for him and asking him the reasons for his recent coldness. *I know the reason*, Mina wanted to tell her, *he has met me and you are out of the picture, girl, adios.*

She did not have the occasion to snoop in Louis' apartment in Paris because he was always there with her. Nevertheless, she looked in the bathroom. No hair, no other toothbrush, no comb, no creams. A good sign. So, where did he have his amorous adventures? Surely, he must have had some. Or, the apartment had been thoroughly cleaned before Mina's arrival on the scene.

At this point, her relationship with Louis became on and off, because he was being non-committal sometimes and taking her for granted. When he went to Paris on business or for parties, Mina started dating other guys who came into town and sometimes she even told him about them to make him jealous and react. She did not like the idea that he was going to Paris every other weekend for social obligations. Louis admitted to her that he was often invited to parties by women in the aristocratic milieu. He belonged to some kind of matchmaking group, where they held parties for eligible women and men. She had found some invitations in his desk drawer. She resented his going to such parties.

When Louis asked what she would be doing on the weekends he was away, she responded in a flirtatious manner.

"Well, my dear Louis," she would say, "you go to Paris and do whatever you have to do there, and I do whatever I want to do here."

Whereupon he would smile his cryptic smile and ask her out for dinner in a four-star restaurant which she gladly accepted and he would be particularly attentive to her. *It goes to show you that men like competition, and they shun needy women,* Mina thought.

She felt empowered.

GENEVA

Life in Geneva was pleasant indeed. The sisters were having the time of their lives. They had more activities going on and functions to attend to than in Manhattan. First of all, the proximity of the lake and the swimming pools. Secondly, the business conferences swarming with men. Thirdly, weekends in other cities in Europe. Skiing in winter in nearby France or Switzerland and the French or Italian coasts in the summer. But, there is always a 'but'. She was looking for the impossible-to-find man to enjoy these outings with. She was looking for a duplicate of Shoukry. She *did* want to settle down and have kids at some point. She was just over thirty and her biological clock was ticking away. She knew that there was still time but time passes by fast. In fact, it is the most elusive escape artist of all times. Mina did not want to end up a spinster. Well, not a spinster technically since she had already been married once. But she did want children and she did not want to have them alone like some extremely liberated women tend to do in the States. She liked a family atmosphere and always thought a child should have two parents. Her quest was overwhelming her. She had love-sick suitors but their flaws were not negligible and she knew she would get bored with them eventually.

Mina was very conscious of her looks. She always looked at herself in the mirror for telltale signs of aging—wrinkles and cellulite. Luckily, she did not find any of these signs yet but she knew they would appear eventually. She was so scared of losing her looks and not be able to attract the male species. Although she did not look her age, the number was there. She was over thirty.

At this point in her life she wished she had more time to paint. Man-hunting was a tedious endeavor and time consuming. If she only had one man to concentrate on. One man who would blow her mind away. One man who would obliterate all others. Well, there was such a man but he was far away and she had left him behind.

She was interested in so many things that it was difficult for her to concentrate on only one subject. She jumped from one thing to the other. She was avaricious and wanted to enjoy life to the fullest and not be bogged down with the ordinary. She was constantly searching for new ventures and new excitement.

Her art was going well and she had exhibitions in England, France and Switzerland. She also got good reviews about her work in newspapers. She was super busy with the Office, with her Art and with Men.

"You gotta slow down a little," her mother advised her.

"I'll have a lot of time for that when I am old and arthritic," she replied.

And so, she galloped through life at full speed.

MARCEL

Mina was having lunch in town with a girlfriend after having done some shopping one Saturday afternoon, when she met Marcel accidentally in the same restaurant. He volunteered to take her home with his car. She agreed because she had a lot of parcels and had to change two buses to get home. They spoke little in the car. Marcel had a dead pan face. While he was driving on the main street towards her home, she realized that he did not turn off to the left towards the street of her apartment building.

"You missed my street," Mina said.

"We are going to my place," he said resolutely, not looking at her.

"No, we're not," she snapped.

Whereupon he ignored her and kept on driving with a determined expression on his face. She could have slapped him but she refrained her impulse and bid her time. When he drove up to a stop light, she opened the door of the car and jumped out.

"You can deliver my parcels later on," she said calmly, "after which I don't wish to see you ever again. You're obnoxious."

A couple of hours later, Marcel came by and rang the doorbell. Mina opened the door and he just stood there with her parcels with an apologetic expression on his face. She could have punched him but she needed her parcels.

"So sorry, I should not have acted that way," he said in a sheepish voice.

"No, you shouldn't have. I accept your apology but I really mean it. I don't ever want to see you again.

"Are you sure?"

"Of course, I'm sure. How dare you try to kidnap me!"

"Well, I'll give you time to think it over. I'm still very much in love with you," he said with a hangdog look. Mina hated that type of look. At that precise moment she did pity him but she was not going to change her mind and be with a guy out of pity. She just took the parcels from him, thanked him and he went way without any further comment.

She saw Marcel occasionally around town. They just said hello and that was that.

Mina was now free to concentrate on Louis and try to rekindle her relationship with him. It had gotten to be tepid.

GENEVA

Mina often thought of all the men she had met. None of them interested her all that much. She was the type of girl who got easily bored with people. First of all, she liked good dancers because dancing was one of her passions, but none of them matched her ex-husband or Shoukry. Another thing she looked for is humor, someone who made her laugh. In moments of doubt, she often asked herself, *should I have kept Gary on just because he danced well? What a silly thought.* She was surprised at herself for even thinking about it. Also, none of the guys sparked any passion in her. That was important to her. She considered them as nice guys but 'nice' was not enough. She needed excitement. She was sort of auditioning them in bed to see which one would fit better in her sexual orbit. In no way, did she consider them as lifetime prospects.

One thing Mina realized. The way to a man's heart seemed to pretend not to be interested in him. The more she played hard to get, the more they pursued her. She attracted them like gnats to apple cider vinegar. Men did not like needy and clingy women. Well, she was neither.

There was faithful Bernard, who left his girlfriend and was back in the picture. He was still a good friend. He took her to the theater and to dinner sometimes. He was like a patient dog, always there, ready to serve her. Whenever Mina had no escort and wanted to attend some function, she called Bernard who was all too eager to accompany her. He was convinced that she would take him on if he had more money than Louis. She told him that was not the case.

"Why, then? Why are we not lovers?" he persisted.

"Bernard, you seem to forget the fact that I am now with Louis," she replied. She could not have told him that the idea of going to bed with an orange-haired, shortish guy with dull gray eyes and pursed lips did not appeal to her in the least. She did admit, however, that he was amusing to be with. He had humor.

Norbert, the Belgian, was completely out of the picture after she saw him with the pregnant wife. She met him in a cafe in town one Saturday morning. He was alone and he came over to sit with her.

"Where is your wife?" Mina asked.

"At home."

"You are a sneaky one, Norbert," she said. "Imagine inviting me to Paris after impregnating your wife. You really make me laugh."

"That was an accident. I mean my wife getting pregnant. I am more interested in you but I have come to the realization that you need an inattentive man in your life," he said. "Someone who pays no attention to you, then you would not act so aloof. Or, do you just act like an iceberg only with me?"

"Don't be ridiculous," she scoffed and did not comment any further. They parted ways.

ADAM

Adam resurfaced in Geneva a couple of years later with a short-term summer contract at CERN. They had dinner and he expressed the desire to renew their relationship. Did he really think Mina was panting to see him again and restart something that was not that hot to begin with? Mina was busy with her present relationship with Louis. The dinner was at the Bearne restaurant, the only restaurant in Geneva which had a four-star rating in the Michelin Guide. During the dinner, Adam solemnly declared to Mina, "I think I'll import you to New York at the end of next year."

What about this year? You really think I will be available next year when I am not available for you now? Mina wanted to blurt out.

"We'll see, if I'm still available," she replied with an enigmatic smile. She told him about Louis.

Upon learning that Louis was also a mountain climber, Adam asked her to introduce him so that they could go climbing together. Mina then asked Louis if he would like to go climbing with a friend of hers from New York. She did not tell him he was her ex-boyfriend. She thought it would be fun to get them together. Such opposites. He agreed. She was curious to find out how they would get along. She later learnt that it was a disaster and they never repeated the experience. They went to Chamonix, the ski resort she did not particularly care about, otherwise she would have gone with them to sit in a café and do some people-watching. The town did not offer any frivolities. It was mostly for real sporty people and Mina was not the sporty type. Well, she did go to the gym twice a week to keep into shape, did a little swimming in summers and skiing in winters. But that's as far as her sport activities would go. She was more interested in the evening activities.

During their mountain climbing expedition, Adam found out that Louis was not such an expert. He was lagging behind, so Adam suggested that he hire his own monitor and go separately. They never saw each other again.

Mina was not at all physically attracted to Adam and she declined going to bed with him during his stay, telling him that she had Louis as a permanent fixture. The trouble with Mina was that she yearned for a strong physical attraction. She yearned for that electrical charge pulling her to the man irresistibly, like a magnet. Like it was with Shoukry. Always Shoukry. God damn it! Will she ever stop thinking about him? Maybe she was obsessed by him because she had not gone to bed with him. No, that was not it. Shoukry was different. He had an undeniable charisma.

She liked Adam's mental attributes. And she liked Louis' knowledge on a vast number of subjects and his refined upbringing. But then what? All the men she met had serious flaws and acted immaturely sometimes. She knew she had some flaws too and she was working on them. Mina needed fire in their eyes and passion in their hands. She had auditioned several by now and she had to choose the most marriageable. Louis came out on top of the list. She had to have a reliable and dependable father to the children she intended to have. And, most of all, someone who would not bore her to oblivion. And, she also decided that, if the husband she chose did not satisfy her one way or the other, she would have a string of lovers, like some French women do.

She imparted her newly formed decision to her mother and sister.

They just shook their heads.

"You'll do whatever you have set your mind to, so what we say is of no consequence," said her mother. Vera agreed with her.

"Why don't you get in touch with Shoukry?" Vera asked.

"How can I do that? It would sound so silly. I wouldn't know what to say."

"Think about it. You're miserable and you're not really enjoying yourself with all the guys you meet. You jump from one to the other like a chicken without a head. They don't satisfy you so why not take up with Shoukry?"

"No, I couldn't do that." Mina replied. "What then? Would I be willing to go and live in Egypt? How do I know if he is still available? And, what about you guys? If I go and live in Egypt, will you follow me or stay here?"

There was no response and the subject was closed.

A HORRIBLE EVENING

Mina had a harrowing experience one evening which traumatized her for almost a year. She had gone with Vera to the Club 58 for dancing and were seated with a bunch of people they met that night. Mina danced a few times with some of the fellows then she got bored and wanted to leave. The music was not to her liking. She preferred the Latin beats but those were not being played that night. Also, she did not like dancing slows with just anyone. She liked dancing slows with guys that she really wanted to feel close to. Unfortunately, there were none on the horizon these days.

The sisters shared one car. Vera's date, Sven, told her not to worry, that he would bring Vera home safe and sound. As Mina was about to leave, one of the guys in the group got up also and asked her whether she could drop him off on the way home. As this guy's home was on her way, Mina agreed. She had danced with him that night. They had not had an unforgettable conversation. He seemed to be a boring guy.

The guy's name was Tony. He was British and a journalist at the United Nations. Mina had met his parents at the Tennis Club. They seemed to be decent folks.

When Mina stopped the car in front of his apartment building in the middle-class district of Eaux-Vives, Tony did not get out of the car.

"Would you like to come upstairs for a drink?" he asked slurring his speech.

Mina knew this meant *would you like to come upstairs and get fucked*.

"Thanks, but no, I'm tired. I'd prefer to go home."

She could not stand the fellow. She wished she had not agreed to drop him off.

"I get very nasty with girls who say no," the jerk came out with and pulled at her arm.

It was a cold winter evening and Mina was wearing her fur coat. She snuggled tighter in her coat, looked at Tony and realized that he was very drunk. Here was this huge guy sitting in her VW beetle trying to make out with her. The smell of the liquor was overpowering. She thought of punching him. She was wearing a square topaz ring on her finger and it would inflict quite a bit of damage to his face if she used it. She would then run out of the car and scream for help. *Could I do that without getting hurt?* Mina asked herself.

"Don't even think of honking to wake up the neighbors. I'll hurt you." he said.

This was getting out of hand and Mina thought of a ruse. She was going to get badly hurt if she did not come up with a plausible solution.

"Why don't we go back to the club for a drink?" she ventured to say, while trembling inside.

"Nah, let's go to your place."

"I live with my mother." She should not have said that. All the more reason to go upstairs to his place.

"Then, come upstairs, come on." He nudged her quite roughly.

"Actually, why don't you come home with me?"

"You said you lived with your mother."

"I lied. My mother lives in the same building but in another apartment. I live with my sister whom you met at the club."

At this point, Mina wanted him to agree so that she would drive off to the police station on the way home and start honking right in front of it.

"Are you a minor?" Tony then asked.

"No, don't worry," was her reply.

Tony agreed. So, she drove off and came in front of the police station on Rue de la Serviette but it was closed. Bad luck. Nothing else to do but drive home. She parked in front of her building and thought of getting out of the car fast and run to the front door of the building which was locked. If she could open it fast enough then close it before Tony got to it, it would be great. But, she realized that would not be possible. The door was very slow on its hinges. She would never make it inside alone.

Tony followed her upstairs to the first-floor apartment. Mina kept her fur coat on in case she had to make a fast exit.

"Sit down and I'll get you a drink," she said.

Tony sat down obediently. Mina filled up a paper cup with water and handed it to him.

"What's this? Water? Paper cup? I'd like a proper drink in a proper glass."

Mina then went to her mom's bedroom and woke her up.

"Mom, wake up, there's a man in the living room who doesn't want to leave. He is quite drunk."

Mina explained the problem to her mom in a hushed tone. Whereupon, her mom got up from her bed, put on a dressing gown, came into the living room and faced Tony.

"What's that I hear? You don't want to leave my daughter alone? Please get out of the apartment right now."

"You lied!" barked Tony. "You do live with your mother, after all."

Mina got scared and picked up their huge Maine coon cat to use as a weapon, just in case.

At which point Tony got up from the couch and came to the door. He saw the mail addressed to them on the table next to the door.

"Armenian sluts," he spat out seeing the name ending in 'ian' on the envelopes. Most Armenian names end in 'ian'. He seemed to be aware of that fact.

Whereupon, Mina's mom raised her arm and, in one sweeping motion, slapped this huge guy who was towering above them like an angry giant ready to pounce.

Mina was scared out of her wits and was ready to throw the cat at his face if he ventured to attack her mother. Surprisingly, he calmed down and went back and sat on the couch.

"Call me a cab," he ordered.

Mina was relieved. She picked up the phone and called a cab. After ten minutes, she told Tony that the cab must have arrived.

"Go tell him to go away. I don't need a cab right now. I want my drink first."

Mina was glad of the opportunity to go out of the building. She told the cab driver to call the police and inform them that there was a belligerent person in her apartment who was threatening them. She then came upstairs and told Tony she had gotten rid of the cab. Tony seemed to be relaxed at this point and just sat on a chair looking at the walls. She and her mom and the cat sat on the couch facing him. No words were uttered.

A few minutes went by which seemed like hours to Mina, and the apartment door opened. Vara and her escort came in. Mina explained the situation to Sven who took Tony downstairs to the lobby by force. Sven was also a big guy and could handle Tony. He told him off. Mina was listening through the doorway. Tony then hit Sven and a scuffle arose. At this time, the police arrived. A young guy and an older one. They controlled the situation. Tony and Sven then left and the policemen came to talk to Mina who explained the problem to them from the beginning.

"Would you like to press charges?" asked the older policeman.

"I certainly would," replied Mina.

"I would advise you against it. If this comes in front of a judge, he will tell you that you invited him—although I know you did it to protect yourself as your mother was at home—nevertheless, the situation would be tricky for you. I gave him a good scare and told him that if anything of the sort happens again, I will have his working permit revoked and he would be obliged to leave Geneva."

"Thanks for your advice."

"He won't be bothering you again."

After thanking the policemen profusely, they all relaxed and went to bed.

From that day on and for about a year, Mina never got in a car with any of her dates. She took her own car and would meet them at the designated rendez-vous. She did not want a recurrence of what had happened with Tony. She met him once or twice at the Tennis Club but she ignored him.

HUNTER

One day, while basking in the sun at their cabana at the Intercontinental Hotel Swimming Pool, Mina and Vera met an American man, an older man, Hunter, who was staying at the hotel for an extended period. His work was in the oil industry in Libya but he had been given time off to loll away in Geneva until things got settled with the oil business in that country. He adopted the Seferians and they adopted him. He was another "Uncle Jimmy," the American naval officer who had stayed with them as a roomer in the 1940s in Cairo. Hunter had a wife, daughter and son living in New York. He was lonely for a family life and was a most generous man, taking them to dinner all over town. He liked to eat well. He had a per diem and he was spending it as he saw fit. He was a great talker, relating stories from his youth in Stillwater, Oklahoma. He was also a great cook. He would do the food shopping and bring the groceries to their place and cook up a scrumptious meal with their mother. When the sisters did not have dates, they played canasta with him. Mina was going out with Louis, then. Hunter told her she should not hesitate and to hook him fast. Everybody said so. But Mina was still dithering. She didn't know what she was waiting for.

For Shoukry to suddenly materialize perhaps?

Another New Year came all too soon. Mina, Vera, Louis and another fellow went to the U.N. Reveillon Ball. It was held at the U.N. What a bore that was. First of all, Louis was not a good dancer nor a good conversationalist with people he did not know. There was nobody else she could dance with and, after midnight, she wanted to go home. Vera was enjoying herself with her escort and she stayed on. Louis wanted to take Mina over to his place to christen the New Year with sex but she feigned tiredness and refused. She was not in the mood. She felt a sadness overpowering her. She would have liked to be with Shoukry.

After about two months, Hunter's family came from the U.S. and they all lived in the Intercontinental Hotel. Hunter's wife, Bea, was an exceptionally nice woman and their daughter, Martha-Nell, was a riot. Their son had a drug problem which preoccupied them a great deal. Then Martha-Nell's boyfriend also came over with a backpack. He had been starving during his travels throughout Europe, so when Hunter took him to dinner on the first evening he was in town, he ate for three people. Mina had never seen a person eat so much steak in all her life.

The sisters had an eventful social life. The U.N. offered gym classes and they took part in that to keep into shape. They also took some language classes to be more proficient in Spanish and Italian. They started playing tennis and badminton. All in all, their agenda was full. The evenings when they did not go out, they read or sewed or knitted or played cards. Life was indeed good.

As for Vera's love life, it was not too brilliant. She was carrying on an affair with one of the Directors at the WMO, an Iranian guy married to a Swede. Vera told Mina that the wife knew about the affair and did not seem to mind his philandering. Vera guessed the wife no longer wanted to have sex with him. Mina would sometimes meet the wife at the supermarket and they would greet each other. Farhad, that was the guy's name, was very much in love with Vera and wanted to marry her if his wife would grant him a divorce. But the wife did not agree. She wanted to keep the existing scenario, having a husband in name only—for the style of life presumably. Vera was not that keen to marry him. She liked him, though.

An unfortunate incident also happened to Vera one evening.

Mina was coming home from a hen birthday party at around 10 pm one evening and, while parking the car, she noticed that Vera was in a car with a man and there seemed to be a scuffle. The guy was pulling Vera to him while she was trying to push him away. Vera was trying to get out of the car but her escort was forcibly pulling her away from the door. Mina walked resolutely to the car and opened the door on Vera's side. The guy looked her as though he had seen a ghost.

"Vera, come with me," she said "and you get the fuck away from here before I call the police, Mina told the fellow." She was surprised at her outburst. Vera came out of the car and uttered a sigh of relief. The guy drove away making a quick exit. Mina had not forgotten the Tony incident of not so long ago.

THE DIVORCE

Getting remarried and having children came into Mina's thoughts often. She did not wish to end up a single lonely woman. Family was important to her. However, before she could get remarried, if the right candidate suddenly made an apparition, she had to ask her husband for a divorce. The right candidate seemed to be Louis at this point. She trusted him in a way. He was dependable, kind hearted and cared for her. He was just too shy to express his feelings.

Gary was still in New York and was doing quite well, she heard. She wrote him a letter.

"Don't ever expect any alimony from me," Gary replied. Mina could sense he was almost growling when he wrote that. They had an acrimonious correspondence going back and forth on the subject of divorce and alimony.

"I don't need your alimony," Mina wrote to him.

"I'll get a Mexican divorce," he said, "it will be quicker."

"No Mexican divorce for me, it is not recognized in Switzerland."

"I'll get a Las Vegas one then," was his next suggestion.

"No Vegas either, just get yourself a New York lawyer and our lawyers will drum up something acceptable to both of us," was her suggestion.

Actually, Gary had borrowed money from Mina during their marriage and she tried to bring this up in their correspondence. Gary categorically refused to pay her a penny if she wanted the divorce that badly.

Mina accepted the conditions and gave up asking for the borrowed money. The divorce proceedings would drag on indefinitely, if she did.

She just wanted to get it over with and be free to remarry. The American lawyer tried to prolong the matter of course to get more funds from Gary. One of her mother's friends told her to hurry up because Louis would not wait forever. "You have the catch the bird when it is cooing," she said, "otherwise it might fly away to other more welcoming nests."

The complication arose from the fact that Mina was an Iranian national through Gary who was Iranian through his father, who had obtained Iranian citizenship after landing in Iran during the Armenian Genocide march. Her life was indeed complicated. Born in Egypt, having an Iranian passport and residing in Switzerland with a husband in New York.

It was necessary to get an attestation letter from the Iranian Consulate. The day Mina went in to get the letter, she was told the secretary was absent on sick leave and she was asked to type it herself. Luckily it was in French and not in Farsi. She agreed without hesitation.

When she was asked for the reason of the divorce, she wrote down "incompatibility." It was accepted by the Consul.

Before the divorce could be pronounced in the Swiss courts however, the final approval had to come from the Ministry of the Interior in Teheran. Under Iranian law, a wife's domicile is that of her husband. That meant Mina had to go back to New York and try to get a divorce there. That would cost her a lot of money and time. She asked the Iranian consul for advice. As the latter was getting a divorce himself and, as he was after Mina's tail, he agreed to help her. Mina did not tell him her tail was not available for him. The Consul volunteered to go with her to her Swiss lawyer and brought the Iranian Civil Code with him. He helped the lawyer find the appropriate code for Mina's divorce in Geneva.

Mina did not trust lawyers, due to her experience with Frank, her lawyer in New York during her separation with Gary. She kept asking her Swiss lawyer how much the divorce would cost. He was a massive, bespectacled, sixty-year old man seated behind an antique desk in a room furnished with somber antique furniture and an expensive looking Persian rug. There were also several bookcases lining the walls full of thick lawyerly books.

"I am not like American lawyers, you know, I don't inflate my hours, you can trust me."

Trust a lawyer? Does he think I am that naive? Mina asked herself. After he corresponded with Gary's lawyer in New York, she came to trust him as he got the job done at a lesser cost than she expected. Not having that much money in her bank account, Louis lent her the money to pay for the divorce. Actually, it was only 1,200 Swiss francs, equivalent of a month's salary at the IEO.

Mina was finally divorced and free to remarry. But was Louis the right candidate? She had a plethora of men friends but they were just that—men friends with some of whom she had sex. There was only Louis in the picture at this time as a plausible marriageable candidate. He seemed to be the most eligible and dependable. The next time he was in one of his amorous moods, she would broach the subject. He just needed a little pushing.

LOUIS

Louis taught Mina a lot about French literature, antiques and classical music. He gave her some books by French authors to read. She enjoyed reading the French classics. He appreciated her being an artist. He even bought a couple of paintings from her. They had fun together going to cultural activities around town. She saw a lot of him and they often had sex. He was always eager. Mina's French improved tremendously. She started to have deep feelings towards him and considered seriously marrying him.

The thing that bothered her the most about Louis, was that he was not affectionate and Mina like to cuddle up to a man like a cat and be caressed. She knew he cared for her and he was sexually heated up every time he saw her. He just was not an ardent lover. He performed sex quite mechanically. Mina needed passion and she was not getting it.

He was not Shoukry. She kept thinking about Shoukry and wondered whether she would ever cease yearning for him or whether she would ever see him again. Unless she went to Egypt, of course, but that trip was not in the picture at all.

The office girls teased her again when they realized the relationship was on seriously again with Louis.

"So, you've made up your mind?" They asked.

"Sort of." She was not forthcoming with any of her innermost thoughts.

Louis planned a party in his apartment in Paris to introduce her to his entourage—his aristocratic entourage. That's good, she thought, that would ward off all the prospective aristocratic bitches who are chasing him and inviting him to parties.

He wanted her to be dressed to kill. He was quite meticulous about clothes. As they were walking to go to the movies one day in Paris, he spotted a fabric in the window of a small dressmaker's shop.

"That's a good fabric, for you," he said. "It matches your coloring."

In fact, it was a gold-colored tweed with some turquoise threads, quite unusual.

"Let's go in and ask them to make you a dress," he suggested, "for the party this weekend."

They went in the shop and Mina designed the dress, a simple sleeveless sheath that would show off her curves.

"Isn't it a bit tight?" Louis asked looking at her up and down while she was trying it on at the shop.

"No, it's not," she said, "and even if it is, she can't let anything out, there is not enough fabric in the seams." And that was that. The dress fitted her like a suede glove.

Mina got the dress the next day.

Louis also asked her to have her hair done up in a chignon. He wanted her to appear sophisticated, ladylike and slightly snobby. That was not *her,* so she refused. She was not at all in agreement that a man change the way she dressed or did her hair. She did not want to change her personality.

"I want to be myself," she told him. "Don't try and make me into something I'm not." He saw that she was dead serious and did not argue any further.

Louis hired a caterer to provide champagne and hors d'oeuvres. He was nervous the whole day of the party but, when he saw her emerging from the bedroom in the slick dress and her hair done on one side like Veronica Lake, he was speechless.

"You look gorgeous," he said and relaxed with a great sigh. She had passed the test. She was ready to be shown off to his people like a prized animal.

He had invited about twenty people over in his small living room. Mina could see the envy in the women's eyes and the admiration in the men's. The party went well and Louis was the charming host. He introduced her as his Armenian friend from Geneva. Her being Armenian from Egypt intrigued the guests and she was asked numerous questions. Again, she had to go into her spiel.

Mina had to be back in Geneva that night to go to work the next day, so she had to leave before the party ended, to catch the train. As Louis could not leave his guests to drive her to the train station, one of his friends, Gilbert Du Barry, a lawyer, offered to drive her. Louis thanked him.

During the drive, Gilbert pushed a pencil and paper in her lap and asked for her phone number. Mina was surprised at the request and it took her about a minute to respond.

"But, Gilbert, I am engaged to Louis."

"Well, maybe things might not take their desired course, and I would like to see more of you."

"No, no, that won't do. What will Louis think?"

"You don't have to tell him," he said with a wink, trying to get hold of her hand.

Mina pulled her hand away.

"You just want to spoil things for me, take my phone number and then brag to your friends about it and then somehow Louis will hear and break off the engagement. And you would have achieved your plan. Sorry, I won't play that game."

"I can always find your phone number from information," he ventured to say.

"You do that, but I will not go out with you, so spare your efforts."

"You're such an obstinate creature but adorable, nevertheless."

Mina felt uncomfortable during the ride which seemed interminable. They finally arrived at the train station. He tried to give her a peck on the cheek but Mina turned her face away.

"Thank you so much for accompanying me but this is where it stops," she said giving him the brush off.

When Mina saw Louis again in Geneva, she told him about Gilbert. Louis chuckled. He liked that other men desired her. It reassured him that he was making the right choice—getting a girl that other men coveted.

Finally, there was a change in Louis' behavior. He began inviting her out with his friends. He was proud to introduce her to them now that he had made up his mind to get married. He would then relate to her their opinion—all complimentary. He was flattered that all his friends and acquaintances liked her. *Did he really need their approval?* Mina asked herself. *Of course, they liked me. I am so different from the cold, uptight aristocratic bitches.*

A week later, Mina received a letter from Gilbert, addressing her as Mademoiselle. He had somehow managed to find her address. It was easy in those days. Everything was in the White Pages. He told her that he would be in Courchevel the two coming weekends and if she was also there, he would see her and, in fact, he would love to see her again. Mina did not tell Louis about the letter. No use making him suspicious or angry. One thing about Louis, he was even-tempered and was never angry.

The following weekend when she was in Courchevel again with Louis, they went to the Bar Equipe from 7 - 9 pm for dancing. Dancing with Louis meant slow dancing and Mina was dying to do the Latin dances.

Lo and behold, Gilbert was there with a group of people. He winked at her and she looked away. He then came over to Mina's table and asked Louis if he could dance with her. Louis agreed of course. After all, he was one of his friends. The dance was a wild cha, cha which Gilbert performed well. Then there was a slow tune, a soulful French song.

Gilbert held her tight and guided her away from Louis' view. He then murmured in her ear.

"You don't belong with Louis."

"Says who?"

"Says I. You're full of fire and he is so placid."

"And so?"

"And so, you're not suitable for each other. You should gently discard him and come with me," he said and kissed her on the cheek.

Mina immediately drew away. "Please stop this nonsense," she said.

He held her closer. "You're so adorable when you are angry."

Mina liked it when men yearned for her. It excited her and Gilbert was a hot guy. However, she was planning on marrying Louis so she did not want anything going wrong at this juncture. She might have accepted his advances if Louis were not in the picture. Gilbert was the playboy type. She liked playboy types. Wasn't Shoukry also that type?

"Let's return to the table," she said. "I don't want to cause a scene by pushing you away brusquely."

"As you wish, madam, but know that I am always available for you. You have my phone number on my letter head."

"Wishful thinking," was all she said and drew away. They returned to the table. She was flushed. He gave a *reverence* and walked away.

That was the end of Gilbert.

Mina never trusted any man wholeheartedly. She did not know what Louis did when he was in Paris although they were about to get married. She knew men were sneaky. All she had to do is count the number of married men who were on business trips to Geneva and who went out with other women, she and her sister included. *The more you trust a man the more he cheats on you*, she always believed. She had seen too many letters of invitation written to Louis by mothers of prospective brides. This was the norm in the aristocratic circles of France. The mothers would send letters of invitations to prospective candidates to present their marriageable daughters. It was some kind of market. In one of his talkative moments—which were not too many— Louis had informed her of this custom. Mina knew, or rather she guessed, that when he went to Paris on business, there was also some business of 'girl-watching.' In Armenian it is called *Aghchig Des*. And, naive that she was, she thought this was only an Armenian custom.

Mina, therefore, kept her options open. She would accept dates from any potential candidate that came her way. And there were plenty. Unfortunately, none of them captured her heart and soul. *What am I saying? Soul? That's not what I mean. I want to say that none of them had that "je ne sais quoi."* She did not consider them as husband material. As boyfriends they would do, but as husbands, not even close. Mina saw no reason to attach herself to someone if that someone was not the right one. So, she was unfaithful to Louis, when he was away going to his matchmaking parties and if the occasion arose. And, she would continue doing so, until such time as a definite marriage date had been set. She had to keep her options open.

Surprisingly, Louis started talking about children before talking about marriage. A good omen. And, wonder of wonders, he told her he loved her. She did not see that coming. He was rather shy in expressing his feelings. Yes, he would make a good, reliable and caring husband. What else did she need? She needed ardor and passion, that's what she needed. She needed her heart to vibrate at the sight of her lover.

Louis had the bright idea to introduce her to his mother, brother and sister-in-law who lived in Grenoble. He had finally decided to take the plunge. Mina had her misgivings, though. Not being of aristocratic descent and knowing these people looked down on the class beneath them, she was not that eager to meet them.

First, they went to visit the mother.

"Do you and Louis have plans?" the mother asked when they went to see her. She was ailing and received them in bed.

"Yes, we do," she replied looking at Louis sideways, waiting for him to reply. *Did she really want to marry Louis?* She asked herself one last time.

Louis nodded to his mother and explained their plans. Aristocratic people talk to their parents in the plural mode. They call it "vousvoyer" in French. The parents, however, would use the singular form "tutoyer" when speaking to their children.

Therefore, they started making concrete plans this time. Finally.

She had her divorce so things would go smoothly from then on.

"You are the only woman I have introduced to my mother," he said afterwards while they were in the car driving to his place.

"Why is that?" Mina asked.

"Because I never considered marrying any one of them," was his reply.

Was this a proposal?

He then bought a sumptuous apartment in a posh district in Geneva which he made her visit and, like a feathered cock, he went from room to room announcing which ones were for the children. Two kids, precisely. At the end of his tour, he looked at Mina for approval.

"*Es-tu d'accord?*" (are you in agreement?) he asked.

"Is this supposed to be a marriage proposal?" she asked.

"What else does it look like?"

"It looks like you want to have kids."

He then laughed. "You know what I mean," he said.

Yup, she got what he meant. It was indeed his marriage proposal and she accepted because he was an excellent marriage material and she had come to love him—almost. Perhaps if time went by, she could love him even more.

But then, he was transferred to Nigeria on a post for one year. He asked her to go with him. She refused, not wanting to leave the comforts of Geneva to be in an unsettled African country. Anywhere south of the Mediterranean coastal countries did not appeal to her in the least. And, in any case, she could not take a leave of absence that long. And what would she do in Nigeria? Twiddle her thumbs? They corresponded often and he sometimes spoke on the phone. He had not given up on them getting married. He told her so in each letter and proclaimed his love towards her which he said was as constant as ever. This was a new Louis.

Mina was touched but she was drawing away from him gradually. He was too far away to keep the momentum going. Just when everything was ready and they had planned to get married, Louis had to go away to Nigeria, of all places. Well, Mina thought, it was not meant to be. Now what?

MARBELLA

Mina and Vera often went on vacations to exotic places. They always chose a posh destination. It made no sense for them to go to a mediocre, inexpensive place where it would be swarming with mediocre people. They had *le gout du luxe,* (taste of luxury).

During the summer of 1966 which was an exceptionally bad summer weather wise, they decided to go to Marbella. They booked a room at the Don Pepe, a posh hotel in Marbella. They were sure to meet classy people or not too classy but certainly people with money, preferably some bachelors.

They flew to Madrid by Swissair and from there they hopped on a local plane to Marbella. What a hassle it was to get their suitcases on the next plane. The scene was chaotic. Suitcases were piled one on top of each other in some corner of the airport terminal. They had to hire a porter to find them and get them out. In those days they travelled with a lot of suitcases filled with a variety of clothes for every occasion. They always expected to be invited to parties, nightclubs and they were dead set to be elegant. Women were extremely clothes-conscious during the 1960s, maybe not all women but the sisters, definitely.

After a lot of trouble locating their suitcases which were piled up with a thousand others that looked similar—a mile high in some corner of the airport—they flew on a local plane to Marbella. The plane was shaking all the time and Mina wondered whether they would arrive safely or die stupidly. They then took a taxi to the Don Pepe Hotel. It was a fabulous swanky hotel in a swanky resort town. Their room had a gorgeous view of the swimming pool and the Mediterranean Sea. They were enchanted with everything.

The minute Mina got into the room, however, she developed a high fever. She didn't know if it was from the excitement or the stress of traveling.

The next morning, she still had a high fever and was shivering although the temperature in the room was a cozy 75 degrees. She was worried, so was Vera. She called down to reception to send her a doctor. A Spanish doctor came along and, after examining her, he said something which she didn't quite understand. He gave her some antibiotic pills and told her she should rest in bed and that she would be okay in a few days.

Mina looked at Vera in dismay.

"In a few days? Is he kidding? This is my vacation. I don't have a few days to waste in bed. I am here for only two weeks and I have to make the most of it. I want to go to the beach and to nightclubs. I'm not in Marbella to rest in bed."

"You might get worse, so you better listen to what the doctor told you," Vera said.

Mina did not heed her advice and also disregarded that of the doctor's. The next day, her fever had subsided a little, so she put on her not too skimpy, gold colored bikini and went down to the pool with Vera. She was feeling rather weak but she persisted in being outside. She stayed away from the sun, under an umbrella.

The hotel was not full. As they lay down on their chaises longue and started to put sun cream, a middle-aged man, in the most God-awful bathing trunks with a design of red hearts (how childish) on it, came up to them and asked whether they needed help in applying the lotion. Mina looked up at him, and saw an ordinary man. Ordinary in every way. He was of medium height, medium weight and had a German accent and his teeth were yellowish and he was balding. This was a no, no. They did not encourage him but he insisted on helping to put lotion on their backs so they allowed him to do so. Mina noticed that he was kind of lingering on Vera's back but Vera was oblivious. The conversation was not memorable and they refused his dinner invitation although they wanted to economize and not spend too much money on food. But he was not doable at all and they certainly did not care for his company. They could not visualize having a boring dinner and hear his horrible German-accented English.

The restaurant of the hotel was expensive but, as Mina was not feeling too well, they could not go gallivanting around to find another restaurant. Therefore, they ordered room service and shared the food which was plentiful.

The next day, Mina was feeling much better. Again, they had room service in the hotel for lunch then took a short nap. The weather was hot. After the nap, they put on their bikinis, wrapped themselves in sexy-looking *pareos* (wrap arounds) and went down to the pool. This time they had a big surprise. There were about fifteen men, around thirty and forty-year old, sitting around two tables at the pool. Mina and Vera were the only girls. The guys whistled and said "Hi."

"What luck," Mina told Vera.

"Yeah, we can have our pick. No competition around either."

The guys invited them to sit at their table and have a drink. They accepted but opted for lemonade. The conversation went on quite smoothly after the usual introductions.

"Where are you from and how come all of you are in this hotel?" Mina asked one of them. "Is there something special going on?"

"We are all from DuPont de Nemours and we're here for our yearly conference," said one guy who turned out to be Scottish. His name was Alasdair. The guys were from different parts of Europe and of different European nationalities. The sisters had a good time with them at the pool, drinking lemonade and having some snacks. A Finnish guy, by the name of Mikko, got stuck to Vera and both Alasdair and Mikko invited them to dinner that evening somewhere in town.

They accepted gladly.

The sisters put on their trendy cocktail dresses and were driven to a cozy beachside restaurant with multi-colored lanterns hanging from the ceiling. They ordered paella and sangria. The food was delicious. Real Spanish paella. There was a guitarist playing soulful love songs. Mina adored paella and guitar music and she really liked Alasdair. He was handsome, looked like Sean Connery and she was immediately attracted to him. Vera was not so impressed by Mikko. He drank too much and talked too much.

After dinner they went to a night club to dance. Mina saw an American couple there and she befriended them. They were from New York on a trip to see the sights in Spain. They had been married fifteen years and they were still lovey-dovey together. She wondered how that could happen. She had not experienced that feeling with Gary. After about four years of being married to Gary, her love for him had gone down the drain.

Alasdair was not such a good dancer but his body felt good against hers. It was firm and embracing. He was manly and Mina enjoyed the closeness and his warm breath against her cheek. Returning to the hotel, she ended up in his room. They stood in the balcony of the room listening to the waves swishing up from the sea. Mina could feel his warmth although they were not touching. He turned her around then and they kissed. Very romantic interlude that was. He led her to the bed and lay on top of her kissing her and caressing her. He was an excellent lover, the best she had ever had. He took time in foreplay.

She later found out that Vera did not accept Mikko's advances. He had not appealed to her all that much.

After Mina went back to her room and fallen asleep, around 4 am, someone was banging on their door. The sisters woke up and stared at each other. Vera got up to look from the peephole.

"It's Mikko," she said. "He looks drunk."

"All Finns drink a lot," was Mina's reply. She had heard this somewhere and as usual she generalized her statement to include all Finns.

"What should we do?" Vera asked.

Mina came to the door and shouted at him through it. "Go away Mikko, we're sleeping."

"Open the door or I'll break it down," he shouted back. He was a bulky, tough-looking guy and looked tougher through the peephole.

The sisters got scared and they did not argue any further with him. They called reception to get someone to take him away. After two minutes, they heard a scuffle through the door. He was being manhandled and asked to leave and not disturb the clientele.

The incident was not repeated.

The next morning, Mina related the incident to Alasdair who did not seem to be shocked.

"He acts badly when he gets drunk," he said.

"I hope he is not your friend. We don't ever want to see him again."

"Don't worry, he is just a co-worker. I'll give him a talking to."

Mina had a marvelous week with Alasdair at the Don Pepe. They went for rides exploring the Spanish countryside, all the way down to Sotogrande, a new seaside resort area being developed for the rich and famous. There was also a yacht harbor. Mina was enraptured by it and would have loved being on a yacht someday. The town was still being built. It only had one hotel for the time being. They stayed the whole day at the hotel beach and frolicked in the Mediterranean. It was an exhilarating and wonderful day for Mina. The whole day was bathed in a flickering glow of a new romance. She had finally found a guy she liked. *Better than Shoukry? No, I don't think so,* she told herself, *but better than anyone else I've met so far.*

The DuPont team departed and Mina felt rather sad. Alasdair told Mina that he would be working at DuPont in Geneva for the coming months. Mina was elated when he took her phone number and promised to call her in Geneva. She was very much looking forward to it.

Vera and Mina then went to Torremolinos to stay there for another week but they did not like it too much. It was quite a few notches below Marbella. It was not an elegant place and was frequented by the English middle class, who were rowdy and uncouth and the guys were drinking the whole time. There were a lot of drunkards, all around. It was not their scene so they left after a couple of days and came back to the Don Pepe. The hotel was not the same without Alasdair.

It was time to fly back to Geneva. They went via Madrid again and stopped over for one night to discover the city. It was a vibrant city but it would have been better with male escorts to take them around. People ate dinner so late, around 10 pm. Mina wondered how they went to work the next day.

Back in Geneva, Alasdair contacted Mina and they became an item. She enjoyed his company and the love-making was great but, how long would it last? He told Mina that he was married and had two children but was living apart from his wife who was in London. He also told her that he had not had sex with his wife for the last four years, right after his second son was born. Mina just went along for the ride with him and did not expect him to divorce his wife and marry her. She really liked him, though. He was hot and cozy, intelligent, well-groomed and cultured but a tad stingy. Mina was used to receiving small gifts from guys who travelled to other countries. They often brought back mementos, nothing expensive. Sometimes the interns at the Annex brought gifts to all four girls in the secretariat. Alasdair happened to be a chemical engineer at DuPont and travelled extensively. Not even a pin from him. Mina knew that Scots were known to be stingy—another generalization.

Mina was whole-heartedly smitten by him—for the first time since meeting Shoukry. She did not like that feeling too much though, because it made her vulnerable. However, she could see that he was smitten by her also. They had a torrid love affair in Geneva. It was a whirlwind romance. She forgot all about Louis who was still on the extended mission for the IEO in Nigeria. It was lucky that Louis was away because it left her free to see Alasdair and re-assess the situation.

A few months went by and Alasdair was transferred to London. That cooled things off. He visited Geneva quite often for DuPont business and saw Mina during those times.

During a candlelit dinner in a restaurant that looked like Aladdin's cave, Alasdair took hold of her hands and proposed in a weird way.

"I would like us to get married, but can you wait until my children get older?"

"How much older?" she asked.

"Well, the youngest is seven years old."

"How old should he be before we can get married?"

"At least twelve," he said. "You see, I'm very close to my children and I don't want to hurt them by marrying another woman. They know their mum and I are separated but we're not divorced and we do quite a few things together. I don't want to disturb their lives."

Mina's jaw fell. *Wait for him for five years? No sir, that would not do,* Mina told herself. She lied however, and told him she would wait. As she only saw him a couple of times a month, she decided to date other men until Louis' return from Nigeria. She kept up a positive approach to life thinking that one day she would meet a replacement for Shoukry, someone who was not married or was not divorced and did not have any appendages. Acting as a mother to another man's children was not in her genes. Alasdair was not readily available and Mina hated waiting indefinitely for things to happen. Her enthusiasm waned and her feelings towards him got to be more and more tepid during his bi-monthly visits.

He noticed her coolness.

"You are being very casual," he remarked during a dinner at a lakeside restaurant.

The best reply was not to give a reply at all. They continued seeing each other sporadically but her heart was not in it. She did not break up with him though. He was too sexy. She could not resist being with him. Alasdair called her a few times a week and wrote love letters. One of his letters said that he had had an accident with the car because he was thinking of her while driving and crashed through a fence in the countryside. Nothing serious had happened to him but the car was in a sad state. *What's the point of all this?* Mina thought. He would not divorce his wife because he wanted to be close to his children. And she did not wish to insist. It was his decision. She would not influence him. It would be the wrong move. She did not want to be blamed for unforeseen circumstances later on. He seriously thought she would wait for him. However, her infatuation for him wanned and she gradually forgot about him. Well, not really forgot, but he was on the back burner.

Vera could see the disappointment in Mina's eyes whenever she brought up the subject of Alasdair.

"You're not lucky, sis."

"The hell with Alasdair, I just want Shoukry. I can't forget him. These men are only temporary flings and they cannot be replacements. Since I want children, I guess I have to settle with Louis. At least he is dependable and caring. I am not in love with him but I love him in a way and can see a life with him."

MADJID

During one of Louis' prolonged absences, Mina met an Iranian PhD student in Mathematics at Geneva University. The way they met was rather amusing. Mina and Vera were on their way to a nightclub one Saturday night and they stopped at a red light. There was a car in the lane next to them. The stop light was rather long and the guys in the other car started a conversation. They asked the sisters where they were heading to. Mina told them they were going to the Griffins Club, whereupon these two guys said they would follow them and meet at the Club. Encounters were easy in those days.

They arrived at the Club at the same time. One of the guys was Iranian, tall, good-looking and impeccably dressed. He spoke excellent French. Mina was impressed by him. Madjid was his name. He was quite an amusing fellow but talked a little too much. The guy with him was Lebanese and he took a liking to Vera. The music at the club was not so great that evening. It was too loud and the psychedelic lights annoyed Mina. Younger people seemed to like that, but she was not so young anymore.

After the encounter at the Club, where they danced all night, Madjid pursued Mina relentlessly but she was not ready to have an affair with him because she guessed there were quite a few women running after him and she did not want to be considered as one of his conquests. He was wealthy and charming to the bone and spent money lavishly. He knew she dated other guys and that made him even more eager to get her into his bed but Mina played hard to get. She enjoyed flirting with him, though.

"How come you're not swooning over me like other women do?" he asked her jokingly on day while having dinner.

"Because I am not the type of woman who swoons. It is usually the other way around," she replied, whereupon he laughed.

"That's what I like about you. You are hard to get and I love the chase. I promise you, however, that you will change your mind and we will become lovers. I am confident."

"Not on your life," snapped Mina. "I'm afraid your confidence will be shattered."

He was fun to be with, a great spender and appreciated the good things in life. He was used to getting what he wanted but Mina was adamant. He would not get her.

She invited him to her birthday party together with a few of her friends. He came with twenty-four red roses and a bottle of Dior perfume. He knew how to court a woman.

He told her mother, "your daughter is like a rose, she wants to be smelled by many but her thorns reject her suitors."

"Even if you had a rich husband, a fabulous home and lots of time to paint, you would still be dissatisfied," Madjid told her in the presence of Vera and her mother, after the other guests had left.

Mina thought about what he said and started to ask herself whether that was true. For sure she would be happy with Alasdair, but he was in London ensconced with his wife and kids. There was always Louis in the background. And, of course, Shoukry, who she adored, was in a far-away place—another world.

So, the search went on.

"What the hell was that about?" Mina's mother asked her after he left.

"He would like to have carnal relations with me, that's all," she replied and they both laughed.

"I hope you're not going that route," said her mother. "He seems to be a charmer but also a heart-breaker."

"No fear, I'm not that daft."

One day, out of the blue, the Moroccan Minister of Foreign Affairs, she had met in New York, called her from Rome. He asked her to fly over to meet him. Another married man who wanted to get into her pants. Mina did not accept, feigning work, because she did not want to have anything to do with him. She had rebuffed his advances in New York and she didn't see why she would start anything with him now. It was around this time that a Moroccan opposition leader was assassinated in Paris and Mina had the faint inkling that this high-ranking official might have something to do with it. All these travels he was undertaking to Paris sounded a bit fishy to Mina. She remembered him telling her that the opposition leader was a traitor when she asked about him during one of their meetings in New York. All future attempts to see her were rejected by Mina. Even going out to dinner would be considered dangerous for her. She told him she was engaged to be married in order to stop any future communication.

Yes, she was engaged, wasn't she? To Louis.

MANHATTAN

In the autumn of 1967, Mina and Vera decided to visit the U.S. They had not returned since they left in 1963. They thought their green cards were still valid but it turned out they were not. They rushed to the American Embassy in Bern to have them revalidated.

The Ambassador was a young, blond, good-looking fellow seated behind his desk with his assistant standing next to him. He had his feet up on the desk.

"Please sit down," he said with a broad smile. "You girls have not followed the rule."

"What is that?" Mina asked looking at him wide-eyed and making herself look ignorant.

"A green card holder has to go back to the U.S. every year, otherwise the card is no longer valid and proceedings have to start all over again. You had to apply for re-entry visas before leaving the U.S but you have not done so. You cannot apply for re-entry from the outside.

The sisters' hearts fell to the bottom of the floor. They looked at each other in despair.

"Is there nothing we can do?" Mina asked him meekly. "After all, we have kept our bank accounts still open in New York, and we would like to spend that money." That was the truth.

"Hmm," said the Ambassador with an enigmatic smile, looking up at his assistant, "well, in that case, why don't we make an exception and give these two charming young ladies their green cards back?"

"Really?" Mina asked incredulously. "You are so kind, we are so grateful."

"Next time, you'll know better, I hope."

"Indeed, we will."

And the matter was settled.

The sisters could not believe their luck. They had their re-entry permits and were prepared to go to New York for two weeks.

It was a big preparation, their first journey back to Manhattan. They stayed at Hunter's place. He was not there, or course, being in Geneva. His wife, Bea, received them and they took over the children's bedroom. Bea told them that brother and sister shared a room until Martha-Nell had gone to college. The son was a drug addict and the parents never knew where he was. He would return home after a few months' absence, completely broke, get his mom to buy him new clothes, then disappear again, peddling his clothes for drugs.

The sisters were in this bedroom which had no shutters and no drapes. How did these young guys sleep in a room that was not darkened at night. Mina took some dark colored towels from the linen closet and scotch-taped them to the windows. Now they could finally sleep. It was surprising that with Hunter making all that money in Libya, Bea had not found it necessary to install some drapes in that room.

Mina and Vera decided to get temporary jobs while in New York, to make some extra money during their trip.

Mina saw an ad in the paper. A modeling agency was looking for models. She was curious. Why not? Gary had never wanted her to be a model but now she could. The sisters went off to be interviewed. There were not too many girls in the foyer. They both went in at the same time for the interview. They were tall, skinny and pretty and were sure they would get the job.

A young guy was seated behind a desk looking at some photos. He looked at them, made them turn around and then said:

"I've got a photo shoot for you girls in Playboy Magazine. It pays very well. I can set up the appointment. Tell me when."

The sisters looked at each other. Mina's jaw practically dropped to the floor but she feigned no surprise and rejected the offer. They were not that desperate and to show nudity was not in their agenda.

"Let's stick to secretarial stuff," Mina told Vera when they left the building.

Whereupon, they went to an agency for temporary office work. The agent found a good job for Vera with a Jewish philanthropic agency and Mina was offered the job of secretary to the President of an advertising agency. His secretary was out on a week's vacation and Mina was hired as the replacement. The executive offices were located in the penthouse of the building. After taking the regular elevator to the twentieth floor, she had to walk a flight of stairs up to the Penthouse. Very private. The President's office and that of his secretary were the only offices in the Penthouse. There was also a restroom and an alcove for a small fridge and a coffee machine. Nothing else. The President was a young handsome guy and friendly-looking. He sat behind an enormous desk, shaped like a wave. There was nothing on the walls.

Mina had nothing much to do at this job. She got bored answering the telephone. A couple of business calls and two calls in the morning both from his wife. *Keeping tabs on him? Wrong thing to do to check up on a husband. He invariably will drift away,* Mina wanted to advise her.

John was his name. He called her in for dictation. He had his feet up on his bare desk, facing her. Mina hated guys who put up their feet on a desk with her sitting across from them looking at the dirty soles of their shoes. First the Consul and now this guy. It seemed to be an American habit.

He dictated something short. That was it for the morning.

At noon, she went downstairs into the street to grab something to eat and buy a book to alleviate her boredom. In the afternoon he dictated a three-line memo. She finished the book after typing and sending out the memo.

There was mostly nothing to do during the whole week that she was employed. *Why did he even need a replacement secretary? For prestige?*

After the end of the week, the Employment Agency called her.

"Would you like to work in your present position permanently?" asked the agent.

"What about his secretary?" Mina asked.

"I suppose he prefers to have you."

"I am flattered but I have no intention of staying in New York, so please thank him for me and decline his offer."

What was that all about? Men are traitors and cheaters, Mina thought. *They are ready to get rid of what they have to try something new.*

That is why Mina had become quite *blasée* (jaded) in her relationships with men. She trusted no man. They did not warrant her faithfulness or her affections. This guy's wife was quite pretty. Mina saw a photo of her on his desk and also one of a small child, a girl. Being pretty did not mean anything. Men always wanted something new.

Was that not what Mina wanted also?

Anna, a childhood friend of theirs, who worked at the U.N. in New York, proposed to go to a singles' dating bar to try out the atmosphere. These bars were newly operating in a few cities in the States. The three girls went and stood at the bar eyeing the merchandise. Nothing earth-shattering. Just the usual young and not so young men hanging around the bar, drinking and looking over the merchandise. There were a few overly made-up young women trying their best to look appealing. The three girls started talking in French between themselves so that these Romeos would not know what they were talking about. They laughed quite a bit criticizing the fellows standing next to them.

One of the guys turned around and offered them a drink. The girls refused. Then he came up with an obnoxious remark, "my father can buy you three cunts in a heartbeat."

They ignored him.

"Frenchies, Frenchy sluts," the guy continued, making a spitting sound.

"Let's get out of here and not respond to him. He seems to be pretty drunk and you never know what he'll do with his glass. He may very well throw it at us. We don't want to get hurt," said Mina to the others in Armenian, this time. They skedaddled out of the club and went home promising themselves to never again venture into a singles bar. It was not their scene.

After two weeks in Manhattan, they took a bus to Washington, D.C.

They rented a residence in a hotel. It was a nice comfortable place. They called their friends to reconnect with them as they had not seen them since about seven years.

Mina also called the American Airlines pilot she had met at the Hilton Hotel in Rome the summer before. His name was Vic. He had tried to get her into bed but she had refused. He had been too sweaty while dancing. After his departure, he had written lengthy love letters to her and he sounded rather sincere, so Mina was curious to meet him again just for dinner, nothing else.

He arranged to meet her and Vera in a restaurant and said he would bring a few friends along. He got drunk during dinner and started acting very possessively with her. Mina saw a side of him that she disliked. Falling all over her and cracking jokes like she belonged to him.

"Vic, please stop, I don't belong to anybody," she told him.

"But you do, my precious one, you belong to me forever," he said trying to hold her hand down on the table and slurring his words. She jerked her hand away.

Mina realized that he was extremely drunk and tried to rack her brain for a way to get rid of him. She asked Vera to accompany her to the restroom. They thought of a plan to ditch him and his party.

When they returned to the table, Vera announced that they were late meeting their cousin who was supposed to pick them up from the hotel.

"Oh my God," Mina explained, "we better go. Let's call a cab."

Vic looked dumbfounded.

"I thought we were going to spend the whole evening together." he said.

"Sorry, Vic, not tonight." *Not any night*, were her thoughts. "We have promised to meet my cousin and his family."

"I'll drive you," Vic ventured.

"No need, you stay and have fun with your friends," she said and they quickly got up and went outside to get a taxi. She could hear him calling after her, "I'll see you tomorrow."

Not on your life, buster, she murmured to herself. They were finally rid of him, or so thought Mina.

They went back to their hotel, made a few more phone calls and got ready for bed. Finally, after making plans for the next day and reading a little, they put off the lights and were sound asleep when they were awakened by a loud banging on the door. They sat up and looked at each other. It was 2 am.

"What the hell, who could that be?" asked Vera.

"Let's check before opening the door," Mina cautioned.

She looked through the peephole and there was Victor, disheveled and drunk.

"Go away, Victor, we were asleep and you woke us up."

"Open the door, I want to see you," he growled.

"You're drunk Victor, please go away."

"If you don't open the damn door I'll break it down," he threatened.

Mina realized that he meant it and was frightened.

"We'll call reception," she told Vera and grabbed the phone asking the sleepy dope at reception—he had not looked too bright when they were checking in—to get a drunk guy away from their door.

"What, what?" the dope asked.

"There's a drunk guy at our door and he will break it down if we don't open it," Mina repeated. "Hurry, do something."

"I'll see what I can do."

"You'll see? You do what I'm telling you to do right now," Mina insisted. She could be extremely authoritative when warranted.

Realizing that this guy was going to be too slow and perhaps incapable, Vera dialed 911 and reported the ruckus. In the meantime, as the sisters were apprehensive that he would break the door before the police arrived, they barricaded themselves in the bathroom. There was a small, white rickety chest of drawers which they put against the door. That would not prevent Victor from barging in though. They waited for the police. After some time had elapsed, they came out of the bathroom and looked through the peephole. They saw two policemen accompanied with the guy at reception. They took Victor away and that's the last they heard of him. Good riddance.

When Mina was back in Geneva, she received an apologetic letter from Vic he about his behavior and he begged her to give him a second chance. Mina ignored the letter and did not write back. She certainly was not going to tolerate possessive, drunk and violent men. She could not imagine how some women put up with them out of love or fright but, for her, being violent was completely unacceptable.

LOUIS

When the sisters returned to Geneva, Louis was back from Nigeria for a fortnight. He invited Mina to dinner and he was extremely sweet all through the dinner. He kept looking at her trying to appraise her, *or is he trying to make up his mind about marrying me?* She asked herself.

"I missed you, you know," he said, looking at her with those sleepy blue eyes.

"I missed you too," she said and she actually meant it. After her American adventure, Louis appeared as a welcome savior. They held hands in the car on the way back and everything was chummy-chummy. She made up her mind to marry him. He was a most decent human being.

The fortnight became permanent and Louis was back in Geneva to stay, so Mina was in the 'on' period again.

Skiing season started soon that year. Louis and Mina often went to ski resorts in France. French ski resorts were closer to Geneva than the Swiss ones. They would go for the day or for the weekend. Mina's favorite place was Courchevel 1850, meaning the resort was 1850 meters high. There was also Courchevel 1650 and Courchevel 1500 but the skiing and the hotels were better at 1850. There were French celebrities staying at the 1850.

Louis always wanted to stay at a posh hotel. The Carlina was his favorite. It was the only four-star hotel in that ski station, situated on one of the ski slopes. The balcony door of the room opened right onto the main ski slope. They would step in their skis and ski down to the chair lift. Mina really loved skiing but hated the chair lifts. She never felt quite secure on them. Skiing gave her a certain kind of freedom, zooming down the slopes—well, maybe not zooming but going at a reasonable speed. She was the cautious type. Vera had broken her ankle during one of their skiing trips and Mina was careful not to have broken bones.

After lunch on the top of the mountain, where they basked in the glorious sun, they would take a nap and then go to l'Equipe, an after-ski drink and dance place from 6 to 9. The only drawback was that Louis only danced to the slow tunes. He did not know how to move with the trendy music. And, Mina wanted to rock and roll and do the cha, cha. Once, while they were at that bar, and while Mina was going to the rest room, a guy grabbed her and took her on the dance floor to dance a wild cha, cha. She did not object. She then came back to their table and sat down as though nothing unusual had transpired.

"Who was that?" asked Louis.

"A guy I know from other times I have been here," she lied.

At dinner during one of their stays at the Carlina Hotel in Courchevel, Mina saw Yves Montand, a famous French singer and actor— a heartthrob and a womanizer—come in to the restaurant accompanied by two guys. She liked Yves a lot. She loved his songs and his films and also as a man—ruggedly handsome and tall. As he was walking over to his dinner table, he looked Mina's way. Their eyes locked and he winked at her.

"Who's that?" asked Louis surprised at the wink.

"That's Yves Montand, the singer/actor."

"Why is he winking at you?"

"I don't know."

Louis then mumbled something unintelligible.

The next day at dinner, the same thing happened. When Yves walked by their table, he winked at her again. Mina looked over at Louis to see if he had noticed it. He had not. He was busy with his food and luckily had not noticed the wink. *What the hell*, she thought. *What next?* She was flattered, of course. She knew he was a womanizer although he was married to the beautiful actress Simone Signoret. Being married did not mean a thing, Mina had come to realize during her own escapades. Men are cheaters and so was she, to some extent.

After a few days of skiing, the time came for Mina and Louis to check out of the hotel. Louis, as usual, was slow in his packing. He had to check everything in the room. *Looking for his condoms under the bed, maybe?* Mina thought. She went downstairs to reception with her carry-on to wait for him. She noticed Yves coming out of the elevator. He saw her waiting at the desk, and approached her.

"*Bonjour*," he said, smiling.

"*Bonjour*," Mina replied, also smiling.

"*Belle journee.*" (beautiful day).

"*Oui en effet.*" (yes, in fact).

Mina was surprised at this banal conversation. People always talked about the weather when they had nothing to say. *Was Yves tongue tied?* Mina wondered. *God, he does look handsome!*

"Would you like to go to the TV room and watch a film with me? They will put on 'La Casse', it's a good French film," he said. He was not one of the actors in the film.

Mina looked at him with an enigmatic smile.

"Actually, we're checking out," she told him, pointing to her carry-on.

"*Quel dommage*," (what a pity), "won't you stay longer?"

"I'm afraid I can't," she replied laughing.

"Why are you laughing?"

"At the absurdity of the situation."

He laughed also. "Sometimes unexpected encounters are life's good moments," he said and bade her goodbye, taking her hand and pecking at it with his lips. His lips were warm.

Mina laughed again. She really hoped she would meet him again at a future stay in this hotel and thought of him during the whole drive to Geneva.

"You are unusually quiet," said Louis.

"I'm tired," she lied.

They arrived home.

With all these encounters she had with other men, she still persisted on seeing Louis with whom she was not in love. The reason was that he was dependable and the only man she had come across who was of marriage material. Well, there had been Alasdair but he was married and divorce prospects were too far away. Mina never lost her focus of getting married again and having children. She was adamant to do so. She thought her life would not be complete without a husband and children. The husband could not be just anybody. The person had to have a solid background and character. She did not expect perfection, of course. Being good in bed was a criterion but it was not the most important one. Being loved and really cared for were more important. She knew that Louis really cared for her but she wished he was more demonstrative. Some guys told her they loved her but it was in an offhand manner and she never believed them. A very important flaw Louis had was that he did not pay enough attention to her and she craved it. Being passionate was just not in his genes. But then, she would never marry a man who was only good in bed. The passion would frizzle away in no time. She had experienced that with Gary.

Sometimes just to spark some life in Louis, she would tell him that an old boyfriend had shown up and invited her out. Then he would get all attentive and try to lure her away from the guy. He would ask her questions. Some of the replies she gave him were invented to make him jealous, and it worked. She was a good actress. She had long since realized that a man likes it when his girlfriend is desired by others.

At this time, Louis finally decided that they should definitely get married. This was after four years of being together on and off. As he had been a bachelor for a long period of time and had never had a long-term girlfriend, he was hesitant and afraid of the commitment. The married state gave him the jitters. It was understandable to Mina. He was so independent, doing what he wanted when he wanted that it scared him to have a permanent attachment. He did not realize that Mina was also very independent and would welcome to be on her own sometimes.

FABIO

Of all the men Mina met in Geneva and during vacations, no one captured her heart except Alasdair. But that episode was now forgotten. He returned to London and to his wife and children. Some of them were great guys but they did not give her any sparks. *Was she ever going to get sparks again, after Shoukry?*

Fabio was one of the guys she fell for. A wealthy Italian industrialist from Milano, a bachelor. But Mina never trusted Italian bachelors. They were the most flirtatious and promiscuous men of all the Europeans. Mina was charmed by Fabio and his debonair stance, but no matter what he did or proposed, she did not succumb to him quickly. She knew that the minute he had her, he would seek other pastures. She played hard to get.

Mina accepted an invitation from Lusi, an Italian girl she had met in New York, to vacation with her in San Remo where Lusi had a holiday apartment. Lusi was a fun girl and they had clicked instantly.

Lusi subsequently invited a few of her friends from Milan to come to San Remo at the same time to meet her two friends from Switzerland. Mina and Vera went to San Remo and met Lusi's friends at a dinner in a seaside restaurant. The food was delicious.

One of Lusi's friends happened to be Fabio. He was accompanied by a girlfriend who was all over him. He, on the other hand, was more interested in Mina and she felt a little embarrassed. Mina did not like monopolizing someone else's merchandise, so to speak. The next evening, while they were having dinner again in another restaurant,

Mina saw Fabio's girlfriend suddenly leave the table throwing her napkin at Fabio's face. Mina turned to Lusi, who was seated on her right, and asked her what the matter was. Lusi told her that Fabio had had an argument with his girlfriend about her the evening before and he had tried to break up with her. At this point, Mina did not realize that Fabio had such a crush on her so as to leave his girlfriend. She looked at him with a different eye and found him quite charming. He monopolized her during the rest of the evening. They conversed in Italian and he did not bring up the problem with his girlfriend.

Fabio came to visit her quite often in Geneva and she finally went to bed with him. The sex was satisfactory but nothing to write home about. Fabio was rather skinny and his lips were dry. Now, she had to juggle two relationships at the same time. Fabio and Louis. Fabio was much more fun than Louis. They had such different personalities. Fabio was flamboyant while Louis was reserved. Mina usually arranged that Fabio visit her when Louis was away in Paris.

"Let's get married, I am tired of these bi-monthly visits," said Fabio, one day while they were gazing at the half moon lying in bed in a luxury hotel in Sestriere, an Italian ski resort where he had a chalet.

"Tired?" Mina repeated. "Is that a reason to get married?"

"No, of course not, you know I adore you and can't get enough of you during my visits. They are very short and nothing gets accomplished."

While Mina was really drawn to Fabio, and his suave sophistication, she could not envision going to live in Milan, a city she did not really care for. She supposed that if she really loved the guy, she would follow him to Timbuktu. Well, not her. She was not convinced the relationship would work out. It was his turf and she would be an outsider. She asked him for some time to ponder the situation, her job, her family, and what not.

"You don't have to work in Milan," he said. "I make good money. You can have all the household help you need and do your own thing."

"I'm not the type of woman who can only play house," she told him.

"Well, you can start a business, if you want to be busy, and I'll help you."

He was offering her a good life but she did not budge from her position. What if it did not work out. She would lose her secure job at the IEO and her Swiss residency papers. She wanted independence. She could not rely on a man for her existence.

"Give me time to think about it," she said, although there was nothing to think about. Her answer would always be No. She had no intention of jeopardizing her secure job and good life in Geneva to follow a man to a city where she had no friends and had to start all over again. His visits to Geneva continued but less often and the affair trickled away after some time. He thought she had met someone else and asked her about it. She denied, of course.

She could now concentrate on Louis again full time. Mina did not particularly care for this see-saw position with Louis but he seemed to be the only doable candidate for marriage. It is just that she was not totally sure whether she would enjoy life with him on a long-term basis. She was sure she would have roving eyes, unless she was bogged down with kids and, even then.

DOGAN

During the summer months the Annex invited about six interns from all over the world to study and work there. Some were given an office and ATS arranged cocktail parties to get to know them.

On the way to her office one day, Mina noticed a guy sitting in the conference room doing some paper work. She did a double take and saw that he was quite handsome. She wanted to meet him so she introduced herself and asked whether he needed anything, like a stapler, paper, pens, etc. He looked up, smiled and thanked her saying that he did not need anything. His name was Dogan and he was Turkish. Being an Armenian, she should not even have considered to befriend a Turk but he was a cute guy. They talked and became friendly and had coffee sometimes in the lounge. He then asked her out on a dinner date. She accepted. The dinners were repeated and Dogan wanted to get intimate, of course, but she rejected him although she was tempted. He looked easy going and she liked his looks and his eyes and his smile. Actually, Mina thought, he himself had not committed any crimes against the Armenians, it was his ancestors. So why blame him?

"I should not even be saying hello to you. You are guilty of the Genocide." she told him on one of their dates.

"So sorry Mina, it was not me, please forgive me. I know the Ottomans were horrible to the Armenians."

She forgave him for his ancestors' sins. Another major problem—he was married. She did not succumb to his charms, although she was tempted to do so. They had a few a hot, smooching sessions in the car and that was it. It was a passing fancy, nothing more. After his stint at the Annex, he returned to Turkey. This was when Louis was still in Nigeria.

All these married guys she met at work. She wondered if their wives knew or suspected that their husbands were philanderers when on a business trip. She also wondered whether, if and when she got married, she would trust her own husband away on a business trip.

THE OFFICE

Mina's work at the Office increased with the new Director. She was still only a secretary with the Grade of G.3. She was quite unhappy with the situation of not being given a higher grade although doing the work of the secretary of a Director at the Grade of D.1 Being the secretary of a D.1 meant his secretary was at least a G.5, if not a G.6. What concerned her most was more pay.

Mina was really fed up from not getting a promotion. She wrote a one-page memo, with the help of Louis, to the Director, stressing the pertinent facts and salient points of her past career, whereupon he promised her she would get her promoted to G.4 at the end of the year.

"I'm doing the work of a G.5, why not promote me to that grade?"

"Things are not done that quickly here."

Yes, in fact they were not. It was a slow-poke organization full of bureaucrats. There was a quota for each country of how many employees in the Professional category they could have from each, depending on the amount of their dues. There was no quota for the General Service category, though.

Mina was discouraged but, as she was having fun in Geneva and sometimes also at the Office with some of the staff members, she accepted their slow and tedious policy. What else could she do? She could not work in the private sector. In any case, the salaries were lower there.

Mr. Drake kept Mina busy with all his correspondence and she did not have time for her private letter-writing to all her friends in the States. Those were the days of long, extremely detailed letters. The days at the Office freakishly repeated themselves, one after the other. Mina was bored. She thought she should have a more responsible position. She wanted to do some important work and not just type gibberish. The problem with the IEO is that a secretary has to start at the bottom of the ladder and every year she goes up one step. No joking. There were twelve steps in the grade of G.3. Mina started with Grade 3, step 4—despite her vast experience—and now she was step 5. They had given her a few of steps to start with. A ridiculous practice. It had nothing to do with one's experience and capabilities. One important factor was that she was bilingual—English and French—that is to say she could work in both languages but that only gave her an additional $ 15 a month. She had to pass a rigorous test in French. Christian, the French guy, a doubting Thomas, had to try her out to see whether she could in fact take shorthand in French and transcribe. Mina came out with flying colors.

No matter how much she showed her competence she would not get promoted beyond G.4 until the end of the year, as promised by the Director.

By this time, almost all employees at IEO knew her to be an artist. Painting exhibitions were organized once a year in the building. Mina happened to be the only professional one. She had already given a few exhibitions in other cities in Switzerland, in London and in Paris. They had been quite successful. She was getting to be known in art circles. One of her drawings was reproduced on the cover of the U.N. magazine that circulated to all the international organizations. So, here she was a good artist, therefore it was presumed she could not also be a good secretary. She had been known to be extremely competent in her previous jobs but the U.N. system was just not for her. Her bosses were all fuddy-duddies. She believed she was over-competent for the job and could put those English girls 'in her pocket'—as the saying goes in Armenian.

At the end of the year, she got her G.4 finally. However, her annual report was not that good. The Director had not really appreciated all her work. No reason given. She went in to see him after she got her report and talked to him frankly. He listened intently and said: "I'll see what I can do."

That's it? He'll see what he can do? The jerk. Well, he better do something, otherwise she did not wish to continue working for him.

He called her in the next day and informed her that he had changed the annual report with a better assessment of her work. He added that he did appreciate her work and also that he liked her a lot.

Wow. That must have been difficult to admit, thought Mina. She did not trust the guy and she wrote a memo to Personnel asking for a transfer.

The Personnel Manager asked her to come in and offered her another secretarial position in another department, that of the Environment. There was one boss and one secretary. She was to be the secretary of that one-man department. It was not a promotion because the boss was only a P.4. There was not much to do in that department because the main office for Environmental issues was at the U.N. Mina did not comprehend why there was even a branch in the IEO. She had a very easy time with her boss, an Austrian/Israeli. He did not have much to do. He would skip work sometimes by coming to the office then putting a pair of reading glasses on his desk on an open document and disappear for the day. If anyone came into the office, it would be presumed that he was present. He also left a spare coat on a hanger. Mina knew of his shenanigans but kept her mouth shut, because she played the same tactic.

One day, he was rather rude to her and she retorted: "Do you treat women like this in your own country?"

He immediately assumed that the country she meant was Israel. *Why not Austria, the country of his birth?* Mina thought. She was called in by the Personnel Manager who told her that her boss thought she was an anti-Semite. Mr. Parker, the Personnel Manager was Jewish himself and reassured her that, as he had known her for quite some time now, he knew she was not an anti-semite. She was transferred to another department, this time with the Grade of G.5. Finally.

The new transfer, however, did not work out well for Mina. The Department was shut down after a few months, because of lack of work and she was asked to resign together with 51 other people.

What happened to "Permanent contracts cannot be terminated?"

Mina was told one of the reasons of her dismissal was that she was redundant, there not being an appropriate opening for her to suit her qualifications in the whole of the IEO. That was bullshit. She requested that the Tribunal take her case. The Tribunal was the body where all conflicts were tried if not resolved within the organization itself.

The Staff Union lawyer offered his services to defend her.

"You are paid by the IEO therefore you cannot do an impartial job. You will never put your own position on the line to defend me. So, no thanks, I don't need your help," Mina told him. He was rather offended. He was one of her clients and had bought two etchings.

Her case came in front of ten high-ranking male employees of IOE and she pitched her case, saying that there was not one secretary in the whole of the IEO who was proficient in English as well as in French and who could also read Spanish. She was asked several tricky questions and she responded logically and confidently. She knew her case inside out and she did a marvelous job of defending it. They could not dupe her. No lawyer would have done a better job. She was pleased with herself. Maybe, she should have been a lawyer, she thought. She had had so many sleepless nights worrying over the dismissal.

The President of the Tribunal researched her case thoroughly and she was reinstated—as his secretary. He was a Frenchman of noble descent. Her lover was one and now her boss. This guy turned out to be extremely impartial and, after trying her out for a couple of weeks, told her that they had done *une grosse injustice envers vous* (a great injustice to you) to kick her out and he apologized on everyone's behalf.

Mina felt good for the first time since the beginning of her employment. She had a boss who appreciated her and she eventually got her G.6.

One funny anecdote was that one day, she was in the elevator with the Austrian/Israeli, and after saying hello to her, he told her that her hair looked very nice and could they have coffee together.

"So, I'm no longer an anti-Semite?" she asked him with a sarcastic smile on her face. She refused the coffee invitation. What a jerk.

THE FATHER

The two sisters were busy trying to find a way to get their father out of Egypt.

At this time, he was not doing well at all. The decorating business had gone downhill with the new Government and he had a limited number of projects. He sold all the furnishings in their apartment, just keeping a few mementos—souvenirs of their past life—and moved to his mother's house in Zeitoon, out in the country.

Getting him out of Egypt was not an easy endeavor. They absolutely needed their family to be reunited. They applied to the Swiss authorities requesting that he be allowed to come to Switzerland as a refugee. Although Egypt was not persecuting Christians, the job situation for them was not promising. Also, their father was getting on in years. He felt discriminated against when he applied for office jobs. Besides the dwindling decorating business, he had two other part-time jobs: One at the Armenian Cultural Club as Manager, bookkeeper and also as teacher at the Armenian Elementary School. Both jobs paid very poorly. Finally, the Protestant Social Center of Geneva took his case, although he was not a protestant. They applied to the authorities. The father had to write a lengthy letter describing life in Egypt for the Christian minorities and how they were being discriminated against regarding job offerings. The family needed a good reason so that the Swiss would accept him as a refugee. The waiting was getting their morale down.

It was now 1968. They knocked their heads all over town, inquiring about other possibilities. Finally, they found out that they could obtain him a visitor's visa for six months to see family. He was given the appropriate acceptance papers and he could finally leave Egypt. They hoped that once he was in Geneva, they could find a way to make him stay for good through the Protestant Social Center. This time his exit visa was refused three times by the Egyptian authorities.

Some time ago, Mina had met a wealthy Argentinian international grain merchant at the Intercontinental Hotel Pool and had told him about her father's predicament. He had promised that he would employ her father as Chief Accountant in Geneva when he came. Mina was rather reluctant about accepting the offer because the guy obviously wanted to get into her pants. There was also one of Vera's old boyfriends, who assured her that he would employ him as his assistant. He owned a large contracting company. Vera was also dubious about this offer.

Finally, he obtained an exit visa to visit family for six months.

The day of his arrival was an exciting day. They went to meet him at the airport. At that time, one could almost approach the plane on arrival. Mina saw an 'old' man with a tattered suitcase, descend the gangplank. She almost did not recognize him. Where was her debonair father? The man who charmed everyone? Their young-looking father, who had looked so young on her wedding day, that he was almost mistaken for her own husband, had aged prematurely.

They hugged and kissed and ushered him home.

The family was finally reunited, minus one Siamese cat.

The apartment was small. One bedroom was for Mina and Vera. The small bedroom, where there was only one single bed (not wide enough for two), was for their mom and their father slept on the sofa in the living room. The apartment situation was not very comfortable but they did not complain.

The father tried to find sponsors in Geneva to obtain a job. Mina and Vera rejected the favors of their two prospects because they knew there would be strings attached. The six-month period of the visa was coming to an end and they had no news of acceptance from any job source yet. The father was crestfallen and started to make plans to return to Egypt. Mother and daughters were frantic and panicky. Then, just by sheer luck, the *Centre Social Protestant* came through and finally vouched for him. Papers were sent back and forth. The family also had to reassure the Swiss authorities that he would be living with them and would not seek to rent a separate apartment—taking one away from the Swiss.

Finally, they received acceptance from the Swiss authorities. Their father had written a long *compte rendu* of the situation in Egypt, exaggerating of course. He was granted asylum and refugee status. He also had a job offer. A miserly job, doing menial tasks. It was at the Bellows Valvair headquarters in Geneva. They dealt in industrial parts. He accepted of course. He had no other choice. His job was to sort out their various products. He remained optimistic that he would find a better job eventually.

Years after their father died, twenty years after, Mina met someone at one of her art exhibitions who introduced himself to her saying that he knew her father at Bellows. "What a personality, he was," this person told Mina who felt so proud and thanked him with tears welling in her eyes. Wherever her father was, he left an indelible mark. People loved his sense of humor and his general attitude towards life. So optimistic and fatalistic, at the same time.

After he found a job, his demeanor changed. The hunchback of doom, that had loomed in his life, disappeared. He became a new person, or rather the person he was before. He had brought very few clothes from Egypt. He, who was one of the best dressed men in Cairo, left Egypt as a pauper. The clothes he had were not in very good condition. As soon as he got his first paycheck, he bought some decent clothes. He bought a new suit, a few ties, not as many as he had when he was wealthy, but still a sizable amount. He rejuvenated. The man, who looked seventy when he arrived in Geneva, now looked fifty. It was a magical transformation. He was never depressed and was now eager to start a new life at the age of fifty in a foreign country. Of course, he was proficient in both English and French. He had had an excellent education at the Jesuits college in Cairo.

Actually, when Louis met their father, he was impressed by his command of the French language for someone having been educated in Egypt. It was not universally known that Egypt had the best English and French schools in the Middle East with professors from England and France.

He still gambled on horses, though. He gambled in Annemasse, a French border town, ten minutes away from Geneva. No gambling was allowed in Geneva. He gambled little and he rarely lost. He always managed to make a little money whereupon, to celebrate, he would take them to lunch on Sundays at the *Jardin Anglais* (English Garden) on the lake. At long last they were one happy family. The rent was paid on time, the food was plentiful and everyone was healthy including the cat. Their mother was happy and less worried for the first time since forever.

It was now time for Mina to find another apartment, preferably in the same building because living quarters were extremely cramped. By this time, she knew the way to do it. She had to bribe the rental agent. She bought a beautiful crystal vase, costing a fortune, and went to see this dour, sour woman of the Agency. The woman smiled when she saw the gift. It was the first time Mina had seen her smile. She willingly found a one-bedroom apartment on the second floor in the same building. It would be ready in a couple of months.

Halleluja! Vera and Mina moved to a one-bedroom, second-floor apartment right above that of their parents and furnished it with IKEA furniture, only the essential, inexpensive but sturdy pieces.

Vera took the bedroom and Mina converted the living room as her bedroom and studio. All guests would be received in their parents' apartment. There was now a proper living room there. Their own apartment was only to sleep in. The kitchen was never used. Their mother continued to cook for all of them. What would they have done without a mother. Precious, she was and she hardly complained. She was so happy having her family with her in one place.

THIS AND THAT

The sisters continued having a busy social schedule. By this time, Mina had a few artist friends and they often went to vernissages together around town and invariably ended up in one of the Night Clubs.

There was a night club called Club 58—which had been inaugurated in 1958. They went to this Club some Saturday evenings, and they sometimes dragged a friend along. The female gender was exempt from membership or from paying an entrance fee. The same went for the Griffin'a Club, which was a newer club frequented by lot of *fils a papa* (father's boys). Another favorite place was La Tour night club in the Old Town. This was a regular night club. It was rather small and more intimate and always had good bands. They went to one or the other every Saturday and met dancing partners. Sometimes they accepted dates and sometimes, not. It depended on the guy.

In her spare time Mina was painting and drawing like mad. She took an etching and lithography course and she loved it. In order to do this, she had to work half-time for three months. Half-time meant half-pay but Mina had saved some money to be able to afford doing this. Etching became her passion and she worked at it non-stop whenever she could make the time. She made the rounds of galleries and got rejected by some. She then thought of applying to a gallery in Paris. Lo and behold, she was offered an exhibition. She worked non-stop to put a good show together. She was jittery about it because it was her first major exhibition. It was a success and she had two write-ups in the Parisian newspapers. She was overjoyed. Applying to Swiss galleries then became easy with the Parisian experience and the write-ups in her background.

One of the exhibitions she had in Switzerland was in a gallery in Hermance, an arty small town along the Lake. The owner of the gallery was an elderly shrew. At the end of the exhibition she was slow in paying her the proceeds. Mina went a couple of times to collect her money but the woman was dithering. Mina then threatened to pick up two of another artist's paintings from the gallery if she did not pay her there and then. The woman saw that Mina meant business and she went to the back of the gallery and got her the money. Never again, would Mina exhibit with her.

That exhibition was the key to her future exhibitions because she got good press reviews in the Geneva newspapers.

She exhibited frenetically from then on. She was making a name for herself.

One day, she had a lucky break. While walking to go on the plane to London with her etchings in a satchel, a guy walking behind her asked whether she was an artist. She turned around and saw a friendly-looking middle-aged man. She stopped and told him that indeed she was an artist going to London to make the rounds of galleries. He turned out to be one of the directors of a London group called Christie's Contemporary Art. He asked her to come around to their gallery and show her work. She was enchanted at this break.

After checking into her hotel upon arrival, she fixed herself up and went to the gallery, where she met the other Director. This gallery was an offshoot of Christie's. They only dealt with etchings and lithographs. They liked her etchings and ordered four of them for their collection. She had to do 150 prints of each image. She gave the work to a Zurich printer who did a fabulous job, rather expensive though. From then on, her career path in England took off. Several English galleries represented her etchings. On one of her London trips, she found a gallery where she exhibited her etchings on an ongoing basis. The funny thing was that an older man came in to buy two of her erotic etchings during the opening reception and he declined to give his name.

The London exhibition led to a Hong Kong gallery where she sold her etchings profusely. All in all, she was quite content with her life and the way things were falling into place.

So now she had two passions: Art and men. There were so many men in her orbit. During one of her skiing weekends in Courchevel, she met an American at the Tremplin coffee shop. He taught semantics in Paris. She met a Swede on the slopes. She had fallen down and he helped her get up. She met a Brazilian millionaire at the Intercontinental Hotel. He was filthy rich and invited her all over Europe. She did not take these guys seriously. She considered them all as *passe-temps*.

Vera had her share of beaux, the most serious one being a Frenchman, married of course, and living in Normandy. She met him at the hotel in Courchevel where they were staying. He was quite a bit older than her and fell head over heels in love with her. He was adamant to divorce his wife and marry Vera but she was not that keen on him and did not encourage him to do so because she was not inclined to move to Normandy. He wrote her love letters every second day. His name was also Louis.

While Mina and Vera were in Paris one weekend with the two Louis, they went out to dinner and Vera's Louis was quiet and reserved. He was usually a verbose fellow but being with Louis no. 1, he restrained himself. It was as though he was in awe of him, being an aristocrat. Frenchmen are funny that way. They change their behavior when meeting a person of a higher class. Vera's Louis was a down to earth type of guy, an extrovert, unlike Mina's Louis. They seemed to get along though and the evening was a success.

Then, lo and behold, Adam came into town again and reiterated his desire to get married. Mina's answer was still no. Mina did not understand why the hell Adam was being so insistent. One day he introduced her to a good friend of his, an American physicist, a world famous one. Graham was an extremely interesting fellow and liked the arts a lot. But he looked like a frog. Mina went for looks. Not stupid/handsome looks, but intelligent-looking good looks. He fell for her and he took her to fancy restaurant to impress her. During the third dinner out, he proposed. He was an excellent conversationalist. Mina enjoyed his company, especially when they talked about art. He seemed to be quite knowledgeable.

"You'll come to New York with me, we'll get married and I shall get you a loft where you will paint all day long. You don't have to work, ever. You can't imagine how you make me feel," and on and on he went, looking at her with adoration in his myopic eyes behind his thick horn-rimmed glasses while chewing his food. Mina listened patiently.

These were words she would have liked to hear from someone she was actually in love with. But that person was nowhere in sight—not yet.

"But, you don't even know me," she said. "How can you propose to someone you have met a few times in your life?"

"I've seen enough. I want *you* and that's that. All the other women I meet fall over me and suffocate me with their attentions, but you are aloof, I like that. You are a woman to be conquered. You'll make me work hard. I know you don't love me yet but I hope you will, soon."

Mina felt sorry for him and could not hurt his feelings and tell him she was not attracted to him in the least. That she just liked his company because they talked about art. The thought of being in bed with a man who looked like a toad repulsed her. She was not one who believed in kissing a toad to reveal a prince! So, she asked that he give her more time. He had to return to N.Y. anyway and that would provide her with the time needed to come up with an excuse not to accept his proposal. He wrote every three days and she replied once in a while. He was away for more than six months before he realized that Mina was not into him. He finally dropped the subject of marriage and always wrote about his impending visit to Geneva, which never materialized. Thank God! Not getting any reaction from her, he finally stopped pursuing her and she never heard from him again.

Right about this time, Mina had an unfortunate incident.

While on the train alone after a Paris trip, she had food poisoning. She had eaten chicken at lunch. It must have been rotten. She had violent diarrhea and vomiting and had to use the two toilets on the train, non-stop. They looked disgusting at the end of the journey. She did not think anybody dared to use those toilets. She felt very faint and could not wait for the train ride to end to be back home safe and sound. It was a horrible experience. The next day, she still felt faint and rushed to her generalist. She was diagnosed as being extremely dehydrated and her blood pressure had plummeted. She was given some antibiotics that made her feel lousy. She stayed home from work for a couple of days until she mustered enough energy to tackle office work.

After this incident, Mina had an aversion to restaurants. The minute she entered one, she felt sick and rushed back home. Her dinner dates felt sorry for her. All she wanted to do is stay in bed and not face life. She had agoraphobia which led to a nervous breakdown. Her doctor prescribed anti-depressants which made her lethargic. Louis tried to cajole her back to life, but to no avail. She just felt miserable. It took her about two months to get over it. For a whole year, she could not eat chicken.

A friend of Mina's from work, had moved to London and they corresponded. This girl suggested that she exhibit also in London. She also told Mina she would help her find galleries. And, indeed, she did. Everything was falling into place except her love life. All these men around her. She needed Shoukry. He overshadowed all of them.

IOS

After much searching for a better job, their father found a lucrative position with IOS—Investors Overseas Services. He was employed in the Accounting Department. He told them the story of how this company came to exist. It was founded by an American financier, Bernie Cornfeld, in Canada in 1955 and was incorporated outside the U.S. with headquarters in Geneva. It employed about 25,000 salesmen who sold several types of mutual funds all over Europe. It geared towards small investors and American expatriates who wanted to avoid paying income tax.

The sisters were neither U.S. citizens nor residents so they did not pay American taxes. As for Swiss taxes, they were exempt because they worked for international organizations affiliated to the United Nations.

"This IOS company raised about $ 2,5 billion due to a brilliant idea called the Fund of Funds," explained the father. The sisters listened attentively and got hooked by it. They bought 10,000 Swiss francs worth of shares. It was a great idea to start with. They hoped to eventually make money. They had big dreams. The salesmen were making tons of money selling these funds and were spending lavishly on booze and parties during their conferences in Geneva.

Unfortunately, it all sounded too good to be true. All good things come to an end. During the bull market times, the company and the shares did very well but when the marked dropped, the guaranteed dividends had to be paid out of the capital. So, during the next bear market, the sisters and most investors cashed in a portion of their fund, as stock values decreased. They lost money. They lost their initial investment by selling the shares at almost nothing. Even the IOS employees and managers sold their shares not knowing what the future was going to be.

The whole scheme collapsed. The news was that another financier by the name of Vesco, came into the picture and carried on some fraudulent business under the guise of helping Bernie Cornfeld. It was rumored that when his scheme came into light, he was going to be arrested, so he fled to Costa Rica.

As for Bernie Cornfeld, he was tried and acquitted. He had not committed any crimes and had not gipped anyone.

Finally, IOS collapsed bringing down some European and American banks in the process.

Mina and Vera were extremely disappointed at the turn of events. They had not sold all their shares and they were now worth zero.

That was the end of IOS, the party company, they called it, for indeed during its heydays, they had attended quite a few of the lavish parties Cornfeld gave in his Geneva "chateau" (castle), and at the Intercontinental Hotel. The parties were fabulous affairs. There was dancing and laughter, with abundant champagne and gourmet food. At that time, the IOS salesmen seemed to have bottomless spending accounts. There were no female sales persons. Bernie was always with a beautiful young woman, a different one each time. Mina and Vera met quite a few interesting guys at these parties and frolicked around town with them but they did not take them seriously.

This was also during an 'off time' with Louis.

Their father had to look for another job and luckily found one soon after.

SOCRATES

One of the sisters' hangouts was the Bar on the roof top of the Intercontinental Hotel. While having drinks at the bar and listening to the orchestra playing dance tunes, Mina met a Lebanese Druze. He worked for IOS. It was during one of their conferences. She did not know what a Druze was until he explained it to her. The Druze consider themselves unitarians. There are the Syrian Druze and the Lebanese Druze, this guy explained to Mina. His name was Socrates. He was no philosopher. He was in Geneva on IOS business with his sister-in-law (his wife's sister) and her husband who was also a salesman. The four of them went out to dinners and parties. He was married but "really" separated. It was not one those phony separations that married men tended to make Mina believe in. The proof was his sister-in-law was in the foursome.

After several outings which led to the couch, Mina dropped Socrates because the relationship was getting to be boring and also because she met a more interesting guy, an American who lived in Norway, also married, of course. This guy was really cute. As he was travelling all the time, Mina was not inclined to go to bed with him, although he persisted. For two years he sent her postcards from all the places he was on business, asking her to join him here and there but Mina refused all the invitations. That chapter had ended in Geneva. There was no future in it for her. He was one of her 'plaything' boy-friends and she refused to sleep with him. He called her his "unfinished business," when he finally left Geneva to return to Norway.

A few weeks after Mina broke off with Socrates, he called her at work one day and invited her to lunch.

"Socrates, I told you I have another boyfriend now."

"I am only inviting you to lunch."

"Lunch or brunch, I'm not free, Socrates."

"I have something very important to tell you. I must see you."

After much cajoling, Mina agreed to have lunch with him.

He took her to a swanky restaurant on the lake, two minutes from the Office, called *La Perle du Lac* (Pearl of the Lake). They ordered *filets de perches avec frites* (perch filets with French fries), the much-appreciated fish fare in all lakeside restaurants in Geneva. It was known that, at this restaurant, the perch was freshly caught and not frozen. They drank a bottle of white wine and she felt rather tipsy. She did not feel like going back to the Office.

"Okay Socrates, what is it that you want to tell me," Mina asked after they were halfway through the meal.

He took out a black velvet box from his vest pocket and handed it to her across the table.

"Here, this is for you," he said with a mischievous gleam in his eyes.

Mina opened the box and there was a beautiful pearl necklace, from one of the prominent jewelry shops in Geneva. There were several high-end jewelry shops in Geneva and they mostly catered to the Middle Eastern and Arabian Gulf markets.

"What is this? Why are you giving this to me? I have no intention to getting back with you, so please take it back." She pushed the box away from her.

"I want to offer it to you anyway," he said and he refused to take it back.

Mina looked at him and saw the candor in his eyes and she accepted the gift.

"Don't raise your hopes, Socrates, this does not change anything."

He shrugged and gave her a smirk and took her back to the office after their lunch was over. He gave her a peck on the cheek before she got out of the car.

"By the way," Mina told him, "you seem to be hard up. I would like to introduce you to an office mate of mine, Gisele, a German girl. She is rather pretty and is desperately looking for a boyfriend. I think you would like her."

"Sure, give me her number and I'll call her," he said.

"Let me ask her first whether she would like to meet you."

When Mina went back to the office, she called Gisele and asked her whether she would like to meet an IOS salesman. She described him to Gisele who agreed wholeheartedly.

Socrates eventually moved in with her for about six months then got bored and moved out. Mina saw him a few times for coffee.

He then went back to Lebanon to finalize his divorce.

Two years later, Mina had a call from a travel agent in Geneva, an Armenian travel agent, who lived in the same block of buildings as she did.

"Socrates Hatoum has sent you a return airline ticket to Beirut," he announced over the phone.

"What?"

He repeated his statement.

"It is available for you. When would you like to pick it up?"

Mina was flabbergasted. Now all the Armenians in Geneva will know that a Lebanese guy had sent her a ticket to go to Beirut and there would be talk and malicious gossip. Her reputation within the Armenian community was at stake here.

Mina was seriously involved with Louis at this time and had no inclination whatsoever to go to Beirut to meet Socrates. She cabled Socrates telling him that she could not accept that ticket because she had no intention of going to Beirut or resuming their relationship.

"Keep it, it's a gift, do whatever you want," he cabled back. "You may change your mind."

He must be in the money, Mina thought.

That was the end of Socrates. She never heard from him again.

GARY NO. 2

After their divorce, Gary became friendlier towards Mina. He wrote to her sporadically. He was doing quite a bit of travelling and even invited her to join him at times. Mina was not inclined to restart anything with Gary so she refused his invitations nicely. No need to antagonize him.

One day a guy materialized on Mina's doorstep. He rang the bell. Mina opened the door and saw this wiry, middle-aged man grinning from ear to ear.

Mina was perplexed. "Who are you?" she asked.

"Surprise," he said. "I met your ex-husband in Paris and he suggested that I contact you when in Geneva."

"Gary? hmmm," she said. "Well, what is your name? Please come in."

His name happened to be Gary also. The resemblance between the two Gary's was uncanny. They were both of medium height, with a dark complexion, jet black hair and big brown bedroom eyes. They both spoke fast with animation and gesticulations. Mina invited him inside as she was curious to find out what Gary had been doing since the divorce.

This second Gary was from the French Secret Service, DGSE (stands for General Body of Exterior Services) in Paris. The French and Swiss Secret Services work closely together as they share a common border.

Mina offered him coffee and Gary No. 2 talked a mile a minute and then asked her out for dinner. They went to dinner. They chatted some more. He told Mina about his secret service life, traveling mostly within

Europe and sometimes to the U.S. on drug related matters. It sounded like a dangerous profession. Mina got interested and listened attentively. He also told her that he had learned all about her by looking at her file at the Geneva headquarters for foreign persons. It is called *Controle de l'Habitant* which means Control of the Residents, pertaining to foreigners. This department kept a file on everyone.

He knew her age, her provenance, how long she had been married to Gary, date of divorce and everything else. Mina did not quite appreciate that someone snooped on her behind her back. She liked to keep some mystery about herself.

He was a rather an interesting companion because of his occupation, and they went out a couple of times while he was in Geneva on business. He did not impart the exact nature of his business in Geneva, or rather the persons he was investigating at that time. He became enamored of her, but she had no such feelings towards him. He was simply not her type. He reminded her too much of Gary no.1.

Gary No. 2 had the habit of always sitting with his back to a wall in a restaurant, darting his eyes back and forth and scrutinizing everyone. In the movies, he insisted on sitting in the back row. He felt uncomfortable having someone behind him. When he walked in the street, he was aware of who was behind him at all times. He was jerky, with constant movements of the eyes and body. It got on Mina's nerves after a while. He was never relaxed and consequently she could not relax when she was with him.

He came from Paris to visit her a few times and they went out for dinners if Mina had nothing better to do. Mina never refused a free dinner, unless of course the man in question was a total jerk. He tried to smooch with her but she avoided all intimate contact. Then one day she received a letter and the letter had an enclosure. It was a draft legal document made out in both their names with *Promesse de Mariage* (Promise of Marriage) and the birth of two fictitious children. Mina flipped. She was shocked at his impertinence of taking things for granted. She immediately wrote to him, rather than calling him, saying that she had no intention of getting married again soon. She told him she was still young and liked her freedom and that she wanted to keep him as a friend only.

Mina could not possibly consider being married to such a character. Another Gary? Not in this lifetime or any other lifetime.

"What is the matter with all these men? How come they all want to get married?" she asked Vera.

"They want to own you, my dear."

"Well, I'm not a piece of furniture."

In any case, she was not attracted to him in the least.

"Why can't men tell when a woman is not into them? This is happening all the time. Just because we accept dinner dates, they take it for granted that we will go to bed with them."

Also, she did not at all appreciate that someone was so inquisitive as to probe into her personal life, behind her back. His response to her letter came immediately. He had high hopes and she had let him down.

"If I cannot have you as a wife, I cannot possibly have you as a friend. It would hurt me too much not to be able to touch you." Then he went on accusing her that she was unkind to him. He loved her so much and as she did not reciprocate, he vowed never to see her again.

Good riddance! No more of Gary No. 2. Mina was relieved. It was over. She never cared for lovesick men who wailed and wailed to be loved.

She filed the two Gary's away in her archives.

During the last two years, Mina had been juggling five men at different intervals.

Louis, Alasdair, Fabio, Dogan and Madjid. That was a plateful. The only one that was still in the picture was Louis with an "on and off" relationship. The others were all *passagère* (passing fancies) well, maybe not Alasdair but she had discarded him because of circumstances.

TUSCANY

The years went by and Mina was thoroughly frustrated with her life at the office and with the men she met. She realized that Louis deserved more attention from her but she got exasperated with him sometimes. They were such opposites.

First of all, her office work infuriated her. She no longer wished to be a secretary. She was an artist but she was not earning enough money with her exhibitions. She knew that very few artists earned their living with their art. One had to be either a famous person who dabbles in art and sells one's name or one is deceased. In any case, she could not leave her job and concentrate full-time on art because of her residence status in Switzerland. The only positive thing in her life was that the family was all together.

Secondly, the men in her life turned out to be disappointing. Thinking about men and relationships, she came to the realization that she had to make major changes in her romantic life. She talked about these two issues with her mother and sister. They agreed. Her mother told her she was like a see-saw.

They were having a horrid spring, bleak and rainy. They did not see the sun for one whole month and decided to go on a family vacation. Mina had heard of a resort town on the Tuscan Riviera called Forte dei Marmi. It appeared to be an up-scale resort on the Mediterranean. She obtained some brochures from a travel agency and the whole family, including the cat, drove there in their VW beetle in May of 1969. The suitcases had to be piled up on the roof of the car. They rented a villa from a local merchant who moved out with his family to live in his sister's house for the month. The villa was spacious but badly furnished. The beds sunk in, so they bought wooden planks to put under the mattresses for firmness.

Mina liked Forte dei Marmi. They all did. It was a laid-back town with a fabulous wide sandy beach flanked by the warm waters of the Mediterranean. The rented a cabana at the beach where they could leave all their beach paraphernalia, and they also rented a *tenda* (a large tent) with lounging chairs. They took the cat to the beach and Timmy enjoyed sitting under a chair watching the people go by on the *passerella* (footbridge). The beachgoers came by and gawked at him. They had not seen a big cat like Timmy before. They thought he was some kind of wild animal. When they tried to pet him, he hissed and drove them away. They were told not to touch him.

The family passed whole days at the beach sometimes. They played cards and back- gammon and befriended some Italians from the adjacent *tende*. There was a small restaurant at the back of the cabanas, run by the couple who rented out that section of the beach, and the woman cooked different types of spaghetti at noontime. It was not expensive and it was always delicious. In the early evenings, sometimes they went into town—a couple of blocks away—and bought pizzas to eat on the beach and watch the sunset. It was a relaxed time and they enjoyed every minute of it. The sisters sometimes went to the night club *la Capannina* to dance. They met Italian guys and had a carefree time in general. Italian men were flirtatious and fun to be with but absolutely untrustworthy, Mina thought. The sisters did not take anyone seriously. This was a holiday. And holiday romances are known to be superficial and fleeting.

One evening, as they were dining in a restaurant along the seashore, Mina got the shock of her life. She thought she saw Shoukry. She pinched herself and blinked once or twice. Yes, she did not imagine it. It was Shoukry seated with a man and a woman. The blood drained from her face and she thought she would faint if she had been standing up. *What is Shoukry doing in Forte dei Marmi? It is unbelievable!* She thought.

"You look like you've seen a ghost," Vera remarked seeing Mina's ashen face.

Mina did not reply. She was comatose.

"Hey, what's the matter?" Vera persisted, shaking her arm.

"It's Shoukry," Mina stammered.

"What Shoukry? You're thinking about him again?"

"Not thinking, he's here," she said in a breathy voice.

"Are you hallucinating or what?"

Mina stared into space and felt paralyzed. "I'm telling you Shoukry is here. He's sitting right there. Turn back slowly and you'll see him."

Vera turned around and looked. She did see him, sitting at a table with two other people.

"My God, you're right," she said. "What are you going to do?"

"I will, I will, well I don't know just yet." She was freaking out and she glanced around nervously.

Mina then saw the woman putting her hand on Shoukry's arm and looking up at him. *She must be his girlfriend or wife*, she thought. Mina felt terrible. She resolved to find out more.

"I'm going to walk past them to go to the restroom."

"Then what?" asked Vera.

"Then, we'll see. I'd like to find out whether he has a ring on his finger. The woman looks too cozy with him."

Mina got up from her chair and walked towards the restroom, trying discreetly to look at Shoukry's hand. She could not see anything. She was too far. On the way back, she felt courageous all of a sudden and stopped in her tracks right in front of his table and feigned surprise.

"Shoukry! what are you doing here?" she exclaimed.

Shoukry glanced up, recognized Mina and got up from his chair. Whereupon, on an impulse, Mina came forward and embraced him and gave him a peck on his cheek. All this to show off to the woman seated opposite him.

"What a nice surprise!" she explained.

The woman was glancing at her *bouche bée* (open mouthed). Mina couldn't care less. She hugged Shoukry closer. He felt so good against her body and she closed her eyes for a minute breathing in his scent. Shoukry was quite taken aback but he hugged her back.

"Mina!" he exclaimed, looking sideways at the woman.

"How come you're here?" Mina asked.

"Long story."

"Hope you'll tell me."

Shoukry looked at the woman again before he thought of responding. For only a second, he felt at a loss for words but quickly recovered.

"Yes."

Darn that woman, thought Mina noticing Shoukry's reaction.

"Let's meet and catch up," Mina insisted.

"Sure."

Was he going to utter monosyllables, or what? thought Mina.

Mina realized that Shoukry was caught in a bind—his eyes were darting back and forth to the woman. *There is definitely something going on between them,* she guessed.

When?" Mina was pushing it. That was the only way to act under the present circumstances.

"I'll call you. Please give me your phone no," Shoukry finally said gaining his composure.

Mina took out a pen and a piece of paper from her purse, jotted down her phone number and handed it to him.

"I'm dying to hear your story," said Mina and winked at him. She was being brazen indeed. With that said, she walked away wiggling her hips, not giving him time to introduce his friends. Her heart was beating like mad and her knees wobbled. She was almost going to fall.

"What was that about? What did you talk about?" asked Vera. Her parents looked at her wide-eyed waiting also for an explanation.

"He'll call me." Mina said feeling euphoric and almost fell down while trying to sit on her chair. She grabbed the table for support. She was excited and apprehensive at the same time. *Please God, let him not be married to that woman,* she prayed. *If she is only a girlfriend, it would be easy to snatch him away,* she assured herself. She was confident. She had to be. There was no other way to handle the situation. One thing she was sure of. She was not going to lose this unexpected opportunity.

This was the most startling evening of her life.

Mina could hardly finish her dinner. All she kept thinking about was Shoukry and his touch and his smell, that she had missed so much.

"You seem to be under a spell," Vera said.

"Indeed, I am. I am euphoric and anxious at the same time."

"How do you propose to handle this?" asked her mother anxiously.

"Oh, don't worry, she'll know what to do," said her father.

They went home and Mina slept fitfully that night. She had horrid fantasies about Shoukry and the woman doing things together in bed. She hated the thought of him touching her. She dreamt and dreamt and dreamt, running after Shoukry in a narrow alley, up some rickety steps, going nowhere, plunging into the sea and not knowing how to stay afloat. She woke up early morning with a jolt from a disturbed sleep. She was all drenched. She gasped for air. She took a shower to calm down and think.

She didn't go to the beach that morning because she didn't want to miss Shoukry's call. She waited until noon. Finally, he called and invited her out to dinner and told her he would pick her up at 7pm. She was beyond happy. She joined the others on the beach and told them about the dinner plan that night. Her family wished her good luck.

Back home, Mina went into a frenzy deciding what to wear. She took out all her clothes and threw them on her bed. She decided on a rusty off-the-shoulder sheath. She blow-dried her hair which fell around her shoulders in golden rivulets. She put on very little make-up and lined her eyes with kohl. She then put on gold spiky-heeled shoes and she was ready. She was giddy with excitement.

"Wow, you're dressed to kill," commented Vera.

"Do I look good?"

"You always do. No worries there."

Shoukry drove up in a dark blue Alfa Romeo convertible. When she opened the door of the house, he stood there a minute admiring her and gave a wolf's whistle.

"You look scrumptious," he said.

"*Grazie signore.* You don't look too bad yourself," was her reply. He looked so handsome in khaki pants and a sky-blue shirt open at the neck. Mina remembered him being a sharp dresser.

He opened the car door for her and she glided in with difficulty—the car being a low seater.

"Where are we going?" she asked as they drove away.

"We're going to seaside restaurant in Viareggio. It is a wonderful place. You'll love it."

They drove along the corniche with the music of Adriano Celentano blasting from the radio. He was one of Mina's favorite Italian singers. She hummed along with him.

The atmosphere was awkward to say the least—meeting him again after all these years.

"So Shoukry, what's your story? How come you're in Italy?" Mina was dying to find out. She was also dying to find out about this woman sitting with him but that would come later. *One thing at a time,* she told herself.

"It's a long story. I'll tell you during our dinner. Let's enjoy the scenery."

Mina looked at him, his profile, his hands, those hands that she yearned for so terribly. She felt like jumping over to him and resuming their petting of such a long time ago. It seemed like it was in another lifetime. In fact, it was another lifetime. Those days were in Egypt. Since then she had lived in the United States and Switzerland. So many flirts, so many love affairs, or sex affairs, rather, because she did not love anyone, except perhaps Alasdair. She had lusted for him. He was so handsome and manly. But Shoukry? There was no one like Shoukry. He was THE ONE and she was not going to let him out of her sight this time, if she could help it and if the other woman disappeared into oblivion. She had to play her cards right and not rush things as she was prone to do. She wondered how Shoukry felt about her.

She had a smile on her face as they were driving along with the summer breeze blowing her hair away from her face.

"What are you smiling about?" asked Shoukry.

"I was just remembering the last time we drove along the Nile Corniche in Alexandria, going to town to see a movie. We were late and you were speeding."

"That was years ago."

"Yes, it was, but the memory has stayed with me. You had a Triumph convertible sports car, a little yellow number, and you drove like crazy, and I was scared we would crash."

"Um," he said, "I remember what happened after the movie," and he gave her a meaningful glance. She blushed and did not look at him.

Mona also remembered that evening distinctly.

On the way back from the movie, Shoukry had suggested they go and walk on the beach at Sidi Bishr No. 2. It was pitch dark, no moon and they walked holding hands. Shoukry had a flashlight and he noticed that one of the cabanas had not taken in the cushions from the wooden bench. He guided Mina in and they sat down on the bench embracing and kissing each other. Shoukry then gently laid her down and he lay on top of her kissing her eyes, her mouth and the hollow of her neck. Her breasts awakened between his kisses and she arched her back. Things got really hot, then. His roving hands were all over her body, seeking, exploring and touching. His mouth was on her nipples and her fingers raked his back feeling his muscles beneath the skin. His hands then travelled down and raised her skirt. "Let me touch you," he said with a hoarse voice and his fingers were between her thighs. Mina gasped. She was wet. She did not know whether to succumb to him after all, but just at that moment they heard some people come up the path singing and being rowdy. Mina and Shoukry quickly straightened out, not that anyone could see them in the darkness. The moment was gone. Shoukry then asked her whether she wanted to come to his house for a nightcap. She refused. They would end up having sex and she had not yet decided on that path.

She felt embarrassed that they were both thinking of that evening.

Shoukry had reserved a table at the Restaurant called *Il Pescatore*. It was a quaint place with blue checkered table cloths and small blue vases of flowers on each table and multicolored lanterns hanging from the ceiling. A soft music was playing in the background and it mingled with the swooshing of the waves. It was a romantic place. *A lovers' place,* Mina thought.

They sat in a corner of the patio facing each other and ordered their food. They started with bruschetta, then spaghetti with mussels, one of Mina's favorite dishes. The wine Shoukry ordered was exquisite. She felt a little tipsy. She was not used to drinking more than one glass of wine during dinner, but here she had two. This was a special occasion.

"So, Shoukry, tell me your story," Mina said, looking at him wide-eyed.

"Okay. After you left Egypt, the political situation started deteriorating. My father did not get along well with Nasser who had drastic ideas about Egypt's future. Father was more inclined to go slowly about making changes. He realized that was not Nasser's goal so he resigned from the Army. Being retired at sixty was not a life for him. He felt useless and was bored. He searched for something useful to do but couldn't find anything appropriate. At this point in time, his health started to fail and he had a heart attack in his sleep and died suddenly. We did not know he had a heart problem. He seemed to be perfectly fit. Mom, of course, was devastated and she was in limbo for quite a while. She then heard that her aunt in Italy had died and she was the only heir to her fortune. The aunt had no offspring so she left everything to mom. She had real estate in Rome and in Tuscany and owned several vineyards."

"What a story!" Mina said, listening attentively.

"Yeah. She then made up her mind to move to Tuscany. She did not fancy staying in Egypt and being surrounded with all of my father's memories. She asked me whether I would go with her and take care of the estate and the vineyards. At that time, I was also getting disillusioned with the state of the Egyptian Airforce. We had lost yet another war which should have been avoided. I decided to quit and join my mother and take care of her business. So, here I am. I live in Rome most of the time and come to Tuscany to manage the vineyards. Actually, the wine you are drinking is ours."

Mina was speechless. "So, you now live in Rome permanently?"

"Yes, and I love it. Life is simpler in Italy. I have left Egypt since about a year now and don't really miss it. Of course, I miss my friends."

"What a change in your life, Shoukry."

"Now it's your turn to tell me all about your career and your boyfriends."

"My career, yes, but boyfriends, no."

"That many, eh?"

"Look who's talking. What about that woman with you at the restaurant? She seemed to be quite chummy with you, or I should say, intimate."

Shoukry smiled enigmatically. His best reply was not to make a reply at all.

Aha, thought Mina. *There is something there.*

The food was delicious and Mina enjoyed every minute of the evening. She wished it could last forever.

"Okay, my turn now. I am now divorced, by the way. So, after I left Egypt I returned to New York and worked as a fashion designer. After struggling to get a good job, which I never did, I quit the design field. I could not stand the dog-eat-dog atmosphere, nor the people in it. A bunch of creeps, very few *comme il faut* people. My sister joined me in New York at this time and she was also disappointed with life in the city, all work and no play. So, on a whim I decided to go to Europe. I ended up in Geneva working for an international organization affiliated to the United Nations as I could not get a residence permit otherwise. And here I am being a secretary all over again. There is one good thing about my life is that my artistic career took off in Switzerland. I have a studio and exhibit all over Switzerland and even in London, Paris and Hong Kong."

"So, all this career talk you gave me back in Egypt fell down the drain?"

"I'm afraid it did," she said sheepishly. She was embarrassed to look at him. "I'm glad for one thing though, my family is all together except for Ted and Nancy who are in Lebanon, as you know."

"Are you happy in Geneva?"

"Yes, I am." *Except for the fact that you are not there with me,* she wanted to add.

"Have you been to Rome?" Shoukry asked.

"Yes, I have. When I decided to go to Europe, I also took a trip to Rome to find out whether I could work for FAO."

"So, what happened?"

"I got a job offer with FAO but I preferred to accept the one in Geneva."

"I could show you the Rome you haven't seen," said Shoukry.

"I'd love that," she said enthusiastically. *So, Shoukry, are we on?* She wanted to blurt out.

The dinner was over and they went for a walk along the beach. He held her hand while walking and that was all. Mina was yearning for his embrace. *Does he still love me?* she asked herself. *After my refusal of his proposal, who knows how many women he has had. Is he still single?* Mina was curious to find out more and, if at all possible, she wanted to restart where they had left off. And what about his companion at the restaurant? Who was she?

The evening ended too soon for Mina. Shoukry accompanied her home, gave her a chaste kiss on her cheek and he drove away. Mina touched her cheek and went into the house. She was disappointed. She wanted to be kissed passionately. She yearned for his lips.

"Well, what happened?" asked Vera. Her parents were also looking at her inquisitively.

"Nothing, we went to dinner in Viareggio, walked on the beach and came home."

"I see a disappointment on your face," said Vera.

"I don't feel like talking about it. I'm tired. I'm going to bed."

Tucked under her blanket, Mina started crying softly.

She had the most sensational evening but it was incomplete.

The next day, Shoukry called and asked her whether she was going to the beach.

"We have a cabana and a *tenda* at Imperia Beach. Do you want to join us? You'll meet my family again," Mina said.

"Sure thing, I'll come over at about noon. I have some business to attend to before then."

Mina impatiently waited for Shoukry's arrival. So were her parents and Vera. He finally made an apparition carrying a cooler with him.

"Hi everyone, how are you, folks? I've brought some beer, soft drinks and some focaccia sandwiches for lunch." They all shook hands and then sat down to have a meal. The atmosphere was congenial.

Mina was a little shy to be showing her bikini clad body to Shoukry who was appraising her discreetly. Her body had changed but only slightly, she hoped. She still retained a youthful figure with curves in the right places.

"You can change into your swimming trunks in the cabana, if you wish," Mina told him.

"Thanks, I will."

Shoukry came out in black swim trunks. Mina loved to look at his body, broad shoulders, a six pack and powerful arms and legs. She wanted so much to be sitting close to him, to feel him, to feel his warmth. *I don't know where this will lead us*, she asked herself. *Are we going to take up where we left off?* She was on pins and needles.

They went swimming together and frolicked in the water. Mina was a good swimmer and Shoukry, a strong swimmer. When he came out of the water, Mina was walking behind him and admired his smooth back. She loved looking at his body and wanted to hug him so badly.

Then they all played canasta on the beach and stayed until sundown.

"I would like to invite you all to dinner," Shoukry said.

"No," said Mina's father, you are invited to our home for a home-made dinner." And it was decided. The mother cooked spaghetti with her special tomato sauce with mushrooms, basil leaves and some other spices.

After the dinner was over, Mina accompanied Shoukry to his car.

"I enjoyed being with your family," he said.

"I'm glad. They're great people, aren't they? I'm so happy to be reunited at long last."

"See you again, babe, I'll call you."

With that said, he kissed her on the cheek.

When will his lips navigate to mine in a passionate kiss? Mina asked herself.

The next day, Shoukry called her up saying that he had to go to Rome on business. Mina was disappointed.

"When will you be back?" she asked.

"I'm not sure. Tell you what, would you like to come with me? You'll have your own bedroom and bathroom, of course."

"Yes, I'd love that." Mina was thrilled at the prospect. However, she would have liked to share the same bedroom. *Well, let's see how things will work out*, she told herself. *He still has not told me about the woman.*

SHOUKRY

When Shoukry was seated at the restaurant in Forte dei Marmi, with his girlfriend, Laura, and a client, he saw a young woman with long honey-blond hair go by to the restrooms and she reminded him of Mina. She looked exactly like her from the back. She had that same swinging stride. He wanted to see her face. He thought he was imagining things and brought himself back to the conversation they were having at dinner.

And then there was Mina coming back from the restrooms. Yes, it *was* Mina. He was not imagining things. Before he could react, here she was, greeting him. His Mina. *What the fuck?* he thought. *How am I going to handle this? Laura is an extremely jealous woman and here I am meeting my old love. My only love.*

He certainly did not feel comfortable and he tried to regain his composure. He pondered on how to handle the situation of having the two women in the same place at the same time. He wanted so much to hug Mina and kiss her but restrained himself. He was rigid and felt like a piece of wood.

He wanted to talk to her some more but Laura was glaring at him. He did not need a showdown in the restaurant. She was known to fly off the handle at the slightest provocation. What an encounter this was. He had to react somehow. He stood up and hugged Mina taking in her unique odor and wanted to bury his face in her hair. He had to think of a plan to meet her alone. Luckily, Mina took care of that by giving him her phone number.

He sat down after Mina walked away from him and faced the fuming Laura. She was an extremely possessive woman. The sex was good with her but his emotions were not involved. It was mindless sex. He did not love her. Actually, he had not loved any woman he had gone to bed with and he had had plenty. They just did not get under his skin like Mina did. His feelings for Mina were sincere and everlasting. She was captivating.

His friend at the table went to the restroom leaving him alone with Laura.

"Who is she?" Laura asked with a scowl.

"An old friend of mine from Cairo," he responded matter of factly.

"You took her phone number."

"Yes, I did."

"Then what?"

"I'll let you know when the time comes. Let's enjoy our dinner and not discuss this in front of Emilio."

With that said, Shoukry continued eating his desert. Laura just scoffed and did not say anything further. She sulked for the rest of the dinner. Shoukry felt uneasy but managed to retain a composed façade. They finished their dinner and Shoukry first dropped Emilio at his Hotel and then drove Laura home.

Laura did not make a move to get out of the car.

"Won't you come in for a nightcap?" she asked coquettishly, toying with his hair at the nape of his neck.

"I'm tired. Let's call it a night."

"I suppose you're gonna call her," she said with a humpf.

"No, I will not call her, not tonight."

"But, you will call her sometime," Laura persisted.

Shoukry did not like being harassed and got exasperated with her. He hated possessive females. He wanted to be alone to ponder about his next move with Mina.

"Please don't harp on this subject any longer. Just drop it, will you?" he said through clenched teeth.

"Okay, we'll talk tomorrow," Laura then said.

"Tomorrow, I'm busy."

"With her, I suppose."

"I told you to stop this, Laura. Goodnight."

With that said, he accompanied her to the door and left without giving her a goodnight kiss. He just didn't feel like it. He drove away feeling guilty in a way. After all, Laura was his girlfriend *du jour* and had been for some months now.

He did not like clingy women. Another clingy one was the last affair he had had in Cairo just before leaving. He had taken up with the American wife of the Hilton Hotel Manager. The husband was a philanderer and the wife felt free to seek her own sexual interests. Besides being clingy, she was sexually aggressive and Shoukry disliked sexually aggressive women. He did not consider them feminine. It had been uncomfortable telling her goodbye but he did not worry too much about it. He was sure she would soon find another sexual partner to replace him.

And now Mina had all of a sudden reappeared in his life. This was a biggie. It was an unprecedented event. He went to bed thinking of Mina. His Mina. He had to find out whether she was married or divorced or what. And more specifically, what was she doing in Italy. Was she not supposed to be in New York? What luck meeting her here of all places. How was he going to handle the situation? He kept thinking about it and decided on a reserved approach. He did not want to appear too eager with her. After all, she had refused his marriage proposal and had gone to the States to pursue a career in fashion design. Why was she here in Italy? He would call her tomorrow and take her out to dinner and talk.

What was he going to do with Laura? He had never had the type of feeling towards her as he had with Mina. She was okay as a sexual partner but he found her too overwhelming sometimes and too demanding. On the other hand, Mina was too reserved. He was surprised she had even kissed him on the cheek when they met at the restaurant. He had a nightcap and went to bed thinking of the next day with anticipation.

ROME

Mina told her family she was going to Rome with Shoukry for a few days. They just looked at her and did not volunteer any comments. She rapidly packed a few things and was ready when Shoukry came to pick her up. The top was up on the car as it was a long ride, all on the Freeway. The conversation was lively, all the way down to Rome. It was about Cairo, the U.S. and Europe. Shoukry patted her thigh once or twice, asking her if she was okay. She was more than okay. She felt like a teenager anticipating a hot, romantic interlude. They finally arrived at his home which was in a sumptuous estate with a gate and all. It was in Aventine where most villas of the rich and famous were located. Mina was in awe.

"What a beautiful place," she said, when they entered the foyer.

"Yes, I love it here."

Shoukry installed her in the second bedroom which overlooked a magnificent garden strewn with fruit trees—figs and guavas and it also housed a gazebo covered in grape leaves. It was stupendous. His bedroom was adjacent to hers and they each had their own bathroom.

They went out to dinner in a trattoria hidden away in the countryside which seemed to be a trendy place. It boasted offering the best homemade cooking in Rome, Shoukry told her. The owners knew him by his first name and they seated them at his favorite table in the corner overlooking a patio with colorful plants. The food was excellent and the wine, divine. It came from Shoukry's vineyards. They drove home after dinner as they were both too tired to venture on a night on the town.

"I'll show you the Rome that you haven't seen, tomorrow," said Shoukry.

"I'm looking forward to it."

"Goodnight, then," he said with another peck on the cheek.

They retired to their respective bedrooms. Mina was rather disappointed that there was not more to the evening, like sitting on the patio close to each other, hugging and kissing. She tried to fall asleep but was too wired up to do so. It was a weird evening, being in the same house with the man she yearned for, and had yearned for several years now, and yet being apart in separate bedrooms. There were a few books on a side table in her room. She picked one up and tried to read but could not concentrate. It was a long-winded story and it was uninteresting. She then had a wild thought. She could be brazen and make the first move towards intimacy. She had to do something to make him react. *Tant-pis* (never mind) if it did not work. She would be greatly humiliated if he rebuffed her, but she had to try. She got out of bed, put on her negligee over her nightgown and went to knock on Shoukry's door.

"Come in."

Mina opened the door and just stood there.

"Do you need anything?" asked Shoukry matter of factly. He was seated at his desk going through some papers.

"Not really."

"What is it then?" He was baffled.

"Well, I feel lonely," she said. There, she said it. She blushed and hated herself for that.

Shoukry looked at her long and hard and pointed to his lap.

"Come and sit here," he said.

Mina gingerly walked over to him and sat on his lap.

"Is this better?" asked Shoukry with an enigmatic smile.

She nodded and waited for his move.

"You, stupid girl," he said and turned her around to embrace her. Mina's heart was beating so loudly that she thought it would burst out of her chest. She put her arms around him and they kissed passionately. His lips felt so good. His mouth tasted her, devoured her.

"You smell divine," he said and started kissing her on the neck. Mina's body undulated beneath his touch as his hands strayed along her breasts. She was in extasy. He then swept her up in his arms and carried her to the bed. It was king size. He lay her down on the bed and her long hair fanned out on the pillow. She arched upward and pulled him against her.

I'm finally going to have sex with Shoukry, she thought. She was giddy with anticipation. She had imagined it so many times when she was away from him.

Shoukry was an expert lover. He took his time. Her whole body quivered and warmed to his touch. She surrendered and lost herself in his embrace. He watched her face and saw the desire in her eyes.

"Your body is that of a seventeen-year-old," he said, while caressing her soft skin languorously. He took off her negligee than brought down the straps of her nightgown to reveal her young breasts. He took one nipple then the other in his mouth and sighed, "gorgeous, so pink and perky."

While Mina was mewing with delight, his lips moved downwards to her navel and further down to the moist space between her thighs. She was wet. He parted her legs and his tongue did the rest. Mina had already climaxed as he entered her. She dug her nails in his back and uttered soft moans of pleasure. She loved the way he smelled: spicy, musky and, most of all, masculine. She wanted to freeze the moment for ever.

"I'd like you to be complete next time," Shoukry said after he climaxed and came out.

"What do you mean by complete?"

"Complete, meaning not to remove your pubic hair. I'd like to be able to twiddle my fingers through them."

Mina laughed.

They could not have enough of each other and were both exhausted after making love three times that night. They then slept the sleep of angels. Mina saw only good dreams this time. She was so enraptured by Shoukry. She did not want to get out of bed, ever.

They woke up around 10 am and Shoukry prepared breakfast. Mina was surprised he knew how to cook.

"I only know how to make breakfast. A woman comes once a day to clean and cook for me during weekdays. I'm still a bachelor."

"Good to know. And the woman at the restaurant?"

He still did not give her any explanation.

After breakfast, Shoukry told her he was going to the office for an hour and then he would come back to show her around *his* Rome.

Mina took a magazine from his library and sat on a lounging chair on the patio flipping through the pages and thinking about their wild night together. Her happiness was complete. She had found her Shoukry. But what about the future? She was in Geneva and he was in Rome.

The doorbell rang and Mina came out of her reverie. *Who could that be? The maid perhaps?* she asked herself. She got up from her chair to open the door. She was surprised to see the woman of the restaurant glaring at her. She was all made up, wearing a tight red dress showing off her ample bosom, and spiky red shoes to match. She was carrying an oversized brown Gucci handbag. Mina admitted that she looked quite sexy and instantly hated her. She hated the thought that Shoukry had slept with her, that he had touched her, that he had entered her.

"Where's Shoukry?" the woman asked, sailing past her into the foyer.

"He's not here."

"Let me look," the woman said and, pushing Mina aside, barged into the living room. Calling his name several times, she stomped from room to room. She saw the unmade bed in the master bedroom.

"Hmpf," she said, "so you're sleeping with my fiancé."

"Is that so?"

"Yes. Don't think you can snatch him away from me. We've got a history together. We will get married soon."

"Is that so?" Mina kept her cool while answering her but she was seething inside.

"You're nothing but a passing fancy, whoever you are. From Egypt I suppose, one of his many sluts."

Mina then slapped her, hard.

"Get out of this house," she barked, and pushed her roughly towards the door.

The woman backed out holding her cheek which had turned crimson. Mina was ready for a fist fight.

"This is not the end, you'll hear from me again, you whore. Wait till I get hold of Shoukry."

"You do that, but in the meanwhile disappear from my sight before I slap you again."

Mina then banged the door shut and went back to the patio slumping on the wicker chair, thinking hard. She would confront Shoukry and come to the bottom of this. *Is he intending to play with two women at the same time? That will not do,* Mina told herself. She waited impatiently for his return. A little more than an hour passed and she finally heard the key in the lock.

"Is my beauty ready?" asked Shoukry coming onto the patio.

"Yup, let's go."

Mina decided to wait for an opportune moment to broach the subject of the woman. She didn't even know her name. She was Italian, for sure. That, she gathered from her accent.

The first place they drove to was Veio Park. Mina was enchanted with what this park had to offer. Waterfalls, woods and pastures. She never knew this kind of place existed in the vicinity of Rome. Shoukry told her that this was the most interesting park north of Rome for its fantasy like nature. They spent a couple of hours there.

Then he took her to the Quartiere Coppede, a charming small neighborhood, where a mixture of Art Nouveau and Art Deco mingled together offering such landmarks as the fabulous Arch at the entrance of the district. The arch was decorated with cherubs and animals. They also visited the Fountain of Frogs and the Spider Palace. Mina only knew of the Fontana di Trevi which she had visited with Diane. She was overjoyed with the sites she saw.

"Shoukry, I'm so thankful you took me to these places. They are magical and delightful. It has been an enchanting time for me. Thanks."

"There's more to see, tomorrow. Now we'll go to Trastevere to eat a 'real' Italian meal. It's a section of Rome full of restaurants."

Indeed, the district of Trastevere was Bohemian and funky, strewn with numerous quaint restaurants. Shoukry headed to his favorite one, called "Giorgio". There was no menu. The waiter just uttered the selection of the day. Mina chose *linguine con frutta di mare,* her favorite Italian dish. Shoukry ordered the same with a bottle of chilled white wine.

Mina thought this would be a good time to talk about the other woman.

"Shoukry, who is this woman who claims to be your fiancée?"

"What?"

"Your fiancée, the woman who was at the restaurant with you when I met you in Forte dei Marmi?" She looked at him expecting a reply.

Shoukry was puzzled. "She's not my fiancée!"

"She thinks she is."

"What are you talking about?"

"I'm talking about the woman who came banging on your door this morning while you were away, and looking for you. She called me a slut so I slapped her."

Shoukry listened to Mina and it was quite evident that he was annoyed. He then guffawed.

"What are you laughing about? What have you got to say? Are you going to sleep with two women simultaneously?"

"I'll take care of her, don't worry."

With that said, they left the restaurant and had another night of passionate love-making. They then slept intertwined listening to Chopin on the stereo. Shoukry was the best lover she had ever had. It was so good that Mina couldn't care less whether he would be sleeping with ten other women as long as he was giving her pleasure.

SHOUKRY

Shoukry had to take care of the Laura problem pretty soon.

Early next morning, he left Mina at the house and went to the Office to take care of some unfinished business before taking off for another round of sightseeing. The phone rang but he did not answer it. He knew it would be Laura. He did not want to confront her on the phone. He decided to go over to her house and break up with her. He drove over and rang the bell. He had a key but he did not want to use it.

"Ah, here you are, I've been looking for you," she said coming over to embrace him and give him a kiss.

Shoukry held her at arms' length.

"What's the matter with you?" she asked, seeing that he looked angry.

"The matter with me is that you were extremely rude to my friend."

"Oh, so she told you what happened. Look, Shoukry, please don't feel bad, I'll forgive you for a night of sex with that *putana*."

Before she could finish the sentence, Shoukry brusquely pushed her away.

"Laura, we're finished you and I," he said in a solemn tone. "I'll not tolerate you insulting my friend."

"What are you saying Shoukry? This can't be over. I said I forgive you," she said holding on to his arm.

"Nothing you can say will change my mind. We were not meant to be, that's all," he said resolutely, pulling his arm away and gave back her key.

"But, Shoukry…" Laura kept saying, unwilling to accept the key. It fell on the floor.

Shoukry left her at the door without another word and walked away towards his car.

Laura slammed the door shut shouting Italian swear words.

Shoukry uttered a sigh of relief and drove away. *Now I can start living again with a positive perspective,* he told himself, *with Mina, I hope. She is all I want. She is the most exciting woman I have ever met and I intend to keep her.*

ROME

Shoukry returned from his unpleasant encounter with Laura to take Mina on another sightseeing tour around Rome. This time they visited Lake Bracciano, a volcanic region some thirty kilometers northwest of Rome. Shoukry told her that it was one of the cleanest lakes in Italy as motor boats were forbidden. It was a picturesque place and the panorama was breathtaking. They swam in the clear lake and had a late lunch in a small trattoria and finally drove back to Rome.

Mina broached the subject of the other woman again as they were driving back. "I hope you don't think that you can sleep with two women simultaneously. I won't stand for it."

"She will no longer be a problem," is all he said and patted her thigh.

Mina was curious to find out what had transpired but she did not dare ask. She didn't want to sound like a pestering woman. She knew men hated that, especially Shoukry who had been a bachelor all his life. She would wait patiently for an explanation. But the subject never came up again.

The evening before Shoukry was to drive them back to Forte dei Marmi, his housekeeper had prepared them a sumptuous meal. They were seated on the patio with soft music playing in the background. It was a starless night and the chirping of the cicadas could be heard close by. It was a perfect setting for a lovers' dinner.

"It's so romantic here," Mina said. "You are lucky to live in such a charming place."

After dinner they lounged on the settee and Shoukry began stroking Mina's hair, as she lay with her head on his lap.

"Do you like Rome?" he asked.

"I love it."

"To visit?"

"Well, um…."

"Would you live here?"

"Well, um…"

Shoukry then took Mina in his arms and looked straight into her eyes.

"I'm going to say this once. You know I love you and I would like us to live together but I don't know how you feel. Now is the time to be decisive. Would you like to live with me in Rome?"

Mina was taken aback. She didn't see this coming, so soon.

"Are you asking me to move down here?" Her eyes were darting back and forth.

"Yes, precisely."

"What about my family and my job? Am I going to be dependent on you?"

"You don't have to be. You can always work if you want to. It's your decision. You leave your job at the IOE, which you don't like anyway, and your family can visit you or you can visit them. Geneva is not that far away. We could have a wonderful life here. I can convert the shed on the grounds into a studio for you and you can paint to your heart's content. There is a lot of natural light coming in through the windows. And there is even a skylight. And we'll have a couple of *bambini* along the way if you don't mind getting fat," he chuckled. "What do you say? This is my second and last marriage proposal," he said with his eyes intensely boring into hers as he was watching her reaction.

"Yes, yes and yes."

NOTE FROM THE AUTHOR

This is not a biography or a memoir. Any similarity between the characters in the novel and persons living or dead is purely coincidental.

The events in this novel are set in the 1960s, a decade which I am very familiar with, when the Women's Liberation Movement was in full swing in Europe. I chose to write about Switzerland because I lived there and had a most enjoyable and adventurous life during that decade. Thanks to second-wave feminism, women were free at last and could think and act like men in their sexual escapades. I am not delving into the injustices of a man-made society because I suffered from it marginally.

Having been born and raised in Egypt was both a curse and a blessing. A curse because young women were not free to do as they liked. And a blessing because my parents were liberal and did not curb my enthusiasm for self-awareness and self-fulfillment. I am grateful to them for what I have become both as an artist and as an author.

That having been said, I am infinitely grateful to my husband for encouraging me wholeheartedly in all my endeavors, however far-fetched they might have been. As for my sons, their existence gave meaning to my life and I was lucky to live it fully, with no regrets.

P.S. All the illustrations inside the book are my own artwork.